THE DARKEST CANYON

By
USA Today Bestselling Author
Roberta Kagan

Book Two in A Holocaust Story Series

CONTACT ME

I love hearing from readers, so feel free to drop me an email telling me your thoughts about the book or series.

Email: roberta@robertakagan.com

Please sign up for my mailing list, and you will receive Free short stories including an USA Today award-winning novella as my gift to you!!!!! To sign up…

Check out my website http://www.robertakagan.com.

Come and like my Facebook page!

https://www.facebook.com/roberta.kagan.9

Join my book club

https://www.facebook.com/groups/1494285400798292/?ref=br_rs

Follow me on BookBub to receive automatic emails whenever I am offering a special price, a freebie, a giveaway, or a new release. Just click the link below, then click follow button to the right of my name. Thank you so much for your interest in my work.

https://www.bookbub.com/authors/roberta-kagan.

DISCLAIMER

This is a work of fiction. Names, characters, businesses, places, events, and incidents are either the products of the author's imagination or used in a fictitious manner. Any resemblance to actual persons, living or dead, or actual events is purely coincidental.

TABLE OF CONTENTS

CONTACT ME..3

TABLE OF CONTENTS..5

PROLOGUE..9

CHAPTER 1..12

CHAPTER 2..22

CHAPTER 3..30

CHAPTER 4..32

CHAPTER 5..35

CHAPTER 6..42

CHAPTER 7..46

CHAPTER 8..50

CHAPTER 9..56

CHAPTER 10..62

CHAPTER 11..65

CHAPTER 12..68

CHAPTER 13..70

CHAPTER 14..72

CHAPTER 15..78

CHAPTER 16..82

CHAPTER 17..88

CHAPTER 18..92

CHAPTER 19..95

CHAPTER 20...99

CHAPTER 21...104

CHAPTER 22...110

CHAPTER 23...112

CHAPTER 24...118

CHAPTER 25...123

CHAPTER 26...133

CHAPTER 27...138

CHAPTER 28...141

CHAPTER 29...148

CHAPTER 30...151

CHAPTER 31...158

CHAPTER 32...163

CHAPTER 33...166

CHAPTER 34...169

CHAPTER 35...171

CHAPTER 36...174

CHAPTER 37...178

CHAPTER 38...183

CHAPTER 39...187

CHAPTER 40...195

CHAPTER 41...201

CHAPTER 42...202

CHAPTER 43...207

CHAPTER 44...209

CHAPTER 45 211

CHAPTER 46 213

CHAPTER 47 217

CHAPTER 48 218

CHAPTER 49 221

CHAPTER 50 224

CHAPTER 51 227

CHAPTER 52 229

CHAPTER 53 234

CHAPTER 54 237

CHAPTER 55 239

CHAPTER 56 242

CHAPTER 57 245

CHAPTER 58 250

CHAPTER 59 256

CHAPTER 60 258

CHAPTER 61 267

CHAPTER 62 270

CHAPTER 63 273

CHAPTER 64 276

CHAPTER 65 278

CHAPTER 66 281

CHAPTER 67 284

CHAPTER 68 288

CHAPTER 69 291

CHAPTER 70 296

CHAPTER 71 299

CHAPTER 72 301

CHAPTER 73 307

CHAPTER 74 310

CHAPTER 75 313

CHAPTER 76 315

CHAPTER 77 320

CHAPTER 78 323

CHAPTER 79 326

CHAPTER 80 330

AUTHORS NOTE 333

MORE BOOKS BY THE AUTHOR 335

PROLOGUE

A Small Jewish Neighborhood, in the Outskirts of Lodz Poland . . . 1938

Lila Rabinowitz lay on her bed panting heavily. Her brow was knitted, and her golden-blonde curls stuck to her neck wet with sweat. She held her breath, unable to speak, until she heard the infant, she'd just given birth to, let out a hearty cry. Lila breathed a sigh of relief as a smile washed over her face. When she sat up on her elbow to look at the baby, a scarlet bloodstain, resembling the shape and color of a red velvet rose, had formed on the white cotton blanket that modestly covered her bare bottom.

It was an early spring morning, and the sun shone brightly through the bedroom window.

"It's a boy," the old midwife, Rivka, said.

"A boy . . . a son! I am so happy," Lila whispered.

The old midwife cleaned the baby with warm water and a clean rag. Then she wrapped him in a blanket and lay him in his mother's arms.

Lila gently removed the blanket and counted her son's fingers and toes. She marveled at the shape of his tiny ears. Then she smiled. "Look at him," she said, her voice filled with awe and just above a whisper. "He's perfect. God has created a perfect child."

Rivka smiled. "Your husband, Ben, will be happy too."

Lila had known Rivka all her life. And if there was anyone she felt she could trust with her secrets, it was Rivka.

"Yes, of course, he will." Then Lila looked down at the baby, and tears began to form in the corners of her eyes. "But he's going to be angry with me."

"Nu? Why?"

"Because I can't allow my son to be circumcised." She was sweating, and there was fear in her eyes as the tears streamed down her cheeks. Rivka wiped Lila's face with a wet rag.

"What? You must. It's Jewish law, Lila," Rivka said.

"I know the law. And I prayed and prayed that I would have a girl so that I would never have to face this decision. But I can't do it. You see, when I was just five, my mother had my little brother. You remember him; I know you do. You delivered him. He was a beautiful little boy. In my childlike mind, I used to make-believe that he was my baby. He was healthy and perfect, just like my son is now." Lila looked into Rivka's eyes. "Do you remember what happened to him? I'm sure you remember, Rivka."

"I remember. He bled to death from a botched circumcision."

"Yes, I will never forget the sounds of my mother screaming and wailing. My father's face, white as alabaster. It was the worst day of my life. So you see why I can't do it to my son. I refuse."

"But what about the child? You want him to be accepted as a Jew, don't you?"

"Of course. But not at the expense of losing him."

"It is unusual that a child will have problems from circumcisions. That was a rare case."

"I can't take that risk. My little boy is perfect right now, just as he is. Just as God created him."

"You're right. Ben is not going to be happy." Rivka shook her head.

"I don't care. He can divorce me if he wants to. He can go to the rabbi and ask for a get, a Jewish divorce. But I can't do it. I won't." Lila's voice was raised. She hugged the child tightly to her breast. Tears ran down her cheeks.

"You're upsetting yourself. Please, don't cry. This should be a happy time, not a sad one," Rivka said, taking the hair out of Lila's eyes.

"I know, and I am very happy to have this wonderful baby boy." Lila smiled through her tears.

"Never mind right now about your concerns with the circumcision. I'm sure you and Ben will work it all out. Have you decided what you will call him?"

"Moishe. I will call him Moishe. I promised Ben we would name the baby for his father who passed last year. Moishe was his father's name. You see, I am not so bad. I am giving the name of our firstborn to Ben's family."

"Yes, that is good of you. And not only that, but it is a good name. A strong name. Moishe is the Yiddish name for Moses."

"Yes, that's right, Rivka," Lila said. "And may God grant him strength. And let him be a strong man—a man with his own mind. A man of God like the deliverer of our people."

"Aliva, from your mouth to God's ears." Rivka smiled. She looked into the blanket to see the baby's tiny, scrunched-up face. "He is a handsome, little fellow, isn't he?"

Lila smiled.

CHAPTER 1

Winter 1939, Berlin

Gretchen Schmidt wound the final pin curl of her friend Hilde's wet hair. She had just finished bleaching Hilde's hair from mousy brown to strawberry blonde. "How do you like the color?" she asked.

"I do," Hilde said. "You did a wonderful job. I was just hoping we might be able to make it a little lighter."

"I tried. This is the lightest it would go." Gretchen had used a hair-lightening product that was produced by a French company known to be sympathetic to the Reich.

"Oh, Gretchen, I wish I was naturally pretty like you," Hilde said.

"Don't be silly. You are very pretty," Gretchen lied. She'd known Hilde for many years, and although she knew Hilde considered them to be best friends, Gretchen didn't. She felt sorry for Hilde. Hilde was an overweight girl with thin, lifeless hair and a less than attractive face. Hilde's father had left her mother when Hilde was very young. Then when Gretchen and Hilde were in their late teens, Hilde was heartbroken when she told Gretchen how her mother committed suicide, leaving Hilde to fend for herself. Most people shunned Hilde, considering her to be strange, overbearing, and broken. But not Gretchen, who, because of her kind heart, found it difficult to say no to Hilde.

"You really think so?" Hilde said, looking in the mirror at her hair again.

Gretchen nodded.

"I met someone," Hilde blurted out. "He's not nearly as handsome as Hann was but he really likes me. And I still can't believe that Hann was so mad about Thea, that Jew bitch."

"It was a long time ago. Forget about Hann. Tell me a little more about your new boyfriend."

"It's hard to understand how a Jew like Thea had that white-blonde hair, and I can't get my hair any lighter than this."

"Let's not worry about Thea or Hann. Come on, and tell me about your new fella while your hair dries."

Gretchen wished she could somehow hurry the drying process. Her nerves were on edge, but she dared not let Hilde see that she was distressed.

"Let's make a pot of coffee and have a couple of those sweet rolls I brought, and I'll tell you all about him. And by the way, I have another surprise to tell you."

Hilde followed Gretchen into the kitchen. "Is this real coffee?" Gretchen asked as she put up a pot of water to boil.

"Yes, it is!" Hilde smiled. "Look in the bag at all the food I brought you," she said, proud and excited to be giving her friend such coveted gifts.

"Oh my! Look at this," Gretchen said. "You brought me sausage again. Bless you. And bread . . . and cheese!"

"And two sweet rolls for us to eat right now."

"How did you ever get all of this food?" Gretchen asked. Hilde had been bringing small gifts of food to Gretchen for several months, but this was more than usual. And what a blessing it was. Gretchen desperately needed the food.

"The man I'm dating's name is Axel, and he is very important in the Nazi Party. He has connections."

"And he got you all of this food? You should have kept some of it for yourself."

"I have more at home," Hilde said. "He also got me an interview for a job. A job that pays very handsomely."

"Oh! That's wonderful."

"You see, we've been talking about getting married. And we both decided it was best if I could leave the factory and find a job that pays well so that we could save some money before we start our family," Hilde said as Gretchen poured them both cups of steaming coffee.

"You've been talking marriage with someone, and this is the first I am hearing about him?" Gretchen asked, pretending to scold her.

"I wasn't sure if I was going to accept."

"But you are?"

"I think so," Hilde answered.

"Oh, Hilde, that's wonderful," Gretchen said. She stood up and felt Hilde's hair; her hands were trembling. It was already beginning to dry. *Good thing her hair is thin; it should dry quickly. I wish her hair was done so she could leave already. Every minute she's here is dangerous,* Gretchen thought.

"Is it dry?" Hilde said, taking a large bite of her sweet roll.

"Almost."

"That's good. We still have a little time together, so let me tell you about my job interview. First off, it's the reason that I wanted you to lighten my hair."

"For an interview?" Gretchen said, sitting down.

"Yes, I wanted to look my best for the interview," Hilde said. "Axel is in the SS. He works as a guard at a place called Buchenwald, located southwest of Berlin. He tried to get me a job there, but because I'm a woman it was not so easy. Then he heard about a camp opening just north of Berlin for women only. It's called Ravensbrück. As soon as he heard about it he made immediate arrangements for me to join the SS-Gefolge, which is a Nazi organization for women. I needed to be a member to get the job."

"When are you going on your interview?" Gretchen asked.

"Next week. But I have so much to do that I probably won't get back here until after I've done the interview."

"I do wish you so much luck, Hilde. I really hope you get it."

"I am very excited about this job. You won't believe it, but if I am hired I will earn 185.68 reichsmarks a month. I will have to live there, so they will take deductions for room and board, taxes, and social security. But, even so, I will still earn about 105.00. And let's face it, that's more than double what we earn at the factory, so we are going to both work for a few years and save as much as we can, and then I'll quit and have children."

"Yes, it is a lot more than we earn at the factory. I make seventy-seven reichsmarks a month. And after I pay my bills, it doesn't go very far."

"That's what I've been earning at the factory too. And if I get this job, it will be so nice to have extra money. But Gretchen, the only thing that makes me sad is I that I will have to move, and I won't see you as often as I do now. I will really miss our coffee chats. You are the best friend I've ever had."

"I know, Hilde. But this job will help you to live a better life."

"And from what I hear, the accommodations for the employees at Ravensbrück are very nice. My family was so poor, I've never lived in a nice place. Even before my father walked out on us, we were always struggling to survive. But at least he was around, bringing in some money. Then as soon as he left my mother, she couldn't afford to keep up the rent, so we had to move into that rat-infested flat where I am living now. You know the truth about my mother; everyone knew she was an alcoholic and a whore."

"It's all right, Hilde, you don't have to talk about this. I know how hard it was for you growing up. We've discussed this many times. And it's all right. It's over now," Gretchen said in a soothing tone.

But Hilde went on talking. She was so wrapped up in the misery of her memories that she didn't even hear Gretchen. "I was always so ashamed of my mother. She was hard on me too. Very mean, when I was growing up. She blamed me for my father leaving us."

"I know, and as I have told you many times before, none of this was your fault. You were just a child, Hilde. You did the best you could."

"Then one day, I came home to find her dead from an overdose. She'd taken some kind of drugs. I don't know what she took. But it was horrible, Gretchen, horrible. She was laying on the floor. Oh, I can't tell you how awful it was." Hilde covered her eyes with both hands.

"Shhh, Hilde. It's over. You're safe now," Gretchen said.

"I know, but when I think about my mother and all the terrible things she did, I can't believe what I went through."

Gretchen took Hilde in her arms and hugged her. "Shhh, don't think about the past. It doesn't do any good to dwell on it. Instead, why don't you tell me about your new job? Come on, smile a little, please. And tell me all about it," Gretchen said.

"Well, as you know, with what the factory pays me I haven't been able move out of that terrible place I've been living. So at least I will have a decent place to live if I get this job."

"I understand. If it weren't for my father's savings, I would have to leave my flat. But I am fortunate he lived very frugally and put aside a little bit of money. So far, between what he had saved and what I earn at the factory, I am able to make the rent every month."

"Didn't your father also work as the handyman here, in the building, so he could pay a lesser rent?"

"Yes, he did. My father made a decent living as a professor, but he wanted to save money. He was frugal like that. And so he helped out in the building. After he left for the army, I started to take on small jobs for the other tenants. Like changing light bulbs, small plumbing, and electricity problems." Gretchen smiled.

"You know how to do all of these things?"

"Light bulbs, yes. Plumbing and electricity . . . well . . . let's just say I am learning."

"Your apartment is certainly nicer than my flat. Every time I try to save even a morsel of bread in the cupboard, the rats get it. So I am happy to leave that place."

"Of course you are. I understand. And you deserve to live in a nice place. I was just wondering, how far is this camp, actually? You did say the name was Ravensbrück?"

"Yes, that's the name. It's in a town called Ravensbrück, which is about fifty miles or so north of Berlin, I think. Still, Gretchen, I know that I'll miss you. But I'll come back whenever I can to visit you. And I'll write when I can too. That's if I get the job, of course. But I am hoping that Axel has enough influence to convince the bosses there to give me a chance. I don't have any real skills or any advanced education, as you know. I hope they won't require any special skills. I have to admit, the idea of a good job is so much more exciting than the idea of marrying Axel."

"What? Why?" Gretchen took Hilde's hand. "Is something wrong between you and Axel?"

"Can I be honest? More honest than I have ever been with anyone? I would only tell you this because you're my best friend."

"Of course, you can tell me anything. You know you can."

"I am still not certain that I really want to marry Axel. And I think the problem is that . . . I never really got over Hann. You know that I loved Hann, Gretchen. I guess I still do. I know he never loved me. But I love him."

"I know you liked him a lot. But he was more of a fantasy. If Axel wants to marry you, he is in love with you. That makes him a much better choice, doesn't it?"

Hilde shook her head. Then she said, "He is in love with me. I know he is. And I know that Hann was in love with that Jew bitch, Thea. But I can't help my feelings for Hann. Even though I haven't seen him in a long time, my feelings refuse to go away."

Gretchen understood this better than she wanted to express. When she and Eli had been apart for several years, her feelings for Eli had not diminished. So how could she judge Hilde for holding a torch for Hann? "Maybe you shouldn't rush into marriage. Maybe you're right; maybe you should wait until you find someone who makes you feel the way Hann did. Still, Hilde, it is said that love can develop over time."

"I don't know if this will make sense to you. But I like everything that Axel brings to the marriage. I like his position in the SS. He earns a good living, and when we walk into a restaurant together, he makes a very nice appearance in his well-tailored uniform. He is also very kind to me, and well, I am lonely. My mother and I were never close. So, except for you, I haven't ever felt like I had any family. Would you believe that I have started to really like the idea of having a child. I know, I never wanted one. But as I am getting older and I see women pushing carriages, I wonder if a baby might be the key to happiness."

"Perhaps you will learn to love Axel," Gretchen said, and again the guilt came over her. She liked Hilde, and Hilde was her friend. But she had never felt as close to Hilde as Hilde felt to her. And she was secretly hoping that a husband might occupy more of Hilde's time and bring out a softer side in her.

"I think I will enjoy our life together. I know I will love being invited to galas where there will be high officials from the Nazi Party. And there is no doubt in my mind that Axel will be a good father. We've talked about children. He is pure Aryan, comes from a good pure bloodline. And as you know, that is so important for the future of our fatherland. And I would never have gotten this interview without Axel's influence. I must admit, I am kind of thrilled to be interviewed for such a good paying, steady job. Quite frankly, I'm sick of the factory with its low pay and lack of opportunity to earn more. I feel so unimportant and disposable there. I hope that I am not hurting your feelings."

"My feelings, why?"

"Well, because you work at the factory as well."

"Nonsense. You're absolutely right about the factory. The employees are disposable and the pay is lousy. But it's a job and I am comfortable there. So what is this place where you are going for your interview?"

"Axel described it as a camp for women. I am not sure what exactly that means. But he told me about the pay. And I love that it's lots of money. He also said that there would be plenty of food. Who could complain, right? And besides, if I get the job, I would see him more often. He was happy about that. He said his superiors will allow him to visit me at Ravensbrück. Everything sounds good. Except for how much I will miss you. I'll come home as often as I can. I promise. Besides, once I have been working at this job for a while and I've proved my worth, I could ask my superiors if they would consider hiring you."

"Oh, I don't know. I want to stay here, at my apartment in Berlin. When my father comes home this is where he will return to. I don't want him to come home to an empty house. I'm sure you understand."

"I was hoping that you wouldn't say that." Hilde smiled. "But I kind of assumed you would. I know how you are about your father."

Gretchen smiled. "Yes, well, when he returns he will need me. I think about him every day. And I worry. I keep hoping to hear news from him. So I must wait. But if you're hired, and I know you will be . . ." Gretchen smiled. "You must take the job. It will be good for you. Do you think it's like a women's prison?"

"I'm not sure what it is exactly. I'll see when I get there. All I know is the pay and benefits are good. And Axel says I'll even get real coffee, sometimes."

"I feel so sorry for the poor women in that place."

"Remember, they are enemies of the state. They are getting what they deserve. Anyway, will you miss me, Gretchen?"

"Of course I'll miss you," Gretchen said. She would miss the food that Hilde brought. And she would sometimes even miss the conversations.

There was a loud noise as if something had fallen.

"What was that? It sounded like it came from below. I think I remember that you have a basement. Don't you?" Hilde asked.

Oh my God, Gretchen thought. *Eli or Rebecca must have*

dropped something. "Oh, I'm sure it's nothing. It happens sometimes. It's just rats in the basement." Gretchen's voice was high and shaky.

"Are you sure? Do you want me to go and check?"

Gretchen's heart was pounding out of her chest. "Oh no. You don't want to go down there. Rats bite and they have rabies."

"I would do it for you," Hilde said.

Gretchen forced herself to smile. "You've done enough by bringing me all this wonderful food. How can I ever thank you?" Gretchen tried to hide the fear in her voice. Then in an effort to distract Hilde she added, "Your hair looks wonderful, by the way. It's almost dry. And it looks much lighter than it did when it was wet." She knew she couldn't trust Hilde. But she wanted to believe that somewhere inside Hilde was a good person. She wanted to believe that Hilde only joined the Nazi Party because she wanted to belong to something, to be a part of something. After all, Hilde had always been an outcast. But even as Gretchen tried to rationalize and trivialize Hilde's exuberance for the Nazi Party, she couldn't help but remember what Hilde had done to Thea to punish her because Hann was in love with her.

"No need to thank me. You're my best friend, Gretchen. No one in my entire life has ever been as kind to me." Hilde smiled broadly. Then she got up and walked over to the mirror. "You're right. My hair does look good. I look so Aryan. Like a Valkyrie, like the perfect Nazi woman."

CHAPTER 2

After Hilde left, Gretchen closed the door behind her, leaned against the wall, and took a deep breath. She sighed with relief. *Safe.* She thought. But she couldn't take any chances. She had to be sure. So she ran to the window as Hilde walked out the door of the apartment building and onto the sidewalk. Hilde pulled her coat tighter around her ample waist. The sun had just begun to set as she turned left at the end of the street and started toward home.

Gretchen watched her carefully. Her eyelids were twitching, and her throat felt dry and raw with worry. She wanted to run down to the basement to see Eli and talk to him, to get his advice. But she had to wait; she had to be patient. It was imperative that she be sure that Hilde was gone.

The problem at hand seemed monumental. With Hilde moving out of Berlin they would be losing a large portion of their food source. Gretchen's rations were small, hardly enough for one, let alone three people. If only she and Eli were alone. She longed to fall into Eli's arms and let him cradle her, let him hold her. If only she could lean on him, hear his soft voice in her ear assuring her that everything would be all right. But she knew this would not happen because neither Gretchen nor Eli would ever show their feelings for each other as long as Rebecca, Eli's wife, was present. Even so, just to see him, just to be near him and hear his voice would be a comfort to her.

Gretchen didn't know if Rebecca suspected that she and Eli were attracted to each other. They did their best to deny their feelings or at least to hide them, not only from Rebecca but also from each other. And strangely enough, Rebecca never asked any questions the night following the horrors of Kristallnacht, when Gretchen took them in. If she wondered how Eli and Gretchen knew each other, she never mentioned it. She was always respectful to Gretchen, constantly thanking Gretchen for everything.

If Gretchen's father had not been in the army, she would not have been able to hide Eli and Rebecca. But with him gone, the apartment was hers, and no one could tell her what to do.

Even so, she missed her father terribly. The last letter she had from him had been about the Nazi takeover of Poland. He'd seemed so frightened, and she knew he wished to come home. But his letter made it clear he was unable to. It was heartbreaking for her, each day, wondering if he was safe and not knowing if he was dead or alive.

And to make matters worse, Gretchen was anxious. How were she, Eli, and Rebecca going to acquire enough food to sustain them? Gretchen forced herself to wait for five additional minutes after she saw Hilde disappear around the corner. Once she was certain that Hilde was gone, she jumped up and closed all the curtains. She moved the rug and opened the trapdoor to the basement. She quickly picked up the candle in its holder and lit it. Then after pulling the trapdoor closed after her, Gretchen began to descend the rickety staircase.

The basement was dark, musty, brutally cold, and deadly silent.

"It's me. Is everything all right? I heard a noise down here."

"Yes, I'm sorry. It was me," Eli said as he came out of the shadows, an old blanket covering his shoulders. "I tripped and knocked over my books."

"Hilde was here. She came to see me. She brought us food."

"Oh no! Did she hear the noise?" Rebecca asked, her teeth chattering as she too came into the light of Gretchen's candle. She was covered in several blankets.

"Yes, she heard the noise, but I told her that we had rats in the basement."

"Do you think she believed you?" Eli asked, his voice soft but trembling with concern.

"Yes, I think everything is all right. I don't think she suspects anything. However, we three need to talk. We have a problem," Gretchen said as she placed the candle in it's brass holder in the middle of the cold concrete floor. Then she sat down beside it.

Eli and Rebecca gathered around the candle and sat. "What is it?" Eli asked.

"Hilde is probably going to be leaving Berlin. She has an interview for a job in a little town that's north of here, so she won't be coming by to visit. She brought a bag of food today. But once she moves we are going to have to find a way to survive without the extra food she has been providing."

"Are you sure she'll get the job?" Eli asked.

"I'm fairly certain she will."

"I have an idea. This is something I have been thinking about," Rebecca said. "I have very fair skin, light blonde hair, and blue eyes. If I could get some fake papers, I could get a job."

The marriage between Rebecca and Eli was an arranged marriage. Rebecca had grown up believing that her life's purpose was to serve her husband, to have a family, and to care for her home. When she and Eli wed, she was afraid of displeasing him, so she kept her head down and never spoke her mind. Many couples they knew who were in arranged marriages found love with their spouses. This was not the case for Eli and Rebecca. As life unfolded for both of them, they discovered that, although their feelings for each other were not those of great lovers, they did have a special bond of deep friendship.

Still, when Rebecca was a child, she'd dreamed of finding her own bashert, the man whose soul was the other half of her own soul. She loved the religious story of the twin souls she'd once read. The story said that in the beginning of time, God had divided souls in half, and then sent them to earth where they would occupy bodies and go in search of their other halves. Somewhere, out in the vast and mysterious world, Rebecca believed that her twin soul was searching for her as much as she was for him. So, when she saw the way Eli looked at Gretchen and the way Gretchen's eyes lit up when she gazed at Eli, although she never told anyone, Rebecca knew Gretchen was Eli's bashert. And this she accepted as God's will.

"I don't think it's a good idea for you to go out and get a job, Rebecca. It's just too dangerous," Eli said, shaking his head "If you're caught it would be disastrous."

"But I don't see any other way," Rebecca said. "I insist. I must get work so I can help. But I am going to need papers. And I am assuming that papers will cost money."

"Money, we don't have." Eli rubbed his chin as he thought.

"But as I said before, I don't like the sound of this. It's just too risky. Not only will you be putting yourself in peril, but what about Gretchen? The laws are very clear that Germans must not help Jews in any way."

"So what else can we do?" Gretchen asked, biting her lower lip. "I could try to find another job where I could work at night."

"You work long hours already. I don't see how it would be possible," Eli said. "But I have an idea. I have two teeth that have gold fillings. I can pull the teeth, and we can sell the fillings. They are real gold. They will buy some food. It's not a permanent solution. However, it will help."

"No," both women answered in unison.

"Please, Eli, don't do that," Gretchen said. Her hand went to her throat as she felt the bile rise. "That's not necessary."

"Gretchen is right. You can't do that to yourself. Besides, you could get an infection, and that would be worse for all of us. The very thought of it is horrific. I still think the best thing for all of us would be for me to get a job. If I have papers I can pass as a pure German. I'll be able to get a ration card. Then the three of us can get by on the rations allotted for two people," Rebecca said.

"It might be the only choice we have, Eli," Gretchen said.

"I don't know," Eli said, shaking his head as he gazed down at the floor. Then he continued. "I don't know what to do. I should be taking care of the both of you. Yet I can't. There is nothing I can do for either of you. I feel so helpless."

"Eli . . ." Gretchen said, "don't do this, please. It's not your fault. You're doing the best you can."

Rebecca watched the two of them, but she said nothing.

"Why don't we all sleep on it. We can each give the problem some thought during the night. Perhaps we'll come up with some kind of plan," Rebecca offered.

"Yes, let's do that," Gretchen said.

"All right," Eli agreed.

* * * * *

Once Gretchen was upstairs she carefully covered the trapdoor with the rug. Then she took a quick bath and went to bed. But she couldn't sleep. She lay in bed thinking and shivering from the cold. It was still chilly upstairs even though she'd turned on the gas heater. But it was miserably cold in the basement where there was no heat at all. Poor Eli and Rebecca. She'd given them all the blankets she owned. Gretchen remembered that tonight, when she saw Eli, he had only one blanket across his shoulders. He'd given the rest to Rebecca. That was what she loved about him; he was truly a kind and gentle soul, always putting others needs before his own. *If only I could bring them upstairs and put them in Father's room. They are freezing down there.* But she knew that she dared not. Hilde might return, unannounced, knock on the door, and demand to be allowed in immediately. She'd done this many times before. Or a neighbor might see an extra shadow on the window curtains. Everything was dangerous.

Gretchen tossed and turned, drifting in and out of fitful sleep until it was almost dawn. Then she got out of bed and headed into the bathroom to wash her face and brush her teeth. There on the cabinet, next to the sink, she found an envelope. It was addressed to her. She felt a bolt of fear go through her as she tore it open. A Star of David on a gold chain, fell onto the floor. She picked it up and held it in her hand. Then she swallowed hard and began to read.

"My Dearest Gretchen,

By the time you read this I should be well on my way out of the city. Since I know you as no one else knows you, I can

27

already see how upset you are going to be that I have gone. I am so sorry. The last thing I would ever want to do is hurt you. However, I know that my decision to leave is the best thing I can do. I have given this much thought, and I feel that you and Rebecca will have a better chance of surviving without me. The two of you don't eat much and can probably manage on one share of rations. And although I tried to control my appetite, I know you two were constantly making sacrifices to be sure I always had enough to eat.

I don't want this. My job as a man is to provide for and look after those I love. However, with the way things are, I've been reduced to a pathetic coward hiding in your basement. Let's face it, the Nazis have stripped away my dignity and made me feel like less of a man. I am unable to do anything for either you or Rebecca. All I am is a weight around your neck. I require too much food. And I have little to offer in return. The necklace inside of this letter was a gift to me from my father for my Bar- Mitzva. It is solid gold. I knew if I tried to give it to you, you would have refused to take it. Now you will have no choice. Please, accept it and sell it. Use the money to buy food.

I want you to know how grateful I am to you for taking Rebecca and I in. Rebecca is a good person, with a big heart. I know she cares deeply for you, and even though I believe she has suspicions about you and I, she regards you as a good friend. After all, she and I have never had a real marriage and we both accept that. Together, I believe that you and Rebecca can survive this. Take care of her for me, Gretchen. You are strong and she will need you.

And most importantly, I want you to know that I love you. That I believe that I might have been in love with you from the first day that I saw you in the park. And even though we come from different worlds, I am Jew, and you are not, I am certain beyond a doubt that you are my twin soul. You are the woman that God has destined to be my one and only bashert. I will love you as long as I live and probably even after I have left this life. Carry my love in your heart. Let it nourish you and give you strength when you feel weak. And please, Gretchen, know that wherever you are I am always there with you in spirit.

"If, by some miracle, I should survive, I will find you when this is over. But for now, I must say goodbye.

"Yours forever, Eli."

Gretchen looked at the necklace in her hand and felt the tears begin to form behind her eyes. She wished she could have had an opportunity to talk to him before he ran off. She would have begged him to stay. She would have gotten down on her knees and begged him. The tears flowed down her cheeks. *Oh Eli.*

The sun had not yet peeked through the darkness. If she hurried, she would still have time to speak to Rebecca. Quickly, she took the candle, lit it, and opened the trapdoor. Then she headed downstairs.

CHAPTER 3

Rebecca was sitting cross-legged on the floor covered in blankets and shivering. In one hand she held a piece of paper. In the other, she held Eli's wedding ring. Tears mixed with dirt from the basement floor ran down her face. She unfolded the paper and began to read.

"Dearest Rebecca,

I know I have not been the best husband to you. You certainly deserved better. I am certain that you have been aware of my feelings toward Gretchen. But please know that my love for her started long before I ever met you. You never did anything wrong. It was not your fault that I loved her. You've always been the perfect Jewish wife, kind, loving, and understanding. In my way, I love you too; I always will. You have been a dear and precious friend to me. And I would never want to hurt you. It was just that once I met Gretchen I knew in my heart that she was my bashert. It was not her fault. It just happened. I know you and I know that you would never resent Gretchen for this. Your heart is too good and too pure.

"As I leave here, I pray that all of this with the Nazis will end, and you will find your own bashert. It would give me great joy and peace to know that you were with him.

"I've left you my wedding ring. Please, don't be sentimental; the memories of our friendship will last forever. A ring is just a material object. Please, sell it and buy food. Take care yourself. Take care of Gretchen too. She tries so hard to be brave. But I know that deep within she is terrified. It was beyond generous of her to take us into her home. She has put herself in great danger. However, I know her too, and I am certain that even once I am gone she will not ask you to leave. In fact she will insist that you stay. Stay with her. Be her true friend. I believe that without me around, the two of you will have enough to survive.

"And so I've said everything that I feel. I will always think of you and always care deeply for you.

"Love, your best friend, Eli."

CHAPTER 4

"Rebecca, it's me," Gretchen said as she came down the stairs into the basement

"He's gone," Rebecca said. "Eli is gone. He cut off his payot and left. Look, they're over there on his bed."

"Didn't you try to convince him to say?" Gretchen asked as she glanced over to see the two side curls Eli had worn at his temples, laying on his mattress.

"He left while I was asleep. He left me his wedding ring. Told me to sell it. And he left me a note."

"He left me one too," Gretchen said, "and a necklace."

"His Star of David?"

"Yes."

Rebecca nodded.

There was an eerie silence for several minutes. Then Rebecca said, in small voice, "I suppose I should leave."

More silence. Then Gretchen said, "No, you must not go. You must stay here."

"Eli said you would say that. But let's face the facts: you were hiding us because of your feelings for him. Now that he is no longer here, you don't have to be in danger."

"You knew about my feelings for him?" Gretchen felt her face grow hot.

"I knew. And it hurt me at first. But then I realized that he and I never shared the love that the two of you shared. He loved you long before he and I met. Our marriage never had a chance. You are his bashert."

"He told me that. He used that word."

"I'm sure he did." Rebecca forced a sad smile

"Do you hate me for spoiling your marriage?"

"I could never hate you, Gretchen. You saved our lives. A person can't decide who they are going to love. Love is something that just happens. And it just happened between you and Eli. Someday, I pray that God will send me my own bashert."

"Oh, Rebecca, I'm so sorry for any hurt you felt. I'm so sorry and ashamed of the Nazis for doing this to your people. I am German, but believe me these horrible people are not the Germans I know. The Germans I know are probably afraid to speak up. They are as terrified of the Nazis as we are."

"I know there still have to be good people here in Germany," Rebecca agreed. Then she added, "I'm going to leave tonight."

"You have no where to go," Gretchen protested.

"I'll be all right."

"I insist that you stay. I think your idea of living as an Aryan is a good one. I'll do my best to get papers for you. I'll sell the jewelry to buy the papers if need be. After all, if we sell the gold and use the money for food, within a few months we will be starving again. This way, you'll have a ration card. Then you can pose as my cousin from the country who has come to the city to find work. You'll move upstairs into my father's room," Gretchen said, trying to be as logical as possible while wiping the tears from her cheeks

"What about when your father returns?"

"We'll worry about that when it happens. For now, I think

33

this is a good idea."

"If you think so . . ."

"I do."

CHAPTER 5

Ravensbrück

Hilde pin curled her hair the night before the interview. The bleached-blonde color had turned brassy. *I wish she had been able to make it lighter, a wheat-colored blonde, like Thea's. Still, at least I am a blonde,* she thought as the alarm clock rang much earlier than usual. She jumped out of bed and began getting ready. *This is going to be a life-changing day!*

The weather was miserably cold. However, Hilde was confident that her heavy, tan wool coat and nicely detailed, black mohair dress would not only keep her warm but would also impress her interviewers. She would never have been able to afford clothes of this quality. But she'd found a way of acquiring all the things that she wanted and needed. It was wrapped around the government's strong acceptance of persecution of the Jews, and the idea had come to her quite simply. She'd wanted a handbag when she was younger. It was a beautiful leather bag in the window of a Jewish shop. She'd been admiring it while waiting for a bus. The more she looked at it, the more miserable she was with longing. Then an idea came to her. Hilde could have the handbag, she realized. All she had to do was go into the shop and threaten the shop keeper. Hilde knew that if she went to the authorities and told them that the shopkeeper had tried to rape her, they would take her word over the word of any Jew. So, with confidence, she walked inside. The owner was a kindly, old man with a hump in his back. He asked if he could help her. When Hilde made her threat, rather than fight, he gave her the handbag. And from that day on, she had discovered a way of acquiring anything she wanted in the Jewish sector of town. Using intimidation, she always had the nicest clothes, shoes, handbags, and even food. And that was how she was able to bring special food to share with Gretchen. *The things I get from the Jews should be mine anyway. After all, I'm a true Aryan, and all of these things were stolen from the Germans by the devious Jews. Just like Hitler said. So I have every right to take back what is rightfully mine. Those slippery Jews are always stealing from us, just like Thea tried to steal my boyfriend. It's my responsibility to make sure they don't get away with this.*

Before she left the house, Hilde rummaged through her mother's jewelry box and found a strand of fake pearls which she hung around her neck. *I should see about getting myself some real pearls. I'll have to remember to make a trip to see Gottlieb, the kike jeweler, when I get back. No reason to be wearing fakes when I could easily make them give me a strand of real, good quality pearls. It's a shame, really, that the Gestapo is taking all the Jews away. Once they are all gone, how will I get the things I need? Well, there's another reason enough to be excited about this job.*

She took a tube of red lipstick out of her handbag and smeared a dab on each cheek. After she rubbed the lipstick into her skin until it was merely a stain, she dabbed it on her lips. After a satisfying glance in the mirror, she donned her wool coat and left the house to take the train heading north to Ravensbrück.

As the train rattled along the track, Hilde's thoughts turned to the two men who had most influenced her life, Axel and Hann. She looked out at the snow-covered landscape and thought about Axel, a man who loved her but whose love she could not fully return because she was still obsessed with Hann, a man who didn't want anything to do with her. And then she thought of Hann, and she burned with that old familiar yearning. Why couldn't Hann love her the way Axel did? If only he could, then her life would be perfect.

Axel was the perfect boyfriend, considerate, kind, and affectionate. But he wasn't handsome or exciting like Hann. And he didn't have that romantic, heroic way about him, the way Hann did. Hann's crazy, obsessive love for Thea, a girl who Hilde knew from the Bund, had caused her to hate and eventually destroy Thea. But it had also sparked a deep and unsatisfied need in her. This undying love was what she wanted Hann to feel for her.

She'd tried everything she could to win him. Oh, how she'd tried to make him love her. Then when she could see no way to come between Thea and Hann, her jealousy swallowed her up, and she invented lies and spread them to destroy Thea's reputation in Berlin. But it didn't affect Hann. Even though all of their friends' parents turned on Thea's family because of the rumors that Hilde started about Thea being half Jewish, due to her mother's affair with the Jewish doctor in town, Hann still loved Thea. He would have gone against the whole neighborhood and married her. He told Hilde as much, and it broke her heart to hear it. But as fate had it, Hann never had the chance.

Thea's family was ruined by the gossip. Her father walked out on her mother. Then one night, just a few days later, Thea and her mother left Berlin. No one knew where they went. Once they were gone, Hilde had tried again to seduce Hann. But he had no interest in her. She tried to befriend him, tried to be there for him to lean on. Hann was too brokenhearted over Thea to give her the time of day. Finally, Hilde heard that he left Berlin to take a job working on the autobahn in Frankfurt. Still, Hilde didn't give up. She wrote him several letters, but he never answered, and she knew it was because he had never gotten over Thea.

Hilde could not reach Hann, but she knew that her dream man was a man as handsome as Hann who would love her as strongly as Hann loved Thea. When she met Axel, even though he was not the love of her life, she felt they were destined to be together. They were both very strong Nazi Party members. He, like her, was from a poor family. His father had served in the Great War, returning from fighting without physical scars, but the memory of death and destruction he had seen on the front lines branded into his soul.

Axel's father didn't sleep well, and he would often awaken screaming and crying in the night. When he was a child, Axel lived in constant fear. He felt like a tender zebra colt hiding just feet away from the jaws of a large hungry lion. Sometimes his father would beat his mother and then apologize while weeping on his knees, on the kitchen floor. Young Axel couldn't protect his mother or his younger brother. He came to grow a hatred for his father.

As soon as he was old enough, he ran away from home to find work in the city. He'd gotten a job with the Nazi Party by begging and pledging his devotion to Hitler and the fatherland. And then by working very hard, he set out to prove himself. Slowly, Axel had climbed up the ladder until he landed a position in the SS. And as he and Hilde dated more and grew closer, he shared all the secrets of his past with her.

It took a cigarette and a full glass of schnapps for Hilde to open up and tell Axel about her own terrible family background. With her face as calm as a poker player but her stomach rumbling in anger and fear, she explained about how her father had left her mother for a younger woman. And how her mother had treated her like dirt. Hilde told him that her mother would tell her she was an ugly child, and she was only deserving of a life of misery. Hilde still did not shed a single tear as she told him of the terrible beatings she endured at her mother's hand. Axel's eyes were full of sympathy. He held her hand as she told him that her mother was an alcoholic and a prostitute. He believed every word that Hilde said.

The more she lied, the more the lies began to take on a life of their own, and Hilde started to believe them. Once she was convinced that her own stories were true, she felt justified in murdering her mother. The murder, she decided, she would keep secret. She had never shared it with anyone. She would not even share it with Axel. As she spoke of her past to him, deep in her gut, Hilde relived every vile moment of her childhood. Some of it was true and some she had invented, but she could no longer remember what was fact and what was made up. Her face and eyes remained emotionless. She stared at Axel as if she were telling the story not of herself but of someone else's life.

However, Axel did not judge her. He seemed to understand her, and as he gently squeezed both of her hands in his, he said, "I love you. We are two of a kind. You are the first person I've ever met who I feel close to. Marry me, Hilde, and I promise you, you will have a life that is good and filled with love. I will prove to you that your mother was wrong when she said you were undeserving of love. I earn a good living. Together, you and I can build a strong German home filled with happy children, who will enjoy all the fruits of our efforts, as we work on creating our new and perfect Germany."

She'd smiled at him. The more he spoke, the more she knew he was right for her. But she thought, if only he were handsome like Hann . . . Hann, tall and strong, with his blond hair, chiseled face, and muscular body. If only . . . Axel was not a handsome man. He was only five feet seven inches, just two inches taller than Hilde, and heavyset like she was. His hair was light brown, almost the same color as hers had been before she'd started bleaching it. And he wore thick glasses. Except for the glasses, they could have been twin brother and sister. Still, she knew he was smitten with her. In her entire life, no man had ever been mad about her, so Hilde buried her feelings for Hann even deeper within her private thoughts and accepted Axel's proposal. Neither she nor Axel had any family they would choose to invite to a wedding. So it was decided they would wait until they had some substantial savings. Then they would invite a few close friends to see them say their vows in a civil ceremony.

It was only a short walk from the Ravensbrück train station to Ravensbrück camp. While Hilde had been on the train the temperature had dropped and it was even colder. The streets and sidewalks were covered in ice, making her glad she'd chosen to wear low-heeled, sensible shoes. Pulling her coat tighter around her body, Hilde made her way through the small town toward the outskirts. Before she left home, Axel had explained that the camp was being erected behind what would look to her like a forest. So she was not surprised by the dense trees and foliage surrounding the building.

When she arrived at the entrance to Ravensbrück, she was surprised to see that there was a wall surrounding it that was topped with barbed wire. *This is a prison,* she realized, feeling a bit afraid that there might be some dangerous criminals inside. For a moment she was angry with Axel for finding her a job where she might be in danger, and she thought about turning around and going back home. But then she thought *I've come all this way. I might as well go on the interview. I don't have to accept the job, if I don't want to.*

Hilde was vacillating between turning around to go back home and going forward, when a young female guard wearing a gray wool skirt, matching jacket, and a white blouse appeared at the gate. She was covered with a heavy, black cape. Hilde eyed her quickly and thought she looked very fashionable in her tailored uniform.

"Who are you, and what do you want here?" the woman asked.

"My name is Hilde Dusel. I am here for an interview for a job."

"Hilde Dusel?"

"Yes, Axel Scholtz arranged an interview for me here for a job."

"Wait here," the female guard said. Then she turned and walked away.

A cold wind whipped out of the north, slapping Hilde across her face and sending a chill through her entire body. She was suddenly frightened, but she had no idea why. For a second, it felt like the temperature dropped at least ten degrees. Her entire body shivered. Something was odd and intimidating about the woman guard with her smart-looking uniform. *Perhaps I am feeling outclassed,* Hilde thought. *I've always felt outclassed. Maybe, I don't belong here.* But she couldn't leave. Her feet felt as if they'd been glued to the ground, too heavy to lift. And before she could force herself to move, the female guard had returned.

"Hilde Dusel," the guard said in a stern voice, "come with me."

CHAPTER 6

Hilde followed the woman. They walked past rows and rows of buildings that looked like long, rectangular houses. And although it was unnervingly cold, there were coatless men in striped uniforms working outside. They were doing construction throughout the entire area. Hilde only had a few moments to observe them before the guard led her through a door into a large building and then down a long corridor.

"Sit," the guard said, indicating a row of chairs, then she walked away.

A half hour passed before a man wearing a clean, pressed SS uniform walked over to Hilde.

"Good morning," he said, his voice soft and his high German impeccable. "I'm Commandant Gunther Tamaschke. Welcome to Ravensbrück. You're Hilde Dusel, am I correct?"

"Yes." She smiled shyly. Even though he was soft spoken, Tamaschke was an intimidating man.

"Come into my office," he said. She followed him into a beautifully decorated room, with a hand-carved wooden desk, a plush sofa, several matching chairs, and a large picture of the führer on the wall. As she stood in this man's finely decorated office, Hilde felt a strong wave of inferiority. As she observed all the fine things, she was reminded of growing up in poverty. The man seemed so well educated. Something she was not.

"Your fiancé spoke quite highly of you," Tamaschke said, tapping a pencil on his desk. "He thinks you have what it takes to work under the SS. What do you think? Do you think so?"

"Yes, Herr Commandant. I believe I do," she stammered.

"Are you of pure German blood? No unsavory ancestors in the mix that we might find if we start digging? A dirty Jew, or a Jehovah's Witness? A filthy Gypsy, perhaps?"

"No, nothing like that. I am pure."

"I didn't think so. Axel would never have recommended you if there were a problem. And, frankly, you seem to be perfect for the job. But, of course, we must run the customary background check. However, don't worry yourself too much. It's routine." He smiled a half smile, and she noticed that one of his eyes seemed to drift.

Hilde nodded. The commandant was not an attractive man. His face was full, jowls hung from his cheeks. His eyes were small, dark, and deep set. His face was not chiseled like a Nordic god, as was the Aryan ideal. But his power gave him an air of authority that she found intriguing. Then he turned his gaze directly on her, and she felt her blood go cold. *I have nothing to hide. Why am I afraid of him?* she wondered. Then she stammered, "Of course, I understand."

"Well, I'll see to it that all of that messy paperwork is taken care of as soon as possible." He gave her a quick smile then walked over to the window and glanced outside. "Cold out there," he said then added, "As you can see, we are under construction. Those men out there are slave laborers from Sachsenhausen. They're lazy and slow, but at least we don't have to pay them anything. But, unfortunately, they take their time in finishing a job. Therefore, I don't expect the camp to

43

be open until May or June. So, if all checks out all right, that is when you will start working."

"Excuse me, Herr Commandant. But is this a prison?"

"It will be a prison camp, yes; that is correct. It is to be the first camp exclusively for women. For female enemies of the Reich, political prisoners, thieves, communists, Roma, Jews. A collection of the earth's most abhorrent women. Quite a miserable crowd, don't you think?" His voice was strong and authoritative. But now he was smiling at her in a way that made Hilde feel like she was a part of the staff already. Hilde was in awe of him. Her father had run out on her and her mother when Hilde was young. And she'd always longed for a father. This man, even though there was something under his calm surface that she found a little frightening, had the potential to be the powerful and respected father figure she'd always wished for. If he were her father, people would look at her as a force to be reckoned with. At that moment, Hilde decided that, if she could find a way to prove herself worthy, the staff at Ravensbrück might become the family she'd never had. And although this man's lips were almost always curved into a scowl when he smiled at her she felt included, as if like he liked and accepted her.

She nodded. "Yes."

"They certainly are." He smiled again, but only half of his mouth curved, the other half remaining downcast. Then he went on to say, "So I must ask you once more, do you think you have a strong and firm hand, strong enough to handle prison inmates? They can be quite manipulative. You will find that they don't appreciate that we are giving them food and shelter. Instead, they will try to make you pity them, so you will let them escape or give them more than they deserve. Extra food, that sort of thing. However, it is your job to make sure that they do not manipulate you or escape, at any cost.

Do you understand me?"

"Yes." She nodded again.

"And no matter what happens, you must always remember that these women you will be guarding are our enemies. They oppose the Reich, and they stand in the way of our vision of a better Germany. Especially the Jews. You will find that the Jews are the most manipulative of all. We intend to bring their children with them to the camp. I assume many of them will tell you that the children need your help. Don't believe them; they want to make you soft. You must never trust them. It is imperative to your work for the fatherland that you never, never allow them to get close to you or to get under your skin."

"I will do as you instruct, Herr Commandant."

"That's what I like to hear. You can go now. After you have passed the background check, you will receive a letter telling you when to report to work."

"Thank you, and I will look forward to hearing from you."

"Very good. I'll have Helga show you out."

CHAPTER 7

Berlin

When Hilde returned to Berlin, she stopped at a café where she planned to have an early dinner. But before she placed her order, she took the most recent letter she'd received from Axel out of her purse and went to call him on the public pay phone.

It took a while for the woman who answered to find Axel. But Hilde waited and continued to drop coins in the phone until finally he came on the line.

"Axel?"

"Hilde! How are you?"

"Very good."

"The interview?"

"I just got back."

"So? Tell me? How did it go?"

She told him all about the interview in detail.

"And once my background check is completed, I will receive a letter with my starting date."

"So you got the job?"

"As long as my purity check comes back perfect, yes, I think I did."

"And, of course, it will."

"Of course," she said.

"That's wonderful news. We must celebrate. Why don't you make arrangements to come here and see me? You'll have some time before you start your new job. Spend a couple of days? I miss you terribly," Axel said.

"I'm still working at the factory."

"Take the time off. Who cares now that you have this new job. The new job pays twice as much anyway."

"Well, I agree. But until I start at Ravensbrück, I will stay at my current job and earn as much as possible. But I will ask nicely if I can take a little time off to come and see you."

"That's my girl. Very smart. We will need every penny to start our lives, once we are married."

"If I come to see you, where would I stay?"

"With me, of course, silly. I have a roommate, but I will ask him if he can find some other accommodation while you're here."

"But don't you have to work?"

"Of course, but I won't take any night watch while you're here. I'll spend every night with you, adoring you."

"It has been a while . . ." Hilde said, wishing she were as enthusiastic as he was about spending the night with him.

"Too long," Axel whispered. "I think about you every day. I want to hold you in my arms. I long to kiss your lips again. Hilde, I yearn to feel myself inside of you . . ."

"Axel!" She felt her face turn hot. She was in the middle of a crowded café, and although no one else could hear her conversation, she felt exposed.

"Am I embarrassing you?"

"Yes, actually, a little."

He laughed. "We are engaged. We are in love. No need to feel ashamed."

"Yes, well, I have never talked about it so openly."

He laughed again. "How soon can you take off a few days from work?"

"I don't know. I'll see if they will allow me to take off in a couple of weeks."

"Talk to your boss and let me know. Then I'll make all the arrangements."

"I will. I'll call you as soon as I have an idea if and when I can come."

"Good! And you'll get a chance to see what working at a camp is like. I assume Ravensbrück won't be much different from Buchenwald."

"Is it hard work?"

"Sometimes. It's a bit dirty; the Jews are filthy people by nature. We fight lice here all the time. And controlling them can get messy, if you know what I mean. It's important that they never see a guard as weak. We must maintain our authority and keep them afraid all the time. Some of the men like it. They enjoy the power. For me, it's just a job. I don't much care for the Jews, anyway. But on the bright side, there is plenty to eat and drink. And we do have fun. Once the prisoners are secured away for the night, all of us guards have a few drinks and a few laughs. It's not bad, not really."

"It doesn't sound bad."

"And, of course, waking up beside you every day, my love, will be the most pleasant thing I will have experienced in a long time."

The operator broke into the call asking for more money.

"There's the operator. I don't have any more change. I'd better hang up. But I'll be in touch as soon as I have any news," she said.

"Goodbye and dream of me until we are together," Axel said.

Hilde hung up the phone and sat down at a table in the back of the café.

"Can I help you?" A young, pretty waitress with long blonde braids asked.

"Yes, I'd like an order of potato pancakes, please."

"Yes, Fräulein. Right away."

"Please make them as crispy as you can."

"Of course."

Hilde watched the sun set as she ate. *I am happy about the job. But it's bittersweet. I'll miss Gretchen terribly.*

CHAPTER 8

Gretchen's Apartment, Berlin

Rebecca stayed down in the cellar during the day. It was dark, and candles were hard to come by, so they used them sparingly. Many evenings Gretchen went downstairs to share a late dinner with Rebecca. However, they didn't want to move Rebecca upstairs until she had papers.

Gretchen brought the gold ring and necklace that Eli had left for her and Rebecca, to a man who she recalled had come to see her father right after he returned from being arrested. It was late at night when the man had come to her home. Her father thought Gretchen was asleep, so he never bothered to close the door to her bedroom. She wasn't able to hear the entire conversation, but she had listened as closely as she could and had learned that the man's name was Otto Brant. He had come to ask her father to join him in the Resistance. Karl Schmidt, Gretchen's father, had refused, using the excuse that he was afraid for his daughter. However, he wished Brant luck and promised never to reveal anything about his visit. Before Brant left, Gretchen had heard him tell her father that if he ever changed his mind he could find Brant at the tailor shop. "Look at you, Karl. They beat the living hell out of you. Your nose is broken. You've got a gash on your head the size of a canyon. Do you think they are done with you?"

"I don't know, Brant. But I can't do anything. I can't put my little girl at risk. I am going to follow my brother-in-law's suggestion and join the army. That's all I can do."

"If you change your mind, just go to the tailor shop and ask for me, Karl."

So when Gretchen needed papers for Rebecca, she remembered the conversation, and she went to find Otto Brant. At first, he was reluctant to speak to her. He denied everything. He denied that he was part of the Resistance. He denied the visit with her father. He firmly denied all of it. But when Gretchen began to cry and told him that she was hiding a Jewish woman in her cellar, the short, slender Brant took a deep breath and invited Gretchen to follow him into the back room. The room smelled of leather. Old shoes, boots, handbags, and belts lay scattered around the room.

"Sit," Brant said, and Gretchen sat. "Where is your father?"

She told him how her father had left for the army. He had done it because he thought it would help if he proved his allegiance to the party. "But he hates the party. You know that. You saw what they did to him when he tried to help the Jewish professors at the university where he worked."

"Yes, I saw him. They beat him badly. But I've seen them do worse."

"I'm sure. That's why I need your help."

"Professor Schmidt, a solider? Oh!" He sighed, changing the subject. "Poor Karl. Have you heard from him?"

"Once, last year. But not since."

"And, of course, you know that Hitler has his claws in Austria and in Poland."

"Yes, I know. He is a horrible man. He has stolen the rights from the Jews and anyone else he doesn't think is fit to live.

And . . . and . . . he is the reason my poor father is off, trying to be a soldier." She felt tears beginning to form in her eyes. "Well." She straightened her back, willing herself not to cry anymore. "I didn't come here for your sympathy. I came for your help."

"What do you want?" Brant asked.

"I told you I am hiding a young woman in my cellar. Two people can't survive on the rations of one. Especially with the rations being as meager as they are. Anyway, the Jewish woman who I am hiding is blonde and looks very Aryan. So we've decided to have papers made for her, so she can get a job and a ration card. I need false papers. Can you help me?"

"Papers? This is dangerous business." Brant rubbed his chin.

"Dying of starvation isn't much less dangerous, is it?" Gretchen asked in a sarcastic tone.

"You have your father's wit." Brant smiled at her.

"Well, can you help us? Will you help us?"

"Perhaps."

"I can pay you," Gretchen said. "I have a gold ring and a gold necklace.

A gentle smile came over Brant's face. 'I don't want your money," he said. "Of course, you do realize that this woman, the one who you want the papers for, will be taking an enormous risk."

"I do. She does too," Gretchen said.

Brant nodded. "I'll do what I can," he said and got up, showing Gretchen to the door.

Weeks passed with no word from Brant. Gretchen was afraid that he'd been caught. There was nothing else they could do, so she and Rebecca did the best they could to survive on Gretchen's measly rations and whatever was left of the food Hilde had given Gretchen as gifts. It wasn't much, but at least they were alive. And then one day, almost a full month after Gretchen's meeting with Brant, there was a knock on the door to her flat. She was just returning from work and wasn't expecting anyone. A quick bolt of fear shot through her. In the back of her mind, she was always afraid that they'd been caught. But when she opened the door, it was Otto Brandt.

"Can I come in?" he asked.

She nodded. "Yes of course. Sit down, please. Let me make you a cup of tea."

"No, thank you," he said. He sat down on a chair by the kitchen table and took several folded documents out of the breast pocket of his coat. "These papers belonged to a woman who lived in Bamberg, a small village in Bavaria. She died quietly in her home at twenty-six. From what I understand, she was a sickly girl and rarely left the house. Because she almost never went outside, no one really knew her in the neighborhood. After her death, her family desperately needed money so they sold these papers."

Gretchen took the papers and read the name aloud. "Eva Teichmann."

"Yes. That's your Jewish friend's new name," Otto Brant said.

"Thank you," Gretchen said, gripping the papers tightly. "You have no idea what this means to us. I can never express the extent of my gratitude in words."

Otto nodded. "I did this as a favor to your father. He was a good friend of mine. I knew him for many years. He wasn't much of a resistant, always went with the flow. But he was a good man, a quiet man. Always stayed out of trouble."

"Are you sure I can't get you a cup of tea or ersatz coffee?" Gretchen asked.

"No, thank you again, but I must be going."

And then Otto left.

Two days later, Rebecca went to the factory where Gretchen was employed to apply for work. She filled out her employment application under the name of Eva Teichmann. There were no openings, but the boss promised to keep her application on hand. Now, two weeks had passed since Brant had brought the papers and Rebecca still had no job. It had been over a month since Hilde's last visit and all the food gifts she'd given Gretchen were gone. There was no extra money to purchase food on the black market. Gretchen and Rebecca talked things over and agreed that Rebecca must apply for her ration card. But they wished they could wait until she had found work. They were still afraid of Rebecca being discovered at the ration office where they might ask a lot of questions. It was difficult enough allowing Rebecca to go out and apply for work, hoping all the while that no one suspected the papers of being false.

The night before Rebecca went to the factory, they ate the two last slices of bread and completely fabricated a story for Rebecca to use when anyone asked questions.

"You will be Eva from now on," Gretchen said. "Even in the apartment, when we are talking, I will call you Eva. That will help you get used to the name."

Gretchen described a christening. She made Eva memorize the steps. Then they found the name of a church in Bavaria where, if anyone asked, Eva would say she had been christened. It all sounded plausible. But if anything went wrong, Rebecca would be arrested. And because she had already said she was staying with Gretchen, the Gestapo would want to speak with Gretchen too. Both of them could easily end up in police custody. It was all an overwhelmingly terrifying plan. And because they were too afraid to go forward, they kept putting it off.

Then one night Eva was upstairs having dinner with Gretchen when there was a knock on the door.

"Who is it? Who's there?" Gretchen asked in a small voice as she quickly collected the plates off the table. Rebecca ran into the back bedroom and hid in the closet

"It's me Gretch. Hilde!"

Gretchen sighed with relief and opened the door. "Come in! It's been a while. How did the interview go?" she asked, trying to sound calm.

"I have wonderful news. I passed the purity test and I got the job! And I just got back from a visit with my boyfriend at his job at Buchenwald.

"I am so glad you got the job. How was your visit with Axel?"

"It was good."

"What was it like at Ravensbrück?"

"It's still not completely finished. But it looks like it's going to be a good job. And look, I brought a half of a loaf of bread and some real butter for us to share. Are you hungry?"

CHAPTER 9

April, Berlin

Hilde turned the key in the lock of her apartment and opened the door.

Before she left him at Buchenwald, Axel had given her a small bag of real coffee and two sweet rolls to take home with her. She took them out of her handbag and laid them on the table. Then she put up a pot of water to brew the coffee. Hilde plopped down while she waited for the water to boil and lit a cigarette. The Nazi Party made it clear that they found it unacceptable for women to smoke. However, she had tried to quit and was unable to. Smoking calmed her nerves. As she let the soothing hot smoke fill her lungs, she leaned back in her chair and allowed her mind to drift.

She thought about the trip she'd just made to see Axel at his job. She had no doubt that Axel was in love with her. The visit with him had more than confirmed that. However, it had also confirmed to her that she was less than in love with him. He was kind and generous and certainly affectionate. And she had to admit he was pretty good in bed. But he wasn't the kind of man she'd always dreamed she would marry. Hilde had always wanted a man who would make her the envy of every other woman. The kind of man who turned heads just by walking into a room. Perhaps it was because she'd always spent her life in the background, reminded by her mother that she was ugly and should not expect much. Maybe that was why she'd always dreamed of having a man who was movie-star handsome, someone considered too good for her. Still, even though she was not in love with Axel, she was logical and practical enough to accept that marriage to Axel was a good choice. And that ugly, little voice of her mother's that sometimes came into her head, told her that he was the best a girl like her could do. That voice made her fearful that if she didn't marry Axel, she would end up alone. So, although she wasn't ecstatic about the relationship, she would go through with the marriage.

Taking a deep breath, Hilde let out a sigh. The water was boiling. She stood up and began to brew the coffee.

Her thoughts turned to Axel's job. She was surprised how unrestrained the guards were in the camp. Buchenwald was no paradise, by any means. It was a dirty, smelly place, filled with rats, lice, and disease. But Axel was right when he said the guards were treated well, and they had absolute power. The guards had plenty to eat and decent living quarters. The prisoners were controlled through fear and violence. And there were no repercussions for punishing a prisoner with or without reason. She wondered with excitement and awe if she would have the same power at Ravensbrück or if the guards would be required to be softer on the prisoners because they were women. Most her visit with Axel she'd spent in the guards quarters.

One day she went to work with Axel. She was watching him shuffle the prisoners out to their work details. One male prisoner, who was moving too slowly on his way to work at the quarries, caught the attention of Henry, one of the guards.

She'd met Henry the night before at dinner, and he seemed to be a rather nice fellow. He'd told her about his parents and his brother. He even made jokes that made everyone at the table laugh. But this man who was shuffling the prisoners showed her a different side of Henry. There was no trace of the humor she'd seen in his eyes the night before. His face was like a mask, expressionless. But his voice was stern, empty, devoid of human emotion, and merciless. He had taken on the persona of a ruler. She would have enjoyed feeling such power.

"Move faster," Henry ordered the prisoner.

The prisoner was all skin and bones. He looked like a walking skeleton in his gray-striped uniform, which hung off his body. His bald head was half covered with a gray-striped hat, and his back was bent.

"Didn't you hear me, Jew pig? I said move faster," Henry ordered again.

The prisoner tried to follow Henry's orders but he couldn't. His legs were bent up, and his body looked like the figure of a broken marionette.

Once more, Henry spoke to the prisoner. He did not raise his voice; he did not get angry. But even from where Hilde stood she could see the prisoner shiver. Then Henry glanced over at Axel and shook his head. "Lazy, aren't they?" Henry said.

Axel didn't have a chance to answer before Henry hit the prisoner in the back of his head with the rifle butt. Blood poured out instantly, and the prisoner fell, silent, motionless. Another man in the same gray prison uniform came to help the prisoner who lay on the ground. Henry glared at the man and threatened to hit him too. So he stood up and walked along with the other poor souls in their gray-striped uniforms. The man who'd been hit lay on his belly in a pool of blood.

"I think he's dead," Hilde whispered to Axel. "Will Henry get in trouble?"

"No, there are no repercussions for killing a prisoner. They're only subhumans, after all. And it's one less mouth sucking on the tit of the fatherland."

The blood continued to run from the man's head, covering the ground. Hilde felt excited about the idea of belonging to a group of powerful guards. For the first time in her life people had better show her respect.

"Let's go," she told Axel. "This has made me so hot, that I want you now," she whispered.

He smiled.

The power, the blood, the very idea that soon she could be a controlling force made her feel heady.

"Henry, Hilde forgot something in my room. We're going to go back."

"Yes, of course. You two go on," Henry said. "I'll take care of this. Hilde will only be here a short time. You two lovebirds should enjoy your time together." He winked.

"Thank you, my friend," Axel said to Henry.

"Of course," he responded with a broad smile.

"Come, Hilde," Axel said. Then he put his arm around her shoulder, leading her back to his bed.

When they arrived at Axel's room, Hilde pulled off his pants and mounted him.

"Does that happen often?" she asked.

"What?" Axel asked.

"You know, do the guards kill the prisoners like that very often?"

"It happens sometimes."

"And no one ever gets in trouble?" she asked in awe as she rode him.

"No one ever gets in trouble. WE are like Nordic gods here.

Aryan Gods."

"Oh." She sighed with pleasure.

"And we get paid. Besides, if you're good at it there is plenty of potential for promotion. You could end up earning even more money. You would like that, wouldn't you?"

She nodded. "Yes, of course. I would love this job."

The wonderful fragrance of freshly brewed coffee filled the kitchen in her apartment, bringing Hilde back to the present moment. She got up and poured herself a cup of the steaming black liquid. There was no sugar. She'd used every single drop before she left to visit with Axel. But she did have the sweet buns that she'd brought back with her from Buchenwald. She took them out of the cloth she'd wrapped them in. *Slightly stale,* she thought. Then she took a bite. It was a little stale, but stale or not it was delicious.

After Hilde finished both of the sweet rolls she went to the bathroom to take a bath before bed. She undressed as she ran the hot water to fill the bathtub. She thought about Gretchen's question, What was it like in Ravensbrück? *It was empowering and exciting. I wonder if I will be permitted to be as powerful as the guards at Buchenwald. Could there possibly be a job where I would be allowed to make women bow to me, where I could make them do whatever I ask?* She smiled. *I've been at the bottom of the ladder all of my life. It's my turn to shine now.* As she reached up and caressed her breast she caught a glimpse of her naked body in the mirror. At first she was repulsed, but then her own reflection disappeared, and in its place stood a Valkyrie. Hilde was no longer a doughy, fat, and shapeless girl with orange-gold hair. In the mirror she saw her reflection as a tall, slender, silver blonde with striking blue eyes the color of sapphires. The Valkyrie sat upon a white stallion that had a long, full mane.

I'm very excited for our future, the Valkyrie said.

"You mean the job?"

Of course I mean the job. The Valkyrie smiled.

"Do you think we will be able to command that kind of power? Do you think the prisoners will do what we say? Sometimes I am secretly afraid that I am weak."

Alone, you are weak, Hilde. But together we are invincible. After all, when we had to get rid of your mother, we did what we had to do, didn't we?

"Yes, we killed her together. But I would not have had the courage without you," Hilde responded to the imaginary image in the mirror.

And then I must say, we were brilliant at convincing everyone, the neighbors, the police, even Gretchen, that your bitch of a mother was a prostitute and an alcoholic who committed suicide, leaving you, her poor innocent daughter, to fend for yourself. I must admit I was quite proud of how taken in they all were with our story.

"You went away for a while. Every time I went to the mirror and called for you, you didn't come. Promise me you won't go away again," Hilde said. "I'll need you once I start this job."

How can I go away, when you and I are one.

CHAPTER 10

The following day, Rebecca took a bath and then braided her long, wheat-colored hair. Then she put on one of Gretchen's dresses.

"I'm going to find work. I'm determined," she said, trying to muster a smile.

"All right, Eva," Gretchen said, biting her lower lip. "I don't suppose we can put this off any longer." The name Eva sounded strange to her. "Don't forget everything we talked about: the church, the christening, all of it, all right?"

Rebecca took Gretchen's hand and squeezed it. "Yes, I'll remember everything. And I am Eva now."

"Yes, Eva. And please, do be careful when you are out today." Gretchen felt her body tremble with nervousness.

"I will. Of course I will." The two women hugged like sisters, then Eva took her Aryan papers and left.

Gretchen didn't have to be at work until the afternoon shift, so there was no point in getting ready this early. Her stomach growled with hunger, and she would have truly enjoyed eating a piece of the bread that Hilde had left the night before. But there were only three thick slices in the cupboard, so she decided against it. She would save it for this evening, when she could share it with Eva.

The teapot let out a shrill whistle. Gretchen got up to pour herself another cup of weak tea to fill her empty stomach, when there was a knock at the door.

"I have a letter here for Gretchen Schmidt!" a teenage boy called through the door.

Gretchen quickly grabbed a coin from the kitchen jar. Her hands were trembling. What if this was a letter telling her the news that she dreaded receiving every day. What if this was the letter that told her that her father was dead. There was no one else who would be writing to her. A wave of nausea came over her as she opened the door and handed the boy the coin. Her fingers felt cold and disconnected from her body as she took the envelope.

The boy left.

But Gretchen felt a wave of relief come over her, and tears fell from her eyes when she saw her father's handwriting on the front of the envelope. *He's alive,* she thought. *No matter what else this letter has to say to me, at least I know he is alive.*

"Dearest Gretchen,

I hope my letter finds you well. I am sorry I haven't written very often, but I have been unable to do so. I have not been in one place for very long. They move us around a great deal, and I am forbidden to disclose our location. I'm afraid that as much as I would like to tell you all about how my days are spent, I cannot. However, please know that I am all right. I think of you constantly. And please know that I miss you and love you. I can't wait until the day when I return home and see your bright smile again. Until then, take care of yourself, my dear daughter. Please, stay safe.

"Your loving father."

Gretchen folded the letter. She had a sudden desperate longing to see Eli, to tell him about the letter. Eli knew that she had been terribly worried about her father. But this letter meant she could put some of her fears to rest. Still, in the back of her mind was the constant terror that at any time he might be killed. She was overcome with emotions and desperate to lay in the arms of the man she loved. But he was gone, and she had no idea where he was or even if he was still alive.

CHAPTER 11

Eva walked through downtown Berlin. She was both afraid and exhilarated. It had been a long time since she had been outside, alone and free. The sun cast a golden light on the sidewalk. Automobiles honked as they sped by. People rushed to their destinations. She squeezed her handbag, knowing that her Aryan papers were inside. She tried to feel confident about the papers, which looked authentic, but she was still a little uneasy. Everything should be perfect. But there was always a chance of something going wrong.

Men in business suits and various Nazi uniforms smiled at her flirtatiously. Eva didn't return their smiles. Instead, she tried to appear poised, as if she knew where she was going. Each time a man whistled at her, it struck terror in her heart, and she walked a little faster. Then she passed a candy store and caught a glimpse of her reflection in the window. At first, it shocked her. *I am not wearing the modest clothing of a Hasidic wife. My head is uncovered, my hair is flowing and blonde. And this dress I've borrowed from Gretchen shows off the curve of my collarbone. I am wearing lipstick and rouge. I hardly recognize myself. But, right now, I am very thankful that when Eli and I were first married he didn't insist that I keep my hair shaved. He was satisfied for me to keep my head covered in public. Anyway, it's a good thing that I have long, blonde hair; it helps me look like I belong. And I have to admit, I do look like an Aryan German woman. There is no trace of Rebecca, the son of a rebbe's wife, in my appearance. And even though I am proud to be a Jew, given the circumstances, that's good.*

Eva stopped in front of the candy store and went inside. The shop smelled of caramel and chocolate. *How do they get these things? I haven't even smelled chocolate since I was a child. I wonder if this is a store that makes candy for Nazi officers and not just regular people.* A big-boned woman, with hair the color of blood oranges, was standing behind the counter.

"Can I help you?"

"Yes, I am here in search of a job."

"We don't have any openings," she said curtly.

"Thank you," Eva said and then she left.

For the better part of the afternoon, Eva went from shop to shop, only to be told there was no work available. She was about to give up when she came to a bakery attached to a small coffee shop.

When she walked inside, Eva was greeted by a man in his midforties. He was of average build, with plain regular features, except for a deep cleft in his chin.

"Good morning, Fräulein. What can I get for you, today?" he asked with a smile.

Frustrated, Rebecca said, "Please, I need a job."

"Have you ever waited tables? Or done baking?"

She hung her head. "Only baking at home, Herr Baker."

He nodded. "But you need to work?"

She looked down at the floor holding her breath as she waited for his answer.

"Well, then. Let's give you a try. Are you a fast learner?"

"Yes, I am. A very fast learner," she quickly assured him.

"Be here tomorrow morning at five a.m. We start the

baking for the day very early. Everything must be ready when we open."

"I'll be here."

"And by the way, what is your name?"

She almost said Rebecca but she bit her lip. "I am Eva Teichmann," she said. And she thought it sounded strange. *Can he tell I am lying?* she wondered, but he seemed to accept what she told him without question. *I must start to think of myself as Eva, so I never make the mistake of uttering the wrong name.*

"Welcome to my humble café, Eva. My name is Albert Weber. If you can learn fast and keep up with the pace, you will like it here."

"Thank you, Herr Weber. Thank you so much," Eva said, then she left and walked all the way home feeling as if a weight had been lifted off her shoulders. Now, she was certain, things were on an upswing. Soon she would be earning money, and there would more food for both of them.

CHAPTER 12

Herr Weber had been a widower for the last two years. His wife had been a childhood friend, a girl who grew up only a few houses away from his own. They'd had a good marriage. His wife was a good cook, an excellent housekeeper, and his best friend. But he knew when they got married that she had a heart condition. And the doctors did not expect her to live a long life. Still, he liked her so much that he was willing to marry her anyway, regardless of the fact that they might have only a short time together. Everything was fine until she was actually gone. Then he was devastated, broken, and lost. He'd never been a very social person and neither was his wife, so he didn't have many friends. Although he knew all of his regular customers by name, who came into his bakery each week, he never knew them on a personal level. As long as he was busy kneading dough or making jams, he was able to cope with the loss.

But once he left work and went home, he felt an overwhelming loneliness. Even though he knew how scarce food was, he still managed to bring a bag of crumbs with him from the bakery to feed the birds. Watching them eat gave him a sense of purpose. He would have liked to remarry as soon as possible. He knew that was what his wife would have wanted for him. But he never felt comfortable around any of the women he met. And none of them ever touched his heart the way his wife had, so he filled his time with work.

However, when the girl came into his shop today, the blonde who said her name was Eva, he found himself thanking his lucky stars. She was by far the prettiest girl he'd seen in a very long time, maybe the prettiest he'd ever seen. He was already taken, and he'd just met her. That night, Albert went home to his lonely, sparsely furnished flat, and for the first time in many years he found himself smiling. It was cold outside, but his bed was warm. And there was bread in the bread box, and a block of cheese for his dinner. But most of all, a beautiful, young woman named Eva would come to work at his café tomorrow. She would spend the day beside him. "Eva," he whispered as he washed his hands and face before eating. "Eva." *Perhaps it is a miracle that she came in looking for a job today,* he thought. *Perhaps God has finally heard my prayers and sent me a wife, so that I will not be alone forever.*

CHAPTER 13

June, Ravensbrück

Hilde arrived at Ravensbrück on a bright sunny day, when the sky was cornflower blue, and the sun was so golden that it was almost blinding. As she walked from the train station to the camp, the warm sun caressed her shoulders and head, leaving her with a feeling of well-being. She'd gone to see Gretchen the night before to say goodbye. But instead of crying and telling Hilde how much she was going to miss her, Gretchen had seemed distant, distracted, and in a hurry for Hilde to leave. This was unlike Gretchen, and it had left Hilde feeling disappointed and sad. She wondered if it was because Gretchen was jealous of her job, or if Gretchen was feeling bad that she was going away. Either way, there was nothing she could do; she had committed herself to taking this job. A warm breeze caressed her hair, and she decided she would bring Gretchen some coffee or sugar, or anything she could get her hands on the next time she returned home.

After her train ride, Hilde arrived at the newly built camp. It was much cleaner than Buchenwald. That was probably because it was new. But when she saw the facilities she felt better about the job.

Once again she was ushered into the administration building and told to wait there. But this time the commandant did not greet her. Instead, a young woman came into the room where Hilde sat. As soon as she entered, Hilde stood up.

"Heil Hitler." The young woman saluted.

"Heil Hitler." Hilde saluted too.

"Welcome to Ravensbrück. I'm Ilsa Guhr. You are Hilde Dusel?"

"Yes, that's right," Hilde said. *This woman is incredibly gorgeous. I don't trust her already,* Hilde thought, as she felt the old familiar jealousy seeping over her.

Ilsa Guhr was a petite girl with perfect features—big blue eyes; high cheekbones; a perky, little nose; and curly, silver-blonde hair like a movie star. A whip made of some sort of clear but strong plastic hung from a belt at her waist. She wore a fitted skirt uniform that showed off her delicate but curvy figure and shapely calves. Ilsa smiled brightly at Hilde. She cautiously returned the smile.

"It's not so bad here. We do whatever we want. It's not a hard job. You just have to make sure that you keep control of the prisoners and that no one escapes," Ilsa said, putting her arm around Hilde's shoulder as if they had been friends for years. "The women who work here at Ravensbrück are under the direction of the SS, but the SS officers don't come here very often. And they don't really care what we do to make the prisoners comply with their rules so long as we keep order."

Hilde nodded. "It's very clean. I recently visited my fiancé in Buchenwald, and it was filthy: all lice and disease."

"Yes, well, this camp is new. Just give those dirty Jews some time, and we'll be fighting off disease here too. Anyway, follow me. Let me show you to the guard's barracks where you will be staying."

CHAPTER 14

On Hilde's first day of employment at Ravensbrück, Ilsa took her to the administration building to pick up her uniforms. "What size do you wear?" Ilsa asked.

"I'm not sure," Hilde said, because she'd never looked at the sizes when she stole clothing. She could just tell by looking at something if it would fit.

Ilsa studied her for a few seconds. "You are a solid one, aren't you? A bit on the hefty side."

Hilde was appalled at the blatant insult. But she didn't say a word.

"All right, give me a minute," Ilsa continued, then she turned and spoke quietly to the guard who was in charge of distributing uniforms to new recruits. Next, Ilsa returned with a smile and handed Hilde a pile of neatly folded clothing, on top of which was a pair of gloves, a field cap and two pairs of high, black leather boots. "You have two complete uniforms here. There is one for summer and one for winter. I think you'll like them; they are very smart as you can see. You have stockings, two skirts, two blouses. Everything is waterproof and very well made. I trust you will find them to be quite durable," Ilsa said, turning around in a circle like a model to show Hilde her clothing. Then Ilsa giggled like a child. Hilde found it very strange and out of character, but she said nothing.

"Yes, the uniforms are very nice," she responded cautiously.

"Of course, we are not permitted to wear the SS insignia, only the imperial eagle because we are women. But the uniforms are very attractive. Don't you agree?"

"Yes, absolutely," Hilde said.

"Now, let's go to the barracks, and I'll show you to your room."

"Will you be my roommate?"

"No, you will have your own room. A private room."

"I have my own room?" Hilde asked. "Really?"

"You do! Our wonderful reichsführer has made this camp very nice for us women guards. Just wait until you see your quarters. I think you'll be quite impressed." Ilsa smiled and led the way. They walked through a building with several private rooms. Then Ilsa stopped. She took a key out of her pocket and opened the door.

Hilde gasped when she saw the lovely room with its small bed, pretty bedcovering, a brand new washbasin, and brown wooden dresser.

"There is a bathroom and a kitchen at the end of the hall. We have one on each floor, so you will find they are rarely overcrowded. You might want to go and get washed up after you unpack. Then come and join me and the rest of the guards for dinner."

"Where are the cleaning products so I can clean the shower and the kitchen after I use them?"

"You are not required to clean at all. We have the prisoners take care of that. In fact, they will clean your room as well. And they do all the cooking. It's wonderful. We live like royalty here," Ilsa said. She glanced over at Hilde who was shocked at how nice everything seemed to be. Then Ilsa continued. "I know. At first this is all very shocking, overwhelming even. But after a while you begin to understand that this is our birthright. We are Aryans. We are meant to be served."

"Thank you so much for showing me around. I am in awe of this place. I just can't believe the beautiful furniture here . . . and would you just look at this down comforter. I've never seen anything so lovely," Hilde said, touching the comforter.

"Everything that you see here has been confiscated from enemies of the Reich. Jews stole everything they had from Germany in the first place. And let's face it . . . they always had so much more than anyone else. So it's about time we Germans took back what is rightfully ours."

"That's very true," Hilde said. "These living quarters are much more than I ever expected them to be when I took this job. I visited my fiancé at Buckenwald and it was not nearly as nice as this." Hilde was starting to feel comfortable with Ilsa. In fact, she was even starting to like her in spite of the jab about her being hefty.

"It is nice, isn't it? Come on, follow me down the hall. Before you go ahead and get settled in, let me introduce you to some of the other girls." Ilsa brought her into the kitchen on Hilde's floor, where several of the other female guards were seated, sipping coffee and tea. "I'd like you all to meet our new colleague, and my new friend. This is Hilde."

The camp doctor happened to be present when Ilsa introduced Hilde to the other guards. He'd been visiting with one of the guards who lived on the same floor. Everyone smiled and welcomed Hilde. She returned their smiles.

"Thank you all for welcoming me. I am happy to be here." She felt a twinge of pride at being introduced as Ilsa's friend. After all, Ilsa was the prettiest girl that she'd seen at

Ravensbrück so far.

"I love this shade of rouge, and it would look just magnificent on you with those lovely eyes of yours," Ilsa said, handing Hilde a half-used rouge as they walked back toward Hilde's room.

"You really think I have nice eyes?"

"Of course. They're beautiful."

Hilde smiled then blushed. Coming from someone who looked like Ilsa, that was quite a compliment. "Thank you," she said simply.

"Oh, come on and try it," Ilsa said, spreading a thin line of rouge on each of Hilde's cheeks then rubbing it in until it left a natural looking glow. "Pretty, no?" she said, pulling a compact with a mirror out of her pocket and showing Hilde how the rouge looked on her cheeks.

"Yes," Hilde said. "Yes." She was almost in tears. *Does Ilsa see the girl that lives inside of me? The one who looks back at me from the mirror? Is it possible that Ilsa looks at me and sees the beautiful Valkyrie whom every man longs to kiss?* In Ilsa's compact, the Valkyrie was there staring back at her. She winked and Hilde quickly closed the mirror.

"What is it, dear? Don't cry," Ilsa said.

"Nothing. It's just that when I was a child my mother always told me I was ugly. So I created a fictitious Hilde. She was a beautiful blonde Valkyrie who rode a white horse. I see her in my mirror."

"Every child has fantasies. I had them too. Mine were a little different than yours. Perhaps a little darker," she said then adding, "Someday, when we become good friends, I might just share them with you." Ilsa let out an unnatural-sounding laugh. It was high pitched and harsh. And, for one moment, Hilde was worried about sharing her secret with Ilsa because she felt there was something unnerving about her.

"Anyway," Ilsa added, "you know what?"

"What?"

"You're an adult now, and you have grown into a beautiful woman, so you don't need to invent an imaginary self anymore. Your real life is about to unfold."

Hilde smiled and wiped a tear that spilled down her thick cheek. "Thank you," she said. "Do you really think I'm beautiful?"

Ilsa let out a laugh, then she patted Hilde's shoulder. "Go and get yourself ready for dinner. Your training will start tomorrow. That's when you'll meet our oberaufseherin, Anne Zimmer, the chief wardress. She can be tough. And I can tell you right now that the training here is quite demanding. That's because Ravensbrück is sited to be the training camp for the female guards at all of the camps. So you'll need to be on your toes if you want to succeed here. It's very important that you make a good impression tomorrow."

"I want you to know that I appreciate everything you did for me today," Hilde said

"Of course. We are friends, aren't we?"

"Yes, we are friends," Hilde said as a broad, open smile came over her face.

Once Hilde was alone in her room, she hummed softly to herself as she hung the mirror, she'd brought with her, on the wall next to her bed. But when she caught a glimpse of her reflection it was not Hilde that she saw, but the Valkyrie who stood angrily next to her white horse.

What are you so happy about? the Valkyrie demanded.

"Ilsa! She likes me. I feel like I could actually belong here. I believe she is one of us, another beautiful Valkyrie."

The Valkyrie shook her head. *Fool! How can you be so trusting? Are you an idiot? You don't even know her.*

"You're angry because she told me to give up on childish

fantasies. And that would be you, my glorious, brave Valkyrie, wouldn't it?"

There is no me. There is only us, Hilde. Us! You and me. We are one.

"Perhaps we are not. Perhaps Ilsa is right, and I don't need you anymore."

You are dumber than I thought. And you're right; I am angry. I'm angry because you are letting your guard down too soon. You are trusting her instead of us. You will regret this.

"I want her to be my friend."

And so put all of your trust into a stranger, like a silly child.

"Just look at her. She is beautiful and so powerful. When she walks into a room she commands respect from everyone. And I can't believe that someone like her would accept me as a friend."

You are acting naïve. You are in awe of a dangerous woman. Be careful, Hilde, that she doesn't hurt you like everyone else always has. That is, of course . . . except for Gretchen. She is the only real friend we have, the Valkyrie said, and then she disappeared, leaving only Hilde's sad reflection in the mirror.

CHAPTER 15

The following morning at breakfast, Hilde sat at a table with a group of women who were all new recruits. They were chatting nervously about the upcoming training.

"What do you think will be expected of us?" one girl with curly chestnut hair asked.

"I don't know, but whatever they ask, I will do it," another answered, then she went on. "It's nice to be able to get away from home, earn a decent salary, and live in such a nice place."

"That it is," Hilde agreed. "And just taste this delicious coffee. It's the real thing."

"Yes," one of the girls giggled. "And the jam is delicious too."

"I love the uniform," a tall, pretty, blonde woman said. "Look at the quality of the wool."

"It's quite flattering, really—"

"Enough talking. Your training is about to start." A higher-ranking guard interrupted their chatter as she stood up. "Finish quickly and then come outside to begin. You have about five minutes. Mach schnell."

The girls quickly cleaned up their trays and reported outside. Hilde was nervous and shivering. She had never wanted to please anyone as much as she wanted to please the oberaufseherin. So far, this seemed like a dream job, and she wanted it to work out.

Then one of the trainers hit the handle of her whip on the side of the building. It made a sharp sound that silenced the new guards. "Get in a line," she ordered.

The girls lined up and waited for further instruction. A woman, with dark hair pulled into a twist at the back of her neck, a slender face, and severe features, came walking across the compound. She had an angry look on her face. Then she stopped in front of the girls and was silent for a few moments. Hilde felt a chill run up the back of her neck.

The dark-haired woman slowly eyed the lineup of new recruits. She nodded and saluted. "Heil Hitler!"

"Heil Hitler!" the recruits, including Hilde, answered enthusiastically, and saluted.

The woman nodded again, tapping her whip against her thigh.

"For those of you who don't know me yet, my name is Emma Anne Zimmer. I am the oberaufseherin of this camp. From today forward, you will answer to me for everything that you do. This is a hard job, but the rewards are good. However, if you are weak, you might as well leave now. If you do not have the courage to do what must be done, no matter how distasteful, leave now. You must be strong here at Ravensbrück; you will become even stronger. Indulging the prisoner is a sign of weakness. And, let me tell you this, weakness will cost you. You do not have the luxury of trusting these people. They are devious. Look what they did to Germany before our führer stepped in to save us. If you should even be so stupid as to and treat them as if they were human, you will find that these rats will walk all over you. They are cunning. And once they see that they can get the better of you, they will never stop. So you must maintain control over them at all times. If this seems difficult for you, then you are not cut out to be here. Over the next several months you will learn how to detect prisoners who are trying to sabotage the camp's operations. Quite often they do this by slowing down their work. These actions must be punished immediately. You are to have no tolerance for this. And you will be taught how to punish effectively. The prisoners here, at Ravensbrück, are the filthiest and most abhorrent of women. There are some Jews and Gypsies, and there are also political prisoners, prostitutes, sexual deviants, and criminals of all kinds. These despicable women flourished during the Weimar Republic, and they tarnished our beloved fatherland. But now our needs our help, so he has put them in our hands. We must see to it that their destruction of our country is stopped forever. Do you understand?"

"Yes, Oberaufseherin," the girls yelled in unison.

"I can't hear you. Do you understand?"

"Yes, Oberaufseherin," the girls yelled louder.

"Good. And so we begin. Now, why the prisoners are here. It is rather simple. If you will take a look, you find that they are all wearing a colored triangle on their shirts, with the exception of the Jews. The Jews are easy to spot; they wear a yellow star. And Jews who are also political prisoners will wear a star that is one red triangle and one yellow triangle forming the star. If there is a letter inside the star, it will tell you where the prisoner came from. Now, on those who are not Jews, red triangles symbolize political prisoners. Common criminals will wear a green triangle. Lesbians, prostitutes, Gypsies wear black. The Jehovah's Witnesses, purple. Memorize these. You will need to know them at a glance. Do you understand?"

"Yes, Oberaufseherin," the girls answered.

"Good. Here at Ravensbrück, we have two daily roll calls for the prisoners, one in the morning, the other in the evening. This constant counting of heads, so to speak, makes escape almost impossible. You will be expected to be present at each of these roll calls when you are working. Starting today, you will be given a work detail. You will be under one of our experienced high-ranking guards who will be expected to teach you how to supervise a group of working prisoners in order to get the most work out of them. Do you understand?"

"Yes, Oberaufseherin."

"So I expect each of you to be outside before dawn tomorrow morning, lined up at the roll call for the prisoners. That is where you will be appointed your work detail," the oberaufseherin concluded. "That's all for now. Heil Hitler!" She saluted.

"Heil Hitler!"

CHAPTER 16

Ilsa came into the dining room after work the first day and walked over to where Hilde sat at a long table.

"So, how did it go?" Ilsa asked.

"It went well! It's all very exciting. I've been assigned to work in the sewing room."

"Oh, so you'll be working under Agna."

"Yes, I met Agna. I started today."

"She's a bit harsh. Was she hard on you?"

"Not so much on me, but on one of the other trainees. She slapped her across the face."

"Why?"

"Agna demanded that the trainee kick a prisoner with her boot, and the trainee failed to do it. The prisoner fell to her knees crying. The trainee looked like she was going to vomit. To tell you the truth, the trainee was a real mess. I don't think she has what it takes."

Ilsa laughed. "Oh, that's nothing. All of the prisoners are manipulators. Agna only slapped the girl to wake her up. It's common here for a trainer to hit a new recruit. You'll get used to seeing it. However, if you don't want to be the victim of an embarrassing assault, then you must do whatever Agna tells you to do."

"I don't want to get on her bad side. She looks like a witch."

"Poor Agna. You're right; she is rather ugly. And she thrives on showing the new recruits how much power she has. However, the longer you are here, the more you will realize that we, the women guards, control the prisoners; however, we are also under the thumb of the male SS. There are only a handful of them, but when they come around, they are the controlling force in the camp. They don't come here very often, but when they do come, they must be obeyed. Even so, they don't worry me much. After all, they're men, and in many ways, that makes them easy to control. Of course, that is if you know how. But poor ugly Agna is always trying to make a good impression on them. Sadly, due to her pathetic looks they don't pay her much attention. Never mind though. While you are working under her, just do what she tells you to do, and you'll be just fine. But don't forget that no matter what, you must never appear weak."

"The men are in control? But they hardly ever come here."

"Yes, the men might not be here all the time, but they have power over us, so they are the ones to befriend. And just wait until another shipment of new prisoners comes in. The men will be here. You know why?"

"No idea."

"Because they like to watch when we do our exams on the prisoners. I like to watch it too. It's fun to see the pretty, rich Jews reduced to the humiliated pieces of shit that they deserve to be."

"Exams?"

"Yes, private exams. When they first come in. The guards put them on a table. Then we insert a speculum to examine their private parts."

"Oh?" Hilde tried to keep the shock from her voice. The

idea of anything having to do with another woman's sexual parts did not appeal to her. But she questioned herself as to whether she was just being small-minded. "Do I have to do any of the exams?"

"You are so innocent; you make me smile." Ilsa touched Hilde's hair. "No, you won't have to do them, if you don't want to."

"Good, I'd rather not."

"I have done them. It's kind of fun. It makes you feel so powerful. It might take you a while before you enjoy the control we have here. However, once you get into the swing of it, I think you will find that you can act more like that Valkyrie of your dreams here at Ravensbrück than you could ever dare to anywhere else but in your fantasies."

Hilde nodded but she didn't say a word.

"And on our days off, we guards sometimes go on picnics together or we go boating. You'll see, it's a good place to work. And as far as the SS, the men?" She let out a small snicker. "Don't let them scare you. I find them rather fun and exciting. I have slept with plenty of them. In fact, I have a date tonight with an SS officer. A very handsome one, indeed."

"Really? I can't believe you don't have a steady boyfriend, or a husband. I mean, you are so pretty."

"Who said I don't? I do have a husband. But I have lost interest in him. I don't even go home to see him anymore. I mean, why would I when, well . . . it's like a sexual paradise here at Ravensbrück. I mean . . ."

"Paradise?"

"Yes, you have your choice. Men, women . . . prisoners? Anything and everything you could ever imagine. You can date the officers, sleep with the other female guards. What I mean is, there are no limits as to what you can do. No restrictions. Especially with the prisoners. They don't dare complain, so you can do as you like."

"Prisoners? You have sexual relations with the prisoners?"

"Of course. I do whatever I feel like doing. We are like queens, and they are our subjects, aren't they? Yes? So we can make them do whatever suits our fancy."

"But they are all women," Hilde said, and again she wondered if she might like the power of controlling these women, of humiliating them.

"Yes, they are. And I find that I have developed a taste for unusual sex games with women."

"Sex games?"

Ilsa laughed, and her laughter rang out in loud and frightening gulps. She was laughing so hard that she had to bend at the waist to try and catch her breath. "You should see your face. Your expression is priceless. I don't think you realize it yet, but having absolute power is intoxicating."

"I have never been sexually interested in other women."

"Neither did I when I first came here. But then I tried something I found rather exciting. Do you want to know more?"

"I don't know, I suppose," Hilde said with uncertainty.

But Ilsa just smiled and said, "I'll tell you anyway." Then she added, "Have you ever played the dominant? Or games of sexual sadism?"

"No. I don't even know what you mean."

"Well, it's all about power. And power is fun. You see, I have found that I enjoy a bit of sexual sadism. It's exciting. Perhaps one day, we will have a little fun together. You and I . . . with a prisoner or two."

"Sadism? You mean like beatings during sex?" Hilde asked, wondering if she might just find this exciting. The idea of beatings didn't bother her.

"Beatings and much more. As I said, there is no limit as to

85

what you can do. Here, at beautiful Ravensbrück, you can explore your wildest fantasies."

"Hmmm," Hilde said, "so what department do you work in?"

"I work in the beauty salon, of course. That's the best place here. I keep those girls in line while I get my hair and nails done every day."

"There's a beauty salon here?"

"Of course. Plenty of the inmates were beauticians before they were arrested."

"I had no idea."

"Once you're all done with training, you can come and use the salon on your day off. Perhaps you want to brighten up that blonde in your hair. It seems that the color is fading to a mousy dishwater. Not very attractive. But then again, you are a bit of a mouse, aren't you? Not a mouse, really, more like a little piggy. You are a bit too fat, aren't you?" Ilsa smiled in a mean-spirited way, and her eyes looked like they'd turned to glass.

It felt as if someone had slapped her in the face or punched her in the stomach. She didn't know what to say. Ilsa's comment was so unexpected. "I'm going to get ready for the evening. I have to go now," she stammered.

"Oh, don't go. I didn't mean anything. I was just joking. You're not angry, are you?" Ilsa said. "I'm sorry. I really am."

Hilde shrugged. "A little hurt, perhaps."

"Come with me. I want to share a secret with you," Ilsa said, winking.

Hilde felt she had lost something of value for the few moments it seemed as if Ilsa no longer liked her. And, in spite of her better judgment, she found that she now longed for this woman's friendship and approval. Perhaps it was the way she'd felt like an accepted member of the group when Ilsa had first introduced her to the others, instead of an outcast, for a change.

"A secret?" Hilde asked.

"Can I trust you?" Ilsa asked.

"Of course," Hilde said, trying to look as sincere as possible.

"Well, come on, then. I'll show you my secret."

Maybe she really does like me, after all, Hilde thought.

CHAPTER 17

Hilde followed Ilsa to a private bedroom behind the hospital. It was much larger than Hilde's room or any of the rooms in the dorm where Hilde lived. And right adjacent to the bedroom was a private bathroom. "You don't stay in the guards' barracks with the rest of us?" Hilde asked.

"No, I don't. That's all part of the secret. Now, you made a promise. You said that I can trust you, isn't that right?" Ilsa looked into Hilde's eyes. Once again, as they did earlier, Ilsa's eyes took on that hard look and when Hilde stared into them they looked dead, like glass. Hilde felt a pang of fear shoot through her.

"Of course," Hilde said, a little less confident than she'd been earlier. *Am I in over my head with this girl? There is something about her that is very unnerving.*

"I am having an affair with the doctor who is in charge of the experiments that are being done on the inmates at our camp hospital. He got me this room so that we can meet in secret and no one will ever know. It is very convenient. I don't care much if my husband finds out what I am doing. I will probably divorce him anyway. But the doctor doesn't want his wife to know about me, so he has secured this room for me. And look over here." Ilsa took Hilde's hand and led her to a small peephole in the wall. "I can look through here and watch when the doctor is doing surgery. He does his operations without any anesthesia. It's fascinating to watch. I am always curious to see just how much pain a person can take. When a woman comes in, I make a little wager with myself as to how long it will be before this one starts screaming."

Hilde was excited by all that Ilsa was telling her. There were many layers to Ilsa. More than she could imagine, and each one was thrilling. *We are like two Valkyries together, she and I. The more I know her, the more I find her enthralling.* Hilde thought.

"So what do you think of my room?" Ilsa said, then she continued. "You're standing there like a fish with your mouth hanging open."

"It's nice. Very private. And you have your own bathroom too," Hilde said.

"Yes, I do."

"That must be very nice."

"And look at these . . ." Ilsa pulled two pairs of silk stockings and several pairs of silk panties out of her dresser drawer. "Gifts from Herr Doctor," she said, winking.

Hilde touched the beautiful fabric. "They are lovely."

"Aren't they? I think they belonged to Jews. I think he stole them." She laughed. "I don't care how he got them. They're mine now."

"Yes, and they are very nice."

"Sometimes, if we are very careful not to get caught, we can take things from the belongings of the prisoners when they first arrive. But if you do, make sure no one sees you because it's considered stealing from the Reich."

Hilde nodded. She was impressed by the beautiful things she saw as she looked around the small but private room. Ilsa had black leather pumps in the closet and lovely dresses besides her uniform. On top of the dresser she had a tortoiseshell brush and a silver comb to secure her hair when she swept it up and back into a bun. There was a glass bowl with a strand of snow-white pearls with a diamond clasp. Ilsa picked up the pearls and ran them through her fingers like a rosary. Then she dropped them on her bed.

"Would you like a drink? I have a bottle of schnapps," Ilsa asked.

"Yes, I actually would," Hilde said.

Ilsa poured her a hefty glass of schnapps. "Enjoy!"

"This is good," Hilde said after she took a sip.

"I'm glad you like it. Let's make a toast."

"All right. What shall we toast to?"

"To our friendship, of course. To two Valkyries together, yah?"

"Yes." Hilde smiled. It was as if Ilsa had read her thoughts when she referred to the two of them as Valkyries together. And it sent warm feelings through Hilde.

"To our new friendship: may it last and grow," Ilsa said.

"Prosit!" Hilde said, downing her entire glass.

"Have another?" Ilsa proposed.

"I really should go." Hilde put her glass down.

"Nonsense, have one more. Indulge me," Ilsa said as she filled Hilde's glass, then she emptied her own glass and refilled it. "To your health," she said.

"To your health," Hilde answered. They finished three full glasses of schnapps that way, over the next hour. And during that time, the alcohol began to take affect, and Hilde began to calm down and relax. She'd always loved beautiful things. Granted, this place was odd, and some of what she'd been told by Ilsa was repulsive to her; still, there was a lot to be gained by working here at Ravensbrück. The pearls were still lying on the bed. Hilde eyed them and wondered how the pearls would look around her neck. It was as if Ilsa had read her mind.

"Would you like to try them on?" Ilsa asked smiling.

"Yes, would you mind?" Hilde asked.

"Not at all. Here, let me help you." The pearls caught the light as Ilsa lifted them out of the bowl and put them around Hilde's neck. She fastened them and then stood up and took a mirror out of her drawer. "Have a look."

"Oh my!" Hilde's breath caught in her throat. They were simply beautiful.

"Lovely, aren't they?"

"Yes, very." Hilde nodded. Then Ilsa touched Hilde's hair, and her other hand caressed Hilde's breast. "Oh," Hilde gasped, shivering. She was afraid of Ilsa, afraid to anger her, afraid to reject her. But also afraid of what was coming next. "I don't know about this . . ."

"Here, have another drink," Ilsa said.

"Thank you." Hilde took the glass and drank the contents quickly.

Ilsa smiled. "Just relax. You're going to like this. This is going to be fun."

CHAPTER 18

Much later that same night, when Hilde returned to her room, she leaned on the door after she locked it and tried to catch her breath. She was unhinged. Her hands were trembling and she felt nauseated. The numbing effect of the alcohol had worn off. *The mirror. I need to talk to the Valkyrie in the mirror,* she thought. But the bathroom was at the end of the hall. She took her compact out of her handbag, sat down on the bed, and stared at her reflection. She winced when she saw her disheveled hair and smeared lipstick. *What did I do tonight? Why did I let her convince me to do it?*

"Come to me, Valkyrie. I need you," she said in a whisper to the image in the mirror. Within seconds, her own face disappeared and in its place was the Valkyrie.

Ilsa scares you. I know she does, doesn't she?

"She is perverse. I did things with her tonight purely because I was afraid to say no to her."

You are absolutely right; she is perverse. However, she is powerful; she has influential friends, so you did the right thing. You don't dare alienate her. Keep her friendship even though you are repulsed by everything about her. You may find that you need her someday. Keep her as an ally.

"Yes, as always, you're right," Hilde agreed.

Don't be afraid; I am here with you. I know what you did tonight and I was repulsed. But I understood your fear of saying no to her. She's a dangerous person. I'll help you. If we find that we have to destroy her, then we'll find a way to do it together. Just like we found a way to get rid of your mother.

"Yes . . ." Hilde whispered. "You always make me feel better. I think I will be able to sleep now."

The following morning, just as the sun was peeking through the dark sky, Hilde was awakened by a loud bell. She jumped out of bed.

That must be the roll call. That woman said it was going to be early, but I certainly didn't think it would be four in the morning, Hilde thought as she glanced at the clock on the wall. She'd only had two hours of sleep. Her head ached from the excessive drinking she'd done the night before. In the pale light of day, what she'd done with Ilsa the night before made her shiver. It seemed obscene and unnatural. *That can never happen again. I just had too much to drink. If I have to get rid of Ilsa to keep her quiet about last night, I can count on the Valkyrie to help me.*

Hilde ran down the hall to the bathroom and splashed her face with cold water, brushed her teeth, and peed. Then she ran back to her room and put on her uniform. She donned the gray culottes skirt, white blouse, and gray wool jacket she'd been given the day before. Quickly, she ran outside so as not to be late. The new recruits were being led to an area where the prisoners were already lined up for roll call. Even outside in the fresh air, there was a nauseating odor of filth and despair that hovered over the camp. Hilde felt bile rise in her throat but she forced it back down. The rapportführer, the roll-call leader, nodded to the recruits. Then she began calling out the numbers of the prisoners. Hilde found it hard to believe that the inmates were so painfully thin. Their heads were bald where their hair had been shaved. But despite everything that had been done to them, some of them were still pretty. And these were the ones that the rapportführer was the hardest on. One young, delicately boned girl who appeared to be about seventeen answered quickly when her number was called. Even though the girl did what was expected of her, the rapportführer walked over to her and shoved her to the ground. Then she began kicking her with her boot. The prisoner let out a cry of pain and fear.

"Shut up, swine. Answer more quickly when I call your number next time," the rapportführer said.

A woman a little older than the first, who had been standing next to the young prisoner, helped her up. The young girl winced. But she managed to stay standing in the line until the roll call was finished. After it was over, Hilde saw the older woman take the young girl's arm and help her as they followed the rest of the prisoners to have their morning slice of stale bread and ersatz coffee.

The guards had breakfast in their own dining room before returning to lead the prisoners away to their work details.

CHAPTER 19

That day, Agna, Hilde's boss, was in a foul mood. Hilde was sure that something had happened in Agna's personal life to upset her. She was yelling and screaming at the prisoners, whipping them with her whip across their upper arms. A few drops of blood landed on the fabric on her table and that sent Agna into a fit of screaming. "Look what you did. You've ruined this perfectly good fabric," Agna yelled. Then she took her foot and knocked the chair out from under the prisoner. The prisoner hit the floor with a thud.

"What are all of you looking at?" Agna said to the others, who'd stopped working for a moment to watch. "You have a quota to make. You don't have time to be watching this. If you don't make your quota today, I'll see to it that you don't eat tonight."

The prisoner got up from the floor and sat back down in her chair. Without looking up at Agna, she began sewing as if nothing had happened.

Hilde just stood back and watched. She was stunned by Agna's fit of rage. But it got worse that afternoon. One of the girls who had been sewing became ill and vomited on the floor next to her sewing table. Agna was so infuriated that she took her plastic whip and whipped the girl's face until it was covered in blood. Blood splashed the walls and fell on the piles of fabric. The girl began crying and begging for mercy. The more she begged, the more furious Agna became. Agna picked the girl up by her arms and threw her across the room. As she fell, she hit her head on one of the sewing machines. The girl hit the floor with her eyes open, but she was unseeing. A river of blood spilled from the newly made wound in her temple. Eyeing the mess, Agna hollered, "Look what you've done. You've made a mess of all of these uniforms. Now, who do you think will be responsible for this? Who?"

There was an uncanny silence in the room, and Hilde knew the girl was dead. Hilde had never had a weak stomach, but between the smell of the prisoners, who were not permitted to bathe often enough, and the dark red blood, Hilde had a physical reaction she couldn't help. She vomited.

"Now, you too?" Agna said to Hilde. Her face was red, her fists clenched around her whip and she was clearly furious. "I am going to have to report you. You don't have the constitution for this job. You're just not cut out for it. Get out of here, now."

Hilde left with her head swimming with worry. She thought of calling Axel, but she didn't think he had enough influence to help her. Then she thought about Ilsa, who certainly had plenty of high-ranking friends with influence. *Yes, I have to go and talk to Ilsa,* she thought as she headed straight to the beauty salon. Hilde's job was at risk; she needed Ilsa's friendship. Without it, she would surely be sent home. And because she'd quit the factory, she knew they would never take her back. The very idea of being unemployed was terrifying. She had to try to keep this job at Ravensbrück. She quickened her step when she saw two prisoners leaning against the side of a building. One of them was weeping, and the other was holding her in her arms like a baby. Hilde knew that she should go over to the prisoners and tell them to get back to work. But she was too caught up in her own problems and didn't want to be bothered with the inmates, so she walked by, acting as if she had not seen them.

There was no way to be certain what Ilsa would do when she would hear what had happened with Agna. She might refuse to help Hilde. Or she might be unable to help her, which Hilde doubted. Because she felt certain that if anyone had the connections to secure Hilde's job, it would be Ilsa. Hilde knew about all the men Ilsa was dating simultaneously. They were all high-ranking members of the SS. Hilde hoped that Ilsa would be willing to ask one of them to put in a good word for Hilde. If not, Axel was a last resort. And the chances of his being able to help at this point, were slim.

"Good morning," Ilsa said from the hairstylist's chair where she was sitting. "I'm getting my hair finger waved today. This is Anna; she is a wonderful hairstylist." Ilsa smiled at the woman prisoner, Anna, who kept her eyes on her work as she was carefully finger waving Ilsa's blonde hair. "Aren't you supposed to be at work?" Ilsa asked.

"Agna got mad at me today. I might be sent home," Hilde said, trying not to sound as desperate as she felt.

"Oh, Agna!" Ilsa laughed. "She is such a bag of wind. Come here. Sit down. Tell me everything that happened. Then we'll find a way to fix it, huh?"

When Ilsa acted this way, Hilde liked her so much. But she had seen that other side of her too, that mean side.

"Come, sit, sit." Ilsa indicated a chair. "You"—Ilsa pointed to one of the prisoners—"get my friend a cup of coffee. Sugar, Hilde?"

"Yes, please," Hilde said.

The inmate handed Hilde a cup of hot coffee.

"Now tell me everything. I think I can help," Ilsa said.

"I hope so," Hilde said, and then she told Ilsa all about her morning in the sewing room. After Hilde finished, Ilsa just shook her head.

"That Agna, she's always such a problem. Don't you worry about a thing, my little butterball. I'll see to it that you don't go home. You amuse me far too much to let you go home quite yet."

"Thank you, I think?"

"Of course. Now, why don't we have someone do something about that brassy blonde in your hair. Gretta, fix my friend Hilde's hair. Make it lighter. Not such a brassy terrible color."

The prisoner named Gretta didn't look up. She ran over to work on Hilde's hair.

"I indulge them," Ilsa said. "I call them by their names here, in the salon, instead of their numbers. It makes them feel human. But they are still nothing but swine."

Hilde smiled, relieved that Ilsa was going to help her.

"Tonight, let's have some fun, shall we? We'll play some games. Let's bring some prisoners to my room, and we can have some real fun with them. What do you think?" Ilsa said as she stood up and walked over to sit under a dryer.

"Oh yes, sure." Hilde said

"It will be such fun. A little bit like last night, only this will be much better."

CHAPTER 20

That evening, after dinner, Ilsa told Hilde to come to her room.

"I have some cake for you, my fat, little butterball," Ilsa said.

Hilde nodded. She hated this nickname that Ilsa called her.

"Oh, come on now, don't be offended. This is affectionate, you know."

"I'll be there," Hilde said, wondering what Ilsa would call fun.

When Hilde arrived at Ilsa's room, Ilsa had two naked, young women standing in the center of the room. Ilsa was walking around them, snapping her whip. Every so often she would crack her whip across one of their breasts. The girls cried out. And the cut was so deep and sharp that it took several minutes for the blood to come flowing to the surface. She was no innocent by any means. She had killed her own mother, but she'd justified killing her as a necessity. Hilde was filled with a mixture of emotions—excitement, fear of being reprimanded, and the thrill of absolute power. Hilde sat down on Ilsa's bed, feeling woozy. Then Ilsa said, "What's the matter, Butterball? You don't like the game? You don't want to play? Well, don't you worry because it's all right. Today, you just watch. It's only your first time. You will need to become accustomed to the feeling of power that this gives you. Once you do, it will be like air for you. You will need it to live."

Hilde nervously watched the spectacle in front of her. Ilsa beat the girls until they were masses of blood. Then she took them outside and made them carry two buckets of cold water, which she doused them with.

"The cold water is more fun in the winter. In the winter, I wet them down, put them outside, and watch them freeze," Ilsa said to Hilde. "But even though we don't have the weather, the water gets the blood off of them for now. Anyway." Then she turned to the girls and forced them to fight with each other. "If you are too gentle I will start beating you both again," Ilsa said to the prisoners. Then she sat with her back against a rock and watched. Hilde couldn't believe her eyes. Could they really do this and not get into trouble? She stole a glance at Ilsa, who had pulled her skirt up to her waist and was masturbating furiously as she watched the two young, terrified prisoners. When Ilsa was done, she stood up and straightened her skirt. Then she told the prisoners to kneel on the ground. They did as they were told. One of them could not stop crying. Ilsa pulled the gun from her gun belt and shot them both point blank in the back of the head.

Hilde crossed her arms around her body. She was shivering with excitement and fear. *Can we really do this without any repercussions. We are all powerful, Aryan Valkyries!* she thought.

"Come," Ilsa said, extending her hand to Hilde to help her get up from where she was sitting.

Hilde took her hand. It felt like her flesh was burning where it touched Ilsa's. *I never believed in the devil until I met her. She can be mean and hurtful, but she is so intoxicatingly powerful,* Hilde thought.

"Let's go back to my room. I'm famished. We can eat that cake I brought," Ilsa said smiling at Hilde, whose face was as pale as winter snow.

"Cake?" Hilde said in a small voice. "I'm not very hungry."

"Trying to trim off a bit of that fat, are we?"

"Yes," Hilde said. Then she waited a few minutes before speaking again. "Ilsa, I think I might just go home."

"Don't you dare. Where will you ever find a job that pays you as well as this one?"

"I don't know, but I might not be cut out for it."

"Don't be silly. You're new. You'll be fine in time. And don't worry about Agna. I'll help you keep your job."

"Are you sure?"

"Of course, my little butterball. I don't plan on letting you leave anytime soon. And . . . I have very good news for you."

"Oh?"

"We have a transport coming in tomorrow."

"Oh?" Hilde said quietly.

"And, well . . . didn't you like my pearls?"

"Yes, they are lovely."

"So, when the transport comes in, we can sneak over and take a few pretty trinkets from the huge piles of things that the new prisoners bring with them."

"Won't we get in trouble?"

"Of course, but only if we get caught." Ilsa smiled. "And I have no plans of getting caught." Then she let out a laugh. "The look on your face is priceless. Do I shock you?"

"A little, yes."

"But you would love to have some pretty jewelry, would you not?"

"Yes, I would. I come from a poor family, and I've never had anything as beautiful as those pearls." Hilde admitted,

101

cheering up.

"Well, my dear, this is your chance. Hopefully, we'll get some rich Jew bitches in the transport tomorrow. They bring the loveliest things with them. And when everyone is busy, we can slip over and take one or two pieces. We can't take a lot because we won't be able to hide it in our clothes."

"I would love to have a nice piece of jewelry."

"And you shall. Besides, wait until you see what the new inmates are put through when they arrive. The spoiled Jew bitches, especially. They are brought down from their high horses, that's for sure. They are forced to have their heads shaved. You should see all that beautiful hair on the floor. And we shave their pubic hair too. They just about die of humiliation when we do that. But, after all, we have to prevent lice, don't we?"

"Lice?"

"Yes, lice. These camps are full of it. You'll see. We get plenty of Poles here and political bitches, but I would love to get my hands on more Jews. I hate their smug, rich faces. They're the reason we lost the war, anyway."

"Yes, they are . . ." Hilde agreed, cringing inside at the thought of what she would witness the following day.

In the morning, after roll call, Ilsa found Hilde and whispered in her ear. "Everything is taken care of. Your job is secure once again, Butterball. You're going to work in the hospital, where you will help Dr. Gebhardt with his rabbits. I can feel safe putting you in there with the doctor because, quite frankly, anyone can see that you are not nearly as pretty as I am. But, of course, you know that, don't you?" Ilsa pinched Hilde's cheek as Hilde's heart sank and her confidence crumbled.

The next morning, following roll call, Hilde reported to the hospital. She was expecting to work with a pen of experimental rabbits. What she found was that the rabbits were a nickname that had been given to eighty-six young women, all of them in good health, being used as experiments by the doctor. When she saw the deep, unhealed scars on the bodies of the women, Hilde felt sick. The smell of rotting flesh and illness turned her stomach. How was she going to be expected to help the doctor? Was she going to be told to clean the wounds? To wipe the pus? The hospital, like most of Ravensbrück, was a house of horrors.

CHAPTER 21

Spring 1940, Berlin

When Eva Teichmann had first started working for Albert Weber, she had found the bakery in disarray. And for the first six months of her employment, without asking for direction, she took it upon herself to clean and organize everything. Albert was always grateful, spending hours thanking her for all her efforts. He told her how his wife, who had passed away, had always kept things in order at the bakery. Then after she was gone, he found it very difficult.

"When she died, I was lost," he said. "She managed everything in our lives, not just the business, but all aspects of our lives. And you know what? I was such a fool when she was alive. Would you believe me if I told you that I never realized how much she did around here, until she was gone? God rest her soul."

"I understand," Eva said. "Don't worry, we'll get this place back in order."

She could see the gratitude in his face. "I am so glad you came here looking for work. It seems we needed each other. You needed work, and I needed your help."

"I'm glad too," she said.

And now, as Eva scanned the back room, she sighed with pleasure. It was clean and in perfect order. She no longer had to search for anything. All the supplies and tools had their rightful place.

The floor was spotless, but Eva picked up the broom and swept anyway. Then she went over to the counter and cut up the cold potatoes she had brought from home and made sandwiches for her and Albert to have for lunch. He had taken to giving her some of his ration cards so that she was able to bring food for the two of them to have lunch every day. It was easier for him than trying to provide his own afternoon meal. Eva didn't mind. She and Gretchen had started a small vegetable garden in the back of the apartment building, so sometimes she was able to bring fresh vegetables to share with Albert in exchange for all the bread he gave her.

"What did you bring today?" he asked cheerfully.

"Cold potatoes and sauerkraut. Is that all right? I tried to get a sausage, but I wasn't able to find one. I'm sorry. They were all sold out."

"Anything you bring is perfect." Albert winked at her. "Really, I appreciate your preparing food for me every day."

Albert Weber was not a handsome man. He'd never been athletic or popular among his peers, either. But none of that mattered to Eva because he was kind and generous. She knew by the way he looked at her that he had fallen in love with her. Sometimes, during the day, as they were working, Albert would glance at her. And from the look in his eyes she could see how much he cared for her. Eva was not in love with him, but she cherished their friendship and cared for him. So she did what she could to make him smile. It wasn't difficult. He didn't ask for much, only that she take her lunch with him when they had a few moments of quiet at the bakery. Or that she talk with him and laugh at his attempts to joke. Albert was not demanding. In return for the attention she gave him, he gave Eva extra bread and baked goods to take home to share with her cousin, Gretchen. The more Eva and Albert talked, the more she found she truly enjoyed his company. Once, he asked her how she felt about him, and she told him that she liked him very much. But not in a romantic way. More in the way a sister cares for a brother. Eva knew Albert was disappointed, so she touched his cheek and said, "It's good . . . what you and I have together. We are best friends. A romance would put that friendship in jeopardy. After all, sometimes, quite often, really, romantic relationships don't work out. And then where would that leave us? I would have to get another job. It would ruin our beautiful friendship. And I value the friendship too much."

He nodded. She could see the hurt and disappointment in his eyes, but then he forced a smile and said, "I'm glad you're here, Eva, and I wouldn't ever want to risk losing you. Your presence and your friendship have made me feel alive. After losing my wife, I never thought I would feel this way again."

So they remained friends. He, perhaps a little too protective of her—she, sweet and attentive to him. Both of them fulfilled in their own way.

Working in the bakery was not easy. Eva got to work before dawn because all the baking had to be done before the customers began arriving. During the winter, the heat from the ovens was pleasant but in the summer it was unbearable. However, Eva didn't mind. When she had first started living in the world as a Gentile woman, she was constantly nervous about making a mistake or saying the wrong thing and being discovered. But as time passed, she began to relax, and living as Eva became natural for her. Sometimes, Eva and Gretchen would meet after work and have a light dinner at a small café. Once in a while, on their days off, they walked around the

106

Berlin Zoo. Sometimes, when they were at home in the afternoon, they would quietly discuss how much they missed Eli over a cup of tea.

"I've never truly been in love," Eva said. "I know how much losing Eli has hurt you, and I wonder if it's all been worth it."

"Sometimes I ask myself if I wish I had never known true love, if I wish I had never met Eli. But you know what? The answer is always no. Although this is all very painful, I am still grateful that I had Eli in my life. Love is so beautiful, so precious. Even if it was only for a short time."

When Eva was alone at night she prayed, giving thanks to God for Gretchen. She prayed for God to watch over Eli too. Then before she finished praying, she would say, "Hashem, I know that somewhere my bashert is searching for me as I am for him. Please, I beg you to watch over him and keep him safe. And if it be your will, please bring him to me."

One afternoon, Eva got off work early and went back to the Jewish sector of town to see if she could find out any information on her parents. She knew it was unwise, and she was putting Gretchen in danger as well as herself. But she had to know. There were no Jews left in the neighborhood. No one recognized her, and she recognized no one. It was as if the little town where she had once lived had never been. It was as if her family, along with all their friends and neighbors, had vanished into thin air.

That night, when Eva confessed to Gretchen that she'd gone back to look for her family, Gretchen was angry.

"You've put us in danger," Gretchen said, her voice angry. "I know you miss your family, but we never know who is watching. You can't go around asking questions about Jews. It makes you look suspicious."

"I'm sorry. I didn't realize. After all, you are always so

worried about your father, I thought you would understand my need to find out what happened to my family."

"A mistake like that could cost us our lives. Not just you but me too. Do you understand me?"

Eva felt guilty, but she was also hurt and angry. "Yes. I understand," she said.

The following day, when Eva returned home from work, she went outside to the back of the building. She knelt down and began picking weeds out of the vegetable garden, working on it for nearly an hour. *How can I blame Gretchen? Of course, she's right. I should never have been so selfish as to put her safety in jeopardy. What if I had been caught and questioned; what would have happened?* Sweat beaded at her brow, and ran down the back of Eva's dress. *So many people know I am living here with Gretchen. This could have started an investigation into my life. And then the Nazis might have found out the truth about my papers.* Eva trembled. *There is no doubt that if they did, they would have taken us both away. And who knows what would have happened. After all, she doesn't need to take care of me. If she wanted to, she could throw me out. But she isn't like that. She has never once made me feel unwanted. In fact, Gretchen treats me like a sister. I owe her an apology.*

Later she found Gretchen scrubbing clothes on a washboard. "Here, let me help you," Eva said, taking out a second washboard and filling it with soapy water. Then she sat down on the floor beside Gretchen and began washing a blouse that had been in the pile of dirty laundry. After several uncomfortable moments of silence with only the squish, squish of the clothing being squeezed dry, Eva said, "Gretchen, I am sorry. I was wrong. I was just worried about my family. I should never have done what I did. Please forgive me."

"I understand. I would probably have done the same thing

if I were in your position," Gretchen said, looking up from the washboard, her eyes meeting Eva's. "These are very hard times for all of us."

"I won't do it again."

"Thank you. Believe me, I realize what you must be going through. I have no idea where my father is, either. And every day I think about Eli."

"Oh, Gretchen. So do I. I pray for him. I am so sorry for being so thoughtless. I don't know what else to say." Eva felt the tears sting the backs of her eyes.

Gretchen put her arms around Eva and hugged her. "Sometimes there is nothing to say," she whispered.

Never again did Eva venture to the Jewish sector of town. But thoughts of her family were always on her mind.

CHAPTER 22

Eli wandered the forests without much human contact. His hair and his beard grew long, and sometimes he felt like Moses wandering through the desert waiting for a sign from God. His empty belly left him weak and tired. He did not know how to hunt or fish. He asked God to show him the way, as he was a man of learning not of physical work. Eli tried to survive by eating roots and wild mushrooms. But soon his thirst overpowered him and forced him to lie down. The grass was cool beneath him. In his mind's eye he thought he saw Gretchen walk up to him.

"What are you doing here?" he asked. "You should be at home safe in Berlin. Are you and Rebecca all right?"

"We are fine, Eli," she said. "But you are not. You are dying."

"I know." He smiled sadly. "I don't mind dying. It's never seeing you again, that I mind."

She touched his face with a cool, wet cloth. His eyes opened, but it was not Gretchen he saw. It was a young Gypsy girl.

"Who are you? Am I dead?"

"You're not dead." She laughed. "My name is Nadia. Who are you?"

"My name is . . ." He hesitated.

"You are hiding in the forest. You must be a Jew."

He tried to get up and get away, but he was too weak.

"It's all right. I am Roma. We have just set up camp only a little ways from here. We won't be staying long. But I'll take you there."

"Yes, I'm a Jew."

"I know. Come, we have Jews living among us. You will meet my husband, Christian. We are part of the Resistance. But right now, you don't need to worry about all of this. What you need is food and water, and we can give you that. Can you stand up and lean on me?"

"I think so," he said.

Eli stayed with the Gypsy camp for several months. But when they were invaded by the Germans, everyone scattered. When he returned to look for his newly found friends, they were gone.

CHAPTER 23

Autumn, Ravensbrück

The entire staff at Ravensbrück was buzzing with excitement and concern. They were expecting a visit from Reichsführer Himmler, and they wanted to please him. The guards worked the prisoners extra hard, commanding them to clean every inch of the camp. There was no tolerance for what they considered to be laziness, and they beat the women inmates mercilessly. The guards' quarters, which housed fourteen guards, were scrubbed from top to bottom, including the toilets, bathrooms, and kitchens. Everywhere that Hilde went that week, she saw someone in a gray-striped uniform working. They were on their hands and knees scrubbing the floors. They were washing down the walls and sanitizing the toilets. Sometimes the sight of them gave Hilde feelings of anxiety. She didn't trust them. How could they not hate the guards? The guards were vicious to them. She found it unnerving that the staff allowed the prisoners to cook for them. Had she been a prisoner, she knew, she would have poisoned the guards. And just that very thought made her anxious. After she finished her shift each day, she wanted to be as far away from the inmates as possible. But this week, with the reichsführer's upcoming visit, there was no place to go even for an hour where she could escape seeing them.

Himmler arrived with an entourage. He was impressive, smiling at the staff who were lined up for his arrival. He asked some of the guards how they liked their jobs. Everyone he spoke to offered him enthusiastic responses. Then he walked by Ilsa and stopped.

"Who is this lovely girl?" he asked.

"My name is Ilsa Guhr."

"Aren't you a pretty picture?" He smiled. Then Hilde saw him whisper something in Ilsa's ear. She nodded, and he moved on through the line. That night, Hilde saw the reichsführer disappear into Ilsa's room and she thought, *She is so beautiful that even the reichsführer is caught in her wicked spell.*

The first time Hilde saw Ilsa she was instantly jealous of her. Hilde had always felt that way around pretty girls. To make matters worse, there was something about Ilsa that instantly reminded Hilde of Thea. Even though Ilsa was short and Thea had been tall, they both had that same stunning type of beauty. It was the kind of striking looks that Hilde had always envied. The kind of beauty that left handsome men breathless. But now, as Hilde was getting to know her better, she was finding that she really did like her. Ilsa could be very charming, and she had the ability to make Hilde comfortable and accepted. Not just accepted but really a part of things. When Ilsa spoke to Hilde, she had a way of making Hilde feel like an insider, like she was one of the pretty girls.

Since Hilde had begun working at Ravensbrück, she'd seen plenty of transfers coming into the camp. Now it was overcrowded and dirty. The hospital was always filled with dying prisoners, many of which were the rabbits who smelled like pus and decay from the wounds left by the doctor's experiments. Wounds that never healed.

Hilde hated her job at the hospital. The smells of the infected wounds and the cries of pain sickened her. She begged Ilsa to help her find work elsewhere. And because the camp was crowded, Ilsa was finally able to have Hilde moved to the beauty salon.

As time passed, Hilde came to know that Ilsa was as strange as she had originally thought. She could be kind and generous, but she could turn on Hilde in an instant. Still, there was no doubt that Ilsa was a good friend to have. Certainly, she would be better off to have her as a friend than an enemy. So Hilde often swallowed her pride and bent over backward to keep the friendship at all costs.

When Axel came to the camp to visit Hilde, she was afraid that he would detect something strange and unnatural about her friendship with Ilsa. It wasn't that she really cared what Axel thought of her, but she was truly ashamed of the things Ilsa sometimes demanded of her. Axel, however, was oblivious to anything out of the ordinary. Before Axel arrived, Hilde had been worried that Ilsa's mean and crazy side might come out when she was introduced to Axel. Then Hilde would be forced to explain why she kept the friendship with her and what the friendship entailed. But Ilsa surprised Hilde by pretending to be a perfect lady when she met Axel, looking pretty in her gray wool suit with her pin-curled hair.

"It's a pleasure to meet you," Ilsa said, with a voice that was a little overly sweet and alluring.

Is she trying to seduce Axel? Hilde thought. *Why would she ever want a man like him? He's unattractive. He certainly doesn't have a rank as high as most of the men she's dated. Maybe she just wants me to think she is trying to seduce him. She probably thinks I am in love with him and that would hurt my feelings. Typical Ilsa, she loves to cut me when she can. But not this time because I am not in love with him. I'll marry him, but he is certainly not the man of my dreams.*

"The pleasure is mine," Axel said. "I am so glad that my fiancée has made friends here at Ravensbrück."

"Hilde is such a lovely girl. And wouldn't you know it, she and I have become the best of friends. Now, haven't we, Hilde?" Ilsa smiled a strange and threatening smile. No one but Hilde could see the malice behind that smile. Hilde knew that at any moment Ilsa could blurt out embarrassing information about her, if she chose to. It made her nervous. And although Ilsa never said a word that was out of line, Hilde could see that Ilsa enjoyed watching her squirm.

"Yes, the best of friends," Hilde stammered.

"So, Axel, you have traveled quite a distance to be here with Hilde. Let me leave the two of you lovebirds alone. Yes, Butterball? Would you like that?"

Hilde hated that obnoxious nickname even more now that Axel had arrived, but all she said was, "That would be very nice of you, Ilsa."

Axel was thrilled to be alone with his fiancée. Hilde was the love of his life, and he had exciting news to share with her. As soon as Ilsa was gone, he put his arm around Hilde's shoulder and pulled her close to him.

"They are planning to build a men's camp close to Ravensbrück. I've already requested a transfer. As soon as the camp is open, I will move here and we can be married," Axel said, smiling broadly.

"I would like that," Hilde said. To her surprise she was glad he was coming there. Not that she missed him or wanted to be with him. Hilde was planning to use Axel as an excuse to stop participating in the night games with Ilsa. It would be worth putting up with Axel's constant devotion if it meant she could get out of the mess she was in with Ilsa.

115

"Like it? All you can say is you'd like it?"

"I am truly happy, Axel. This is good news. Very good. Now we can get on with our lives together," Hilde said, trying to sound more loving.

She wanted to feel affection toward him, but when she looked at him there was just no magic. Perhaps, she thought, it was because she had never really gotten over Hann.

When Hilde thought about Hann she felt a strong longing that filled her with despair. She remembered the first time she had seen him. It was when she was just a girl, in the Bund Deutche maidels. His good looks had bowled her over. He had such an effect on her that even now, so many years later, she could still imagine his smile and his bright eyes, or hear his soft voice. Hann was everything Hilde had ever wanted in a man. However, no matter how hard she tried to make him see that they belonged together, he had never cared for her. In her heart she was still certain that he was her one true love. Even now, so many years later, she thought of him at least once a day and considered how different her life might have been had he loved her too.

"So we will start a family right away?" Axel asked, bringing her back to the present.

"Yes, I would like that," Hilde said, thinking that she would like to be at home raising a child even though she'd never really craved motherhood. It would certainly be better than working at this camp exposed to disease and foul odors every day and bending over backward to Ilsa's strong and undeniable will.

"So you would like that as well! I think we should get married in Berlin. Maybe we can even have a honeymoon; take a little bit of time off."

"Berlin would be nice. My best friend, Gretchen, lives there; she could come to our wedding," Hilde said eagerly.

"We could invite your friend, Ilsa. She would come, I'm sure. She seems so devoted to you."

Hilde's head snapped at the mention of Ilsa's name. "I doubt she will be able to get away from work."

"Should we try and make other arrangements? Don't you think Ilsa would be hurt if she were not able to attend. She is such a good friend to you. Perhaps we could get married nearer to Ravensbrück. Would you like that?"

"It's not necessary, really." Hilde shuddered. "Let's just plan to have a nice civil ceremony in Berlin. I'll call Gretchen and invite her tomorrow."

"Whatever you would like, my love."

CHAPTER 24

The guards were in high spirits when the reichsführer returned two months later. He greeted them warmly as if they were his family. This time he smiled directly at Hilde. She felt her face glow with pride when he asked her name. Hilde hadn't expected to be in awe of him the way that she was. He was not a handsome man, but he had an air of confidence that the women guards were all responding to.

Ilsa admitted to Hilde that she had slept with the reichsführer when he had last visited. "I know he is attracted to me. But I am sure you have heard that his mistress, Bunny, lives very close to the camp, so when he comes to Ravensbrück he always goes to visit her. I've seen her pictures. She's nothing special. I would make a more suitable mistress, don't you think? Now, I just have to find a way to convince him." Ilsa winked.

"I'm sure you'll find a way," Hilde said, trying to keep the envy from her voice.

"You really think I can steal his attention from Bunny? You are so sweet, my little butterball. I hope he will find me irresistible."

"Of course he will. Everyone does. Don't they?" Hilde said.

"They do." Ilsa kissed Hilde's cheek. "You are such a good

girl. You're my very best friend, aren't you?"

"Yes, I am," Hilde said cautiously. She could never trust Ilsa, who had a way of making Hilde feel on top of the world one minute, and in the next minute could tear her to pieces.

Immediately after she finished work and the evening roll call was done, Hilde went to the main office and telephoned Gretchen to tell her about the wedding. As Hilde predicted, Gretchen was happy for her and couldn't wait to see her. "Of course I will attend your wedding!" Gretchen said.

Just talking with Gretchen made Hilde wish she could go back to life before Ravensbrück, before she'd met Ilsa. Things were easier to understand then. Back then Hilde had always been the person who was in control. It was she who learned the secrets of others to use as blackmail when necessary. But now Ilsa had beaten her at her own game. And although sometimes she was in awe of Ilsa's beauty, her important friends, and her confidence, she was also afraid of her.

After Hilde and Gretchen finished their telephone conversation, Hilde went to tell Ilsa about her wedding. She knew she could not go to Berlin and get married without telling Ilsa, but she was dreading her reaction.

"Ilsa, it's me," Hilde said, as she knocked softly on the door to Ilsa's room.

"Come in, little Butterball," Ilsa said.

Hilde walked into the room to find Ilsa lying on her bed.

"I was just relaxing. I am surprised to see you tonight. You still want to play games even though your man is here? I could go and find us a couple of prisoners to have a good time with tonight. You know, I was thinking that we could even include Axel in the fun, if you'd like."

"No, please, let's not play the night games while Axel is here."

"Eh, I knew he was a drip. I could tell. But of course, every

119

German woman wants that respectable marriage and children. And you, little Butterball, are no exception. You're just not pretty enough to be confident enough to be on your own. I must say…you do rather disappoint me."

Hilde glared at her. She wanted to tell Ilsa to go to hell, but the strongest protest she could muster was "I really don't like it when you call me Butterball."

"Oh sure, of course you don't. How thoughtless of me," Ilsa said, sitting up a little but leaning back on her elbow. "No more Butterball. So . . . perhaps I'll just call you fatty. Or sow? Now, which do you like better?"

"Please, don't be like this, Ilsa. I've come to tell you something."

"Don't be like what? Like what, Hilde? Go on, tell me. Go on . . . what is it that you really think of me?"

"Ilsa, I think you're one of the most beautiful women I've ever met. I don't have anything bad to say about you."

"Well, good. Go on, then. What is it that you came here to tell me?"

"Well, as you know, Axel and I are engaged."

"Yes, so? Go on. I am getting bored with you and this conversation. Tell me already before I send you back to your own room."

"We are getting married in Berlin next month. I just wanted you to know. And . . . if you can get off from work, I would like to have you attend."

Ilsa let out a laugh. "Would you, now? You are so transparent. Such a terrible liar. You can see the way your Axel looks at me, can't you? He would fall on his face for a night in my bed. You don't want me at your wedding. I am a threat to you. That's why you're having the wedding in Berlin and not here. Now, isn't that right, Butterball?" She hesitated then winked and smiled, her eyes turning to glass. "Oh yes, I forgot. You don't like that name, now, do you?"

"It doesn't matter. You will call me that anyway, won't you? I'm hurt by you, Ilsa. You don't treat me like a friend. You insult me all the time, and I don't know why."

"Stop with your bleeding heart, please. I have had quite enough. Don't you worry yourself. I won't be at your wedding. And I promise not to tell your half-wit of a man our little secrets . . . at least for now." Ilsa looked away from Hilde. "Well, I am going to get some rest. I'll see you at the salon in the morning. Let's have our eyebrows tweezed. What do you think? Have you seen that new recruit with the caterpillar eyebrow running across her face? She has one eyebrow. Has anyone ever told her how unattractive that is? Eh, well, anyway, I am going to get some rest. I'll see you tomorrow," Ilsa said.

She's a monster, Hilde thought when she got back into her own room. *She treats me terribly. Her friendship is so unreliable. And I know she is dangerous. I have seen how dangerous. She wouldn't hesitate to use anything she knows about me to embarrass or destroy me if she felt like it. I know I did cruel things in the past, but I never knew anyone as diabolical as Ilsa. I just wish she would disappear from my life somehow. I would kill her if I thought I could get away with it. But she has too many friends and plenty of high-ranking officials among them. I dare not do anything to harm her. Yet in the back of my mind, I am always afraid of what she might do.*

Hilde looked in the mirror and searched for the Valkyrie. She was feeling weak and alone. It took several moments before the vision of the beautiful blonde woman on the white horse appeared.

"I am scared of Ilsa," Hilde said to the imaginary vision in the mirror. Her heart was racing.

Don't be afraid. Remember who we are. We are the Valkyrie warrior. She can do nothing to us. We are strong, and if we have to, we will get rid of her, the image answered in Hilde's mind.

"But everyone loves her. If she wanted to, she could destroy me."

We won't let her. Don't be a fool. Find ways to make yourself useful to her. Play those perverse sex games with her. Trap her so that you have information you can use later to blackmail her. Homosexuality is against the party. Remember that. We've done this sort of thing, blackmail I mean, in the past with other girls and it's always worked. Once we marry Axel and become pregnant, we will leave Ravensbrück. Then we will not have to see her anymore. We will be able to leave the camp on good terms. When we leave, you'll kiss her goodbye. Thank her for her friendship. And then retreat far away from her.

"Yes . . . yes . . . you have always known what to do."

Of course I have. I am the better, smarter, part of you. The beautiful Valkyrie. As long as you have me in your life, nothing can harm you.

Hilde felt her heartbeat slow down. She was calm enough to sleep now.

CHAPTER 25

Spring 1941, Lodz Ghetto

Benjamin Rabinowitz asked every one of his non-Jewish friends if they would help him and his family. He offered them what little money he had. They all turned away. Some started crossing the street when they saw him coming and avoided him at all costs, while others outright replied that they could not be of any help. He didn't blame them. They were frightened. The Nazis were ruthless, and the Polish people whom he'd known all his life were just not willing to put their loved ones in danger for the sake of Ben's family.

Ben, his wife, and his three-year-old son, Moishe, had been in the Lodz ghetto for over a year, when Moishe became lethargic. Young children were the most vulnerable to the diseases and malnutrition that plagued everyone in the ghetto. Perhaps it was because Moishe never had enough to eat, that he was very small for his age, and weak. But lately he seemed to be deteriorating quickly and his parents were afraid. Still, everyone who knew him thought he was a beautiful child with golden hair the color of sunshine and eyes as blue as the sky on a hot summer day. When he smiled, the dimples in his cheeks were deep and defined. His parents loved him more than life itself, so they were willing to risk everything to save his life. By now all the savings they had smuggled into the ghetto, when they were arrested, were gone. So Moishe's mother, Lila, sold every material possession she owned to provide a small amount of additional food. His father traded with the Polish people selling goods on the black market inside the ghetto, struggling to provide. However, once little Moishe began to look pale and he stopped wanting to play, they knew that if he was to survive, they had to get him out of the ghetto. Ben begged the Polish people he bought goods from for help.

"Please, if we can get my family out of the ghetto, we will need safe houses where we can stay for a day or two along the way . . . until we can get out of Poland. I beg you, please. Can you help me?"

No one offered any help.

When Ben had exhausted all the possibilities, he went to his wife, Lila, and told her. "We must get our Moishe out of here if he is going to survive. Children are dropping like flies. I see small dead bodies on the streets every morning. It makes me sick. And I don't know what to do. We don't have any money left; we don't have anything left of value that we can sell, so even if we could find someone who was willing to take him, we can't pay for his keep."

"You're right. I too have often feared that he would die here, if we don't do something."

"But what? What can we do?" Ben asked, wringing his hands.

"I don't know. You always say that you are the man and that men have all the answers. So where are your answers now, Ben? What should we do? You tell me." Lila glared at her husband.

"I don't know," he said.

"You have never been able to help me when I need it most. I will find a way on my own." Lila turned away from her husband, repulsed by the very sight of him.

"Lila, we are a married couple. This is our son, our only child. You know that I will do whatever I can to help you."

"But that's the point, Ben. You can't help me. You never could. And now, I have to find a way myself." Angrily, Lila walked out of the room and slammed the door. She would have to take matters into her own hands. *At least I stood my ground when he was a baby, and I never allowed Ben to have Moishe circumcised. Now, if I can get him out of the ghetto, he and I can pose as Polish non-Jews. My refusal to have him circumcised might very well save his life.* She was a beautiful woman, only twenty-eight years old, with golden hair and azure eyes. And Moishe looked just like his mother. She would use the gift of her beauty to save her precious only child.

There was a middle-aged Nazi guard in the ghetto whom Lila had often seen looking in her direction. She learned that his name was Werner. He was a tall, thin man with a hook nose and a wart on his chin that was so large that Lila had to force herself not to stare at it whenever she saw him. She knew, from the way his eyes scanned her body, that he lusted for her. So far, he had made no attempt to seduce her. Perhaps it was because the laws forbade him to copulate with a Jew.

One afternoon, seeing him walking the streets, she went to him. She dropped her handbag and bent over to pick it up. She'd purposely worn a very low-cut blouse. When he saw her ample breasts, she noticed the bulge growing in his pants. So it was that she wooed him. She smiled at him, complimented him, and told him that she knew he had the power to take her against her will. However, she gave him her most alluring smile and touched his cheek. In a breathy voice she whispered in his ear that if he decided not to force himself on her, but instead took her as a willing lover, she would fulfill all his fantasies. Lila knew she was taking a risk. After all, he could have had her arrested right then and there. But he was drawn to her beauty, and the words she spoke to him sounded like the melody of a tender violin. Werner was mesmerized when he gazed into her sparkling eyes. She went to his bed willingly. She gave herself over to his every wish. This happened four times. They met in alleyways and behind buildings. After sex Lila lay with him and listened as he told her how when he was younger he'd been engaged, but the girl had broken it off, and he had never had a serious relationship since. She wove a careful web around him that was so dense that when she told him she wanted to run away with him he excitedly agreed.

"You must allow me to take my son with us," she said.

It was late, many hours after curfew. The factories were closed for the evening. But Werner had the keys to several of them and in the shadow of darkness he snuck Lila inside one. The two of them were alone in the basement lying on the floor in the corner.

"Your son? You want me to smuggle a child out of the ghetto with you?"

"I can't leave without him." She leaned over and kissed Werner behind the ear.

"But a child will slow us down. Leave him here with your husband. He'll be safe with his father."

"I won't leave the ghetto without him, Werner," she said firmly. "If you won't let me bring him then I am not going."

He looked into her eyes; he was completely taken with her. "All right. If you insist, then. We'll take him with us."

They made a plan. Werner would put Lila and her son in the back seat of his automobile. He would pack extra clothing, food, and blankets which he would use to cover Lila and

Moishe. They would drive out of the ghetto in the middle of the night. He knew the guard at the gate, and he was certain that the man would not check his back seat. Once they got out of the ghetto, they both agreed it would be best if Lila sat beside Werner in the front seat and posed as his wife.

It took less than a week for Werner to gather everything they would need. Then he sent a note to Lila's apartment asking her to meet him outside the factory where they had last made love. When she arrived he whispered, "We will go tomorrow night. Be here at midnight with your boy."

"Thank you, Werner, for gathering everything together so quickly," she said, her voice barely a whisper. "I can't wait until we can be together forever."

"I feel the same way," he said.

She felt bad because she had to leave Ben behind.

That night she sat Ben down at the table in the small kitchen of the apartment, that they shared with two other families, and told him she was leaving. "I have to get Moishe out of here or he will die. It's filthy in this ghetto. And he is so small, Ben. I have the help of someone very high up. He is going to help Moishe and I get out of here." She hesitated for a moment than drew a deep breath. "I don't know when or if you and I will see each other again. We haven't had the best marriage. I realize this. And for the most part, it's been my own fault. I'm stubborn, I know. But I will miss you. Ours may not have been the greatest love of all time, but in my own way, I care for you, Ben."

"I know. I care for you too. You are all that I have left of the life we knew before we ended up in this ghetto. And believe me, if there is a way, we will find each other again. But for now, you're right. It is best if you take Moishe and go."

"I will. I wish I could I take you with us. But I can't. The man who is helping me won't allow it. Still, I am worried about you."

"Don't worry about me. You have enough to worry about," Ben said. "It won't be easy when you are in the woods alone. But you must do whatever you can to survive and to save our son. Go to a farmhouse. Try to appeal to the farmers. Tell them that you need help."

"I look Polish, so does Moishe. I'm going to change his name and mine too. As soon as I leave the ghetto I am going to pose as a non-Jew. I'm going to call Moishe, Anatol, and myself Felicia. I will use the surname Bankowski."

"That's a good idea. When you go to the farmhouses, tell them that you and your husband were farmers. Tell them you owned a farm but that you had a fire; your husband was killed and you couldn't do all of the work alone so you lost the farm. Now you don't have any money or food to live. Tell them this story; make them believe you."

"Thank you for understanding, Ben."

"I don't have any choice. I wish you could stay here. I don't want to lose my son. But you're right. You must get him out of this place or he will die. So, go, and God be with you."

The following evening, Lila and Moishe got into the back seat of Werner's car. Lila held her child close to her as the engine roared to life. She felt his small body rack with sobs as he wept quietly.

"You must be silent, now, Moishe," she whispered softly into his ear. His hair was stuck, with sweat, to his tiny skull, but he grew quiet and listened as she spoke. "I know you are feeling a little frightened, but your mama is here. I am here, right here, beside you. Shaaa, my sweet boy."

The child burrowed into her and fell asleep. She lay him on the back seat and covered him with a blanket. Then she joined Werner in the front seat, and they kept driving, making their way out of Lodz.

Ten miles outside of the city they were stopped by a roadblock. "Don't be afraid. You are my wife, remember?" Werner whispered to Lila.

In that moment she was on edge. Her fists were clenched, and her nails dug into her palms. *Moishe, please don't wake up right now.* The motion of the car had rocked him as he slept, but now the car was stopped. Lila held her breath as another fearful thought crossed her mind: *Perhaps we have been discovered, and they have set up this roadblock because they are looking for us.*

"Yes, I am your wife," Lila answered Werner, but she was shaking as the policeman at the roadblock came up to the car window.

"Good evening," he said. "Your name, please."

"Gruppenführer Werner Richter and my wife, Magda."

The guard looked into the car and eyed Lila. Then he saw the SS symbol on Werner's uniform and smiled. "Go ahead, Gruppenführer, and have a nice evening.

Lila breathed a sigh of relief as Werner maneuvered the automobile back onto the road, and they continued on their journey.

It was not yet morning when they reached the forests. Lila's entire body was stiff from not moving for hours. Moishe awoke, startled at the strangeness of his surroundings. He let out a small cry, but before he could make another sound, Lila reached into the back seat and lifted him into her arms. "Mama is still here. I have not left you. You are all right," she whispered.

"I have to pee pee," he said, putting his thumb in his mouth.

Lila looked at Werner. "He has to go make pee. If we don't

stop he may pee in the car."

Werner nodded. "I understand." He pulled the car off the road.

"I'm going to take him into the woods. But I'll need to take the gun in case there are wolves lurking in the forest."

Werner handed her his gun. "Do you know how to use it?"

"I think so. Show me quickly."

He showed her how to fire the gun. Lila led Moishe into the woods. She kept her eyes on him until he was done. Then they headed back to the car. Lila had purposely arranged it so that when she returned to the automobile she would be behind Werner, and he would not see her as she approached. "Be very quiet, Moishe," she said.

Once she was close enough to make the shot, Lila pointed the gun directly at Werner's head and fired. He never saw it coming.

The sound of the gunshot was loud, and Moishe began to cry.

"Shhh," she whispered. "Everything is going to be all right."

Moishe stared at Werner. The little boy was trembling with fear. Even in the moonlight it was easy to see the blood and the part of Werner's head that was now missing.

"I want to go home," Moishe said, but Lila ignored him. She gathered all the blankets, clothes, and food out of the back seat. Then she led Moishe into the woods.

Once they were hidden by the forest, Lila stood still for a moment and surveyed the situation. She took a deep breath.

"I'm scared," Moishe said.

"There is nothing to fear, sweet boy," Lila answered and wished she could believe it. She picked him up and hugged him tightly.

The woods were dense and frightening, like the horrible forests of a fairy tale. But there was no time for fear of imaginary monsters. Lila had to save her son from real live monsters. The kind who wore beautifully tailored uniforms and black, shiny boots. She set Moishe back down on his feet. Then picking up the supplies with one hand and taking his hand with other, she led him deeper into the forest.

"This is a scary place. I want to go home, Mama," Moishe said.

"It's all right. We are going on an adventure. It will be one, yes? In fact we are going to play a game. You will have a new name. Your new name will be Anatol Bankowski. I will have a new name too. My name will be Felicia Bankowski. We will never use our old names again. It will be fun." She squeezed his hand gently. "You are with me, so there is nothing to fear. And you know what? We have some food, so we can have a picnic later."

"I'm hungry now."

"I know you are. But let's wait to eat. We have to try to make this food last as long as we can."

"Mama?"

"Yes, my sweetheart."

"Where is Daddy?"

Until now, Lila had forced herself not to think about Ben. "He had to stay behind for a while," she said.

"Will he be coming to see us soon?"

"Yes, soon."

"Tomorrow?"

"I don't think tomorrow. But soon."

"But when?"

"I don't know, Moishe. Please stop asking questions," she said, sounding curter than she'd wanted to.

They walked for a while and then Moishe said, "I'm cold

and my feet hurt."

"All right, why don't we lie down and try to get some rest. I'll put my coat over you. It's not really that cold outside."

The little boy curled up into his mother's lap and put his thumb in his mouth. She sang quietly to him. Within a half hour, his breathing slowed down and he'd fallen into a deep, restful sleep. *How wonderful it is to be a child, to be able to sleep in the woods because he trusts in the words of his mother. I envy him,* she thought. The hard ground hurt Lila's back, but she dared not move least she wake Moishe. Instead, she held him in her arms and prayed silently.

"Dear God, please watch over Ben. He's alone now and not nearly as strong as he thinks he is. But, most of all, please watch over my little Moishe. Keep my son and me in the palm of your hand, as we find our way through these dark, desolate woods. I need you, dear God, now more than I ever have before in my entire life. Please walk with us. I know I have made many mistakes. I've broken your commandments many times. But . . . please forgive me . . . I beg you . . . somehow, someway, bring my family back together again."

CHAPTER 26

February 1942, Ravensbrück

Hilde and Axel's wedding was not fancy. It was a civil wedding. Gretchen was present, and that made Hilde happy. But she was disappointed because there was no fancy wedding dress or lovely flowers. It was just a very practical, quick ceremony. After they were married, Hilde and Axel returned to Ravensbrück. Ilsa was cold and distant toward Hilde because she had not been able to take the time off from work. Hilde had been relieved that Ilsa was not at the wedding and even happier that Ilsa and Gretchen had not met. *I've always believed that Gretchen had a good opinion of me. She knew me when we were just young girls. And I've always been careful to hide things from her that I thought she wouldn't approve of. I've always made sure she saw me in a good light. If Gretchen and Ilsa had a chance to talk, who knows what abominations Ilsa might tell her. I can just imagine the terrible secrets Ilsa might reveal to Gretchen about Ravensbrück. And I would be so ashamed.*

By the middle of June 1941, the men's camp had been built. It was located right near Ravensbrück and was open and running. Axel and Hilde moved together into a small house, right in the Furstenberg Lake District, not far from where

Ravensbrück was located. They both worked at their respective jobs during the day and returned home in the evening. Hilde cooked and kept the house as was expected of a good German wife. And within three months, she was pregnant. When she announced her pregnancy at work, all the female guards and the commanding SS officers cheered for her. After all, this was what was expected of a good German couple. Everyone, except Ilsa, who glared at Hilde after she'd made the announcement then walked out of the room. They drank all night to the health and welfare of the baby. Meanwhile, less than two hundred feet away, the prisoners were starving, sick, and dying.

By February, Hilde was in her fifth month. The cold bothered her and so did the filth and smells at the camp. She vomited often but she planned to work until the baby was born. Then she would quit and leave Ravensbrück forever.

One night Hilde awoke to find blood in her underpants. She was panicked as she tugged at Axel's arm.

"Axel, I am bleeding. I am afraid I might be having a miscarriage."

He got up and without washing his face or brushing his teeth, he drove her to the nearby hospital.

At 2:45 in the morning Hilde had a miscarriage.

"The job is too much for her. She is overworked. She needs to rest," the doctor declared.

After that, Axel insisted that she quit. There was no protest from Hilde. She was glad to leave her job. She'd had enough of the filthy, disease-ridden camp. And she was glad not to have to work with Ilsa and endure the uncertainty of Ilsa's ever-changing moods.

During the day, while Axel was at work, Hilde played records by Wagner on the Victrola that had been given to the couple as a wedding gift by one of Axel's superior officers.

She knew it had belonged to a Jewish family who had been taken away to a camp, somewhere. But she didn't care. It was a good record player. Hilde loved waking up in the morning and preparing breakfast for herself and Axel. Then he would get dressed in the uniform she'd cleaned and pressed for him. He would kiss her gently on the lips, and she would hand him the lunch she'd prepared for him. Once he'd left for work, she would choose a record and play it while she cleaned her house and then baked bread for the evening. This was the happiest Hilde had ever been. She couldn't say that she was in love with Axel, but during this peaceful time, she had come to enjoy his company, and after working at Ravensbrück she thoroughly appreciated her new lifestyle. And two months later Hilde was pregnant again.

Hilde's relationship with her own mother had hurt her deeply and left her scarred. In fact, until the day she felt the tiny life move inside her body, she had secretly questioned whether she even wanted to be a mother. Sometimes she thought that a child would save her, would rescue her from the pain of her past. And other times, she felt that a child would be too needy, sucking all of her energy. However, once she felt movement within her, she knew that having a baby would fulfill her in ways she'd never thought possible. Each day, as her belly grew larger, she found that she cared more and more for her unborn child. She found herself talking to the tiny life that was growing inside her. Sometimes she would sing lullabies and rub her belly softly. *No one has ever loved me completely. Axel says he does, but I don't believe him. But you, my little one, you are everything I have needed all my life. You will be born, and you will love me as my mother never did, and I will love you.*

Axel painted the baby's room with a nice coat of clean, white paint. Hilde knitted a bright yellow blanket and made

135

drapes for the window out of a pretty cotton fabric that was white with a pattern of large yellow sunflowers. Then Axel put in a request to his superiors for a crib. Not long after, he received one. It was a beautiful, white oak crib that rocked and had a canopy. Hilde knew that this lovely piece of baby furniture had been taken from arrested Jews, but she ignored that fact. Instead, she walked through the little nursery in her home, enjoying the beauty she'd created.

Hilde thoroughly enjoyed her days. She spent hours looking at baby clothes and brushing her hair. Because she was pregnant, the food supply from the party for her and Axel was even more generous, so she spent hours preparing lavish dinners. Sometimes she took long, lazy naps in the golden sun of the afternoon. At first she loved the naps. But then she began having nightmares. Sometimes in her dreams she was fighting with her mother, who would turn into a monster that would slay her. Other times Hilde would dream that she was a prisoner in Ravensbrück, and Ilsa was playing her vicious night games with Hilde as her victim. Hilde would awaken clammy with sweat, her heart racing. A bad dream could leave her feeling frightened for the entire day. Hilde was exhausted but afraid to sleep, afraid of the recurring nightmares. She was haunted and sometimes she wished she could discuss her fears with Axel. But she never felt close enough to anyone, not Axel or even Gretchen, to allow them to know her deepest and innermost thoughts.

As the months passed and the pregnancy progressed, Hilde grew more fatigued as she avoided sleep whenever possible. Dark purple circles formed around her eyes, and she began to find eating difficult. She had trouble swallowing her food and sometimes she choked. So she stopped eating and began losing weight rapidly. On her face, she'd developed an angry, red rash that itched most of the time. Then her already thin

136

hair began falling out in clumps.

Axel noticed that Hilde was having a hard time with her pregnancy, and he wanted desperately to help. "Why don't you and I take a little vacation. I'm sure I can get the time off. I can probably get the whole thing paid for by the party. I can request a holiday in Munich. We've both served our fatherland working in the camps. And we've never had a honeymoon."

"I don't feel well enough, and the weather is too cold," Hilde said.

"Darling, you must take better care of yourself. I don't know what to do to make you happy. Please, you must tell me? Perhaps you would like to go home and see your friend, Gretchen? You could spend a little time with her. It might do you good to get away."

"Gretchen? Yes, I might really like to see Gretchen. But not until the weather is better."

"How about if you plan to go and see her in April, to celebrate our führer's birthday? You could go to Berlin in April and spend some time with her. I'm sure she wouldn't mind if you stayed with her."

"I could do that. But what about you?"

"Don't worry about me. I'll stay here and continue to work. Then I'll see you when you return. And perhaps in the early summer, after the baby is born, we can go away on a trip together. You and me and our child. Would you like that?"

"Yes, I believe I would."

"Then consider it done, my love." He smiled at her. "Now, please, you must eat something. You are getting far too thin."

"Yes, I will try to eat," Hilde said. She considered how much weight she'd lost, and she thought about Ilsa for a moment. *I don't suppose you can call me Butterball now, you lousy bitch.*

CHAPTER 27

Berlin

Gretchen had recently gotten a phone in her apartment in case of emergencies. The only calls that came through were calls from the bakery for Eva or calls from the factory for Gretchen.

When the phone rang early one Saturday morning, Gretchen picked it up.

"Gretchen?" Hilde's voice came through the receiver.

"Yes, it's Gretchen. Hilde, hello! How are you?"

"I'm doing all right. I'm pregnant, again."

"Oh, how wonderful, Hilde!"

"I've quit my job. I stay at home now."

"Like a regular hausfrau!" Gretchen said affectionately.

"Yes, I suppose I am."

"Well, good for you, my friend. I'm glad that you and Axel are doing well. I am sorry you have been ill though. Is it just morning sickness?"

"I am nauseated all the time and have some trouble sleeping. But that's not why I called. I called because I think it would be good for me to get away and come to Berlin for a visit. And I would love to see you. There is nothing I would love more than spending a couple of weeks with my best friend."

"Oh?" Gretchen said, caught off guard. *What am I going to do? How can I let her stay here, with Eva? What if we slip up and say the wrong thing?*

"You don't sound pleased."

"That's not true. Of course I am happy. I would love to see you. When are you coming?" Gretchen said hastily.

"I'd like to come in April to celebrate the führer's birthday with you. Can I stay with you?"

Gretchen hesitated. How could she say no? As far as Hilde knew, she was a single woman living alone. Hilde had not even met Eva. Gretchen's mind was racing. She would tell Hilde the same story she told everyone about Eva. That would probably not be a problem. "Gretchen, are you there?" Hilde asked, and Gretchen realized she'd been silent for too long.

"Yes, I'm sorry. I'm here. I don't think I've had a chance to tell you that my cousin Eva has been staying here with me. She came to the city from the countryside, to find work in Berlin."

"You never mentioned her. I didn't even know you had a cousin."

"I know. I didn't even know of her existence until recently. Well, that's not entirely true. My father had mentioned her a few times, but I never thought much of it. She is on my mother's side of the family."

"She must be staying in your father's old room?"

"Yes."

"Well, that's all right. I can sleep on the living room sofa."

"Yes . . . the sofa. But wouldn't you be uncomfortable, being pregnant ?"

"Gretchen, do you not want me to come?"

"No, no, it's not that, Hilde. I am just so surprised and excited that you are coming," Gretchen said, trying to hide the worry in her voice. "We'll find a way to make you comfortable. Don't worry about a thing. I am looking forward to seeing you."

"I can't wait to see you too!"

After Gretchen hung up the phone, she sunk into the living room chair. It was dusk, and Eva would be home from work soon. Gretchen would tell her what happened, and they would discuss Hilde's upcoming visit.

CHAPTER 28

March, the Forest in Poland

Lila Rabinowitz held her son's head on her lap as she sat propped up against a tree in the forest. Moishe was hungry again. He was always hungry. It seemed that every hour of every day she was consumed with finding food. She'd already worked for a farmer picking potatoes in exchange for food. She'd stolen food when she was able to and during the harsh winter she'd taken her son and hidden in barns and cellars to escape the cold.

Sometimes, out of the blue, and for no apparent reason, Moishe would ask about his father. "Where is Daddy" he would say. "Is Daddy coming here to meet us soon?"

She had no answers, so she would try to distract him by singing a song or telling him a story. Most times it worked. But she wondered if this horrible war would ever end and if she or Moishe would ever see his father again.

At night, Moishe was frightened by the shadows in the forest or by the sounds of wild animals. She was afraid too, but she could never let her son see fear. To help him sleep, Lila would softly sing lullabies. She tried to stay awake as much as possible, in case of danger, but sometimes exhaustion overtook her, and she drifted off into a deep and dreamless slumber. They'd somehow survived the treacherous winter by stealing food from farms at night and sleeping between dusk and dawn in barns or cellars that they found unlocked. Then she would awaken Moishe, and the two of them would steal away before sunrise, to be sure they were not discovered by the owners whose land they had trespassed upon. Once, when they were in a barn, Lila saw a pile of horse blankets on a wooden box. Inside the box she found moldy hay and a bit and bridle. She took all the blankets she had, those that she'd stolen from Werner's car and the horse blankets. Then she wrapped them around Moishe to keep him warm. There were a couple of times during the harsh winter months when she had been outside, and it seemed so cold that they might freeze to death. Perhaps these blankets would be of help in the future. It was still cold outside but not nearly as frigid as it had been the previous months, and she was relieved that the winter was almost over. So if they could not find an open barn or cellar, they could at least use the blankets to sleep in the forest.

There were so many ways that death could claim them, and the bitter cold of winter was only one of them. Starvation was always peeking its ugly head around every tree and shrub. When she could find a farm, she would pick a few pieces of fruit or a bunch of vegetables during the night, feeling like a thief, sneaking away in the darkness, careful not to get caught. Many times there was no farm in sight. But they still had to eat to survive, so Lila would try to find wild mushrooms or berries. She did not know which wild plants were safe to eat. She made sure they were not poison by eating them herself first. Once she was sure they were safe, she would give them to Moishe. Every time she had to eat an unusual plant, she said a quick prayer that she would not die. She prayed not so much for her own life but for God to let her live to take care of her son. The very thought of her dying and leaving Moishe alone in the woods made her tremble. Once she'd eaten a mushroom and became sick and vomited. But at least the mild poison acted instantly before she allowed Moishe to eat it.

Wild animals posed a threat too. Lila shuddered as she held her little boy in her arms during the night when she heard the howl of wolves nearby or the hooting of a tawny owl. Once, when she was an eight-year-old child, she'd seen a tawny owl. It was a story that had been branded in her memory.

Her mother had not known it, but Lila had made pets of a family of brown mice who lived under a tree, a few hundred feet behind her home. If her mother had been aware that she was playing with rodents, she would have forbade Lila from touching them. Lila knew her mother, and she knew that her mother would have warned her that mice were dirty and carried disease. But Lila didn't believe it for a second. The mice whom she'd befriended were as soft and sweet as little angels. Every night she carefully broke off bits of bread and matzo from her portions at dinners to bring to her pets. And before she went off to bed, she ran outside and fed them. One Sabbath night, the prayers had gone on longer than usual, and it was already starting to get dark when Lila snuck out of her bed to feed the mice. She ran, carrying the cloth with the bits of bread inside. But she arrived just in time to see the most horrible thing her young eyes had ever witnessed: An owl. In retrospect, the bird was probably not as massive as her younger self remembered it to be. But at the time, it had seemed like a huge mass of black and brown feathers as it swept down and grabbed one of the baby mice with its terrible sharp talons. The mother mouse had let out a squeak of horror.

Lila's eyes had met the coal-black eyes of the owl as she took the baby mouse from its mother's side. Lila looked down at the mother mouse and she swore, even in the semidarkness, that she could see the pain in the mother's eyes. Anger filled Lila. She would have done anything to stop the owl from its flight. She threw stones at the owl, but she was small and not very strong. Her stones missed their mark. Then she began screaming so loud that her mother and father came running outside. But she was powerless to make the great bird of prey release the tiny creature. Her mother ran to her just as the monster owl disappeared into the sky carrying the small, white, furry body. Lila was trembling so hard that her teeth were chattering. Her mother wrapped her arms around Lila and held her as she sobbed for the little rodent and his mother. It was a long time before Lila could stand up and go into the house. But she was amazed that her parents did not reprimand her for having kept the mice as pets, although they insisted that she discontinue playing with rodents. And from that time on Lila feared owls.

Whenever she heard the hoots of the owls as they searched for food, she held her small son close to her. He was more vulnerable than she. And even though she knew he was too large for an owl to carry off, she was still afraid for him. Lila knew she was defenseless, and because she was well aware of this fact, her heart always beat a little too fast, and she was constantly plagued by her own silent terror. She had the gun that Werner had brought with them, but after she shot him she had been so anxious to get away that she'd forgotten to take the extra bullets. To make matters worse, there was always the danger of being caught and arrested. Three times now she had clamped her hand over her son's mouth to keep him silent as they hid behind the trees, while soldiers marched only a few feet away.

The following afternoon, as they were traveling through the forest, they passed a pond. The water had melted in spots. Lila had never been fishing, and she had no idea of how to go about it, but they needed food. She took off her skirt because she didn't want it to get wet. Then in her slip, she sat Moishe on a rock and told him not to move. "The water is still very cold," she told him, then she took his little face in her hands and lifted his eyes to meet hers. "And we don't know how deep it is, either. So, please, stay here and wait for Mommie to take care of things."

Lila walked into the water and waded up to her knees. She was terrified that there might be a sudden drop at any time, and she didn't know how to swim. There were fish swimming in the pond, but they were fast and always eluded her grasp. She slid and almost fell. But she tried again, until she heard splashing behind her. Moishe had followed her into the icy water and he was drowning. Her feet would not move as fast as she willed them to. *What if he disappears under the patch of ice? Please God, please help me.* By the time she got to Moishe, he was coughing furiously, but at least he was still alive, still breathing. His body was trembling from the cold water. She stripped him naked and laid his clothing in the sun. Then she wrapped his shivering body in the blankets and held him close to her breast. Lila felt the hot tears sting the backs of her eyes. *I almost lost you. You are the most important thing in the world to me, and in a single moment you were almost gone forever.* She rocked Moishe softly and the tears began to flow down her cheeks. She thought of her husband. *Ben, I am so alone here. I never thought I would say this, but I need you. I need a friend, someone I can talk to, someone to help me make some of these decisions that I am faced with every day. Oh, Ben. We wasted so much time fighting. Strange, isn't it? I guess maybe I loved you. I can't say for sure. But maybe I did. I always thought I was so*

145

strong, but now I find that I wish you were here beside me, so we could go forward together. There are times I think I can't go on anymore. I just want to give up. I know it's a sin, but I have thought of taking our lives: Moishe's first and then my own. If I could do this in a way that would be painless to him, I would do it. I would do it because I don't know what is in store for his little soul. Will he die a painful death by starvation? Will he be taken from me and ripped apart by wild animals? Will the Nazis capture us and torture our poor, innocent boy just because he's a Jew? She glanced down at Moishe. He was staring up at her, his eyes wide with fear. *Oh, poor child you must have read my mind. You look like you are afraid of me, your own mother. You're eyes are huge, staring at me. You are afraid I will kill you. What have I come to?*

"Shaaa, shaaa, little Moishe. No one is going to hurt you. Mommie is here. Mommie would never hurt you. I will care for you, give my life for you, if need be. But you must listen to me from now on when I tell you to do something. If I tell you to wait outside the water you must do as I ask. Do you understand?"

"Yes, Mommie."

"What a good boy you are. What a very good boy." She bent down and kissed the top of his wet, blond hair.

"Will you tell me the story of Moses again?" he asked.

She smiled at him. He loved that story because he and Moses shared the same name.

"Yes, of course, I will tell you. Are you ready?"

Moishe put his thumb in his mouth and nodded.

"Moses was born to Jewish parents, but when he was just a little boy, there was a pogrom and Moses was in danger. So his mother took him to the river and wrapped him in a Hebrew blanket, so that he would see the blanket when he got older and know that he was a Jew. Then she put him in a basket and pushed the basket down the river. As the river's current took little Moses, his mother said a prayer to God that someone would save him."

CHAPTER 29

April, Berlin

Three days before Hilde was to arrive, Gretchen and Eva went over the entire apartment, cleaning and checking everything. They went over Eva's story several times to ensure they would not slip up while Hilde was staying with them.

"I am so afraid I will call you Rebecca. Once in a while I still slip up when we are in the apartment. And what happens if I say something about Eli by accident? I am so worried," Gretchen said to Eva.

"I know. We have to be very guarded. Before we speak we must weigh everything we say. She will be here all day, every day; there will be no time when it will be safe to speak openly in this apartment until she leaves," Eva said.

"I am dreading this."

"Me too."

Hilde arrived very early in the morning; she looked thin and sickly. She brought a suitcase filled with gifts for Gretchen. She hugged Gretchen and then sat down on the sofa.

"I brought you coffee, real coffee, of course, and sugar, a

whole box full, and chocolate too! I even brought you a gold necklace. I think you will love it."

"It's good to see you," Gretchen said, and it would have been true had it not been for the fact that she had to be very careful of every word she said.

"I'm happy to see you too. I'm afraid I don't look very well though. The pregnancy has been hard on me."

"You've lost weight," Gretchen said. "I mean, not your belly, of course, that's baby weight." Gretchen mustered a smile. "But your face has grown thin."

"Being pregnant takes a toll on your body. But do you remember how I used to say that I thought that if I had a child I would be able to give it up to the Lebensborn?"

"I do."

"I had no idea how bonded a mother can become with that tiny life growing in her womb. I couldn't imagine giving this child away. You were right."

"Having a baby is going to be wonderful for you."

"I think so too. The further along I get in the pregnancy, the more I can't wait to give birth. I had a terrible relationship with my mother and because of it, I didn't think I would make a good mother. But now, I believe that having my own child will help me to work through some of the pain I felt growing up. I want to give my baby the best life I possibly can."

"Oh, Hilde, I am so happy for you. I think that having a baby will bring you so much happiness. And to Axel too."

"Yes, Axel and I have grown closer since I got pregnant. It's still not a fairy-tale marriage. Sometimes I look at him and wish he was handsome and suave. He's really rather ordinary, but in my own way, I care for him. And I realize that he is very good to me."

"He loves you very much. He told me at your wedding. He

149

said you are his reason for living."

"Axel." Hilde smiled and shook her head. "Now, why can't Axel look like Hann?"

"You still think of Hann?" Gretchen asked incredulously.

"Sure, sometimes. You have to admit, he was devastatingly handsome."

"Yes, he was. But you're married now, and you couldn't ask for a better husband than Axel," Gretchen said, then she changed the subject. "You must be tired from traveling. Why don't you go and freshen up while I make us a pot of coffee. I told the foreman at the factory that I might be late this morning because I had a friend coming to stay with me from out of town. I told him I wanted to make you comfortable before I came in to work. But, of course, if you are tired . . . maybe you would prefer to lie down?"

"I think I would like to lie down, if you don't mind. I'm very tired."

"Of course. You know where the bathroom is, don't you?"

"Yes," Hilde said, "I remember."

"And my cousin Eva has agreed to sleep on the sofa while you are here. She wants you to be comfortable. So let me carry your bags to my father's old room."

"Are you both sure about this? I don't want to put you or your cousin out," Hilde said.

"Of course we are both sure. You are our guest. Now go on and get washed up. I'll leave your bag in my father's room."

Hilde stood up and hugged Gretchen. "I am so glad to see you, my best friend. Just being here with you, I feel better already."

CHAPTER 30

Hilde slept, awakening just as Gretchen was returning from work. Gretchen was laying her handbag down on the coffee table when Hilde came out of her bedroom.

"Did you get some rest?" Gretchen asked.

"Yes, I did. I needed it. I slept better here than I have in a long time."

"I'm glad." Gretchen smiled. "Would you like something to eat?"

"I was thinking that I would like to take you and Eva out for dinner this evening. That is, if you would like to go."

"Hilde, that's so sweet of you. But you don't have to do that."

"I want to. It would be my pleasure. Most of the local restaurants should be having celebrations for the führer's birthday tomorrow. So this will be fun. What time does Eva come home from work?"

"Around seven. Sometimes a little earlier or later. She works in a bakery, and the owner closes when he runs out of bread," Gretchen said.

"So she should be arriving in about an hour or so?" Hilde asked.

"Yes, give or take."

"Then let's get ready to go somewhere for dinner. We can talk and have a few beers. It will be nice. Do you think it would take long for her to change clothes and freshen up?"

"I doubt it. Eva is very good that way. She gets ready quickly."

At five after seven, Eva's key turned in the door and she walked in. Hilde stared at her. Her eyes narrowed. "This is my cousin Eva. Eva, this is my best friend, Hilde," Gretchen offered. As soon as Gretchen saw the look on Hilde's face she knew that Hilde saw how beautiful Eva was.

"It's a pleasure to meet you. Gretchen speaks so highly of you," Eva greeted Hilde graciously.

"Oh? How nice." Hilde's eyebrows rose.

"Hilde has offered to take the two of us out for dinner. How long will it take you to get ready?" Gretchen asked as her gaze landed on Eva.

"Just a few minutes. I'll wash my face and change my dress. I'm afraid this one is covered with flour. Would that be all right?"

"Of course," Hilde said. She sat down on the sofa to wait. Her heavy belly made standing for long periods difficult. After Eva had disappeared into the bathroom Hilde turned to Gretchen. "She's quite pretty. Does she remind you of Thea?"

"No, I don't think so. Not at all."

"She has the blonde hair. They are the same height and hourglass shape," Hilde said. "Well, it doesn't really matter, anyway. She's not Thea. She's your cousin. And any relative of yours, Gretchen, is a friend of mine."

Gretchen smiled wryly at Hilde, a little unsure. Hilde's tone of voice had not been at all convincing.

Within a few minutes Eva returned. Even without a stitch of makeup she was radiant. She turned to Hilde. "It really is very nice of you to take us out for dinner, Hilde."

152

Hilde smiled. "So where should we go? Somewhere in town?"

"Perfect," Gretchen said.

The three women, each so different from the others, walked into town. Hilde was right, the restaurants, bars, and beer gardens were full of people celebrating Hitler's birthday. There was live music and people playing drinking games. They chose a little restaurant. The hostess seated the three girls at a table with a red-and-white-checked tablecloth and handed them menus.

"Let's start with a round of beer," Hilde said. "I could use a cold one." She flagged a pretty waitress in a traditional German folk costume, with a short yellow dirndl skirt, a black vest, and white, ruffled blouse. Her light brown hair hung on either side of her head in two braids.

They ordered thick, dark beer, sausage, sauerkraut, and a vinegar-potato salad.

"This is a feast, Hilde. Are you sure you can afford all of this?"

"I'm quite sure. I earned plenty of money while I was working, and now Axel has been promoted. So he got a raise. A few reichsmarks to celebrate two wonderful occasions is money well spent."

"Two?" Gretchen asked.

"Three, actually. Let's drink to them, eh?" Hilde said, as the waitress put three mugs of dark beer on the table. "To my baby."

The three clinked glasses.

"To lifelong friendships, like the one we have, you and I, Gretchen," Hilde said and again they drank.

"And, of course, to good health and long life for our wonderful führer, on his birthday."

They clinked their glasses again. Eva was hesitant to drink

to Hitler. But she hid it well; no one could have seen it in her face.

Hilde's eyes lit up as she glanced across the room and saw a familiar face. *Hann! Hann is here*, she thought with excitement.

Then as Eva lifted her beer to her lips she caught the eye of a handsome man who was staring at her from across the room. So blatant was his gaze that she cast her eyes down. But before she could even look up again he was standing at their table.

It was Hann.

"Hann!" Hilde exclaimed. She glanced over at Gretchen but went on talking to Hann. "It's wonderful to see you. I wrote to you several times but you never answered. I hoped that you were doing all right. So, dare I ask, what are you doing here in Berlin? I thought you were in Frankfurt. My gosh, don't you look handsome in that Wehrmacht uniform! I'm rambling. I'm sorry," Hilde said.

"I was conscripted into the army, so I had to quit my job with the autobahn. I'm here on leave to visit my mother for the führer's birthday!"

"You must join us for dinner. I insist," Hilde said.

"Would that be all right with you, if I sit here, beside you?" Hann asked Eva directly.

She did not look up at him, but she managed to say, "Oh yes, of course."

"Hilde and Hann are old friends," Gretchen said. There was the slightest hint of a warning in her voice.

"We knew each other when we were teenagers," Hann said, pulling up a chair and sitting down beside Eva, between Eva and Gretchen. "I'm sorry, I didn't get your name?" he asked Eva with a flirtatious smile.

"I'm Eva."

"You must be new here, in Berlin. I don't remember you from the Bund."

"She is my cousin, Hann. She's here from the countryside, staying with me for a while," Gretchen said quickly. She was afraid that Eva might be at a loss for words.

Gretchen saw an unmistakable look of attraction in Hann's eyes as he looked at Eva. This was not good, not at all. Gretchen felt her head begin to ache. *I can't believe that of all people, we had to run into Hann. This can bring nothing but trouble,* Gretchen thought. *I wish we could leave and go home before this goes any further. Hilde will not take kindly to his paying so much attention to Eva. I can't possibly ask if we can leave; the food has been ordered. And besides, who am I kidding? Hilde will not want to go.*

Hilde was talking quickly and incessantly. She was obviously excited to see Hann. She began asking him questions about his life. He, in turn, only gave her one-word answers. Then he grew quiet for a few moments and stared at Hilde directly, as if he were about to say something cruel. Gretchen was suddenly afraid he was going to accuse Hilde of being the cause of all of Thea's misfortunes. She felt a shiver run down her spine as she saw the disgust in Hann's eyes as he looked across the table at Hilde.

"Are you pregnant?" he asked.

"Yes, I am. I didn't think you would notice. I thought the table was blocking my big belly." Hilde tried to smile.

"It's not," he said. "So, are you married?"

"Of course I am," Hilde said, looking like she wanted to say something more, but she didn't.

"Well, good. I am glad you found someone who makes you happy and are all settled down."

"Oh, I wouldn't say that I am all settled down, like an old hausfrau." Hilde laughed a nervous laugh.

But Hann said nothing. His eyes were fixed on Eva, who was slowly sipping her beer, her eyes cast down at the table.

Gretchen and Eva did not speak. They were allowing Hilde to take charge of the conversation. However, Eva's silence didn't detour Hann's attentions toward her. Gretchen was horrified. She knew what happened to Thea, and she could see Hann's unrelenting interest in Eva causing them trouble.

When they were finished with dinner, Hann took several reichsmarks out of his pocket and laid them on the table. "For dinner, because I had such a lovely time."

It was more than enough to cover the bill.

"No, Hann, here take your money . . . please. I am taking everyone out tonight. Isn't that right, girls?" Hilde asked Eva and Gretchen. They nodded.

But Hann did not take the money. "A gentleman would never allow a lady to pay a dinner check," he said. "Please, allow me."

"If you insist," Hilde said, blushing and smiling.

"I do," Hann said, then he turned to Eva. "I would like to see you again, Eva. Would you like to have dinner with me?"

"Oh, I couldn't. I'm sorry." Eva stumbled on the words.

"Please? You wouldn't make a man beg to have dinner with you, who is fighting for our country, now, would you?"

"I'm very sorry," Eva said. "Gretchen, I think I am going to head home now. The three of you should stay and have a few more beers. I just want to get to bed because I have to get up for work before dawn. So, good night." Eva got up and quickly began walking toward the door.

"Wait!" It was Hann. He'd come up behind her. "I will not let a beautiful woman walk home alone in the dark."

"I'm fine, really."

"I insist. I would not be much of a man if I allowed a beautiful, young lady to walk home alone at night, now, would I?"

CHAPTER 31

It was a chilly April evening, and the air was moist from the heavy rain that fell earlier in the day. But even in the brisk weather, one could smell the promise of spring in the grass and the trees. The noise of celebration and live music flooded out of the beer halls. Hann walked on the street side of Eva, and for a few minutes neither of them spoke.

"I just got into town this afternoon. I plan to be here for a week," Hann said. "I really would like to take you to dinner. Anywhere you want to go . . ."

"I am flattered, really I am. But I am staying here with my cousin, and if I went out at night and came in late it might disturb her sleep schedule. Besides, I work all day, and I have to get up early because I work in a bakery, so I am sorry, but it's just not a good idea for me to go out in the evening . . ."

"You have so many excuses. I've known Gretchen for a long time. I will speak to her, if you'd like. I'll ask her if she would mind if I took you to dinner. I will promise to have you home early if that's what it takes." He smiled a fetching smile. "Please, have dinner with me?"

I am walking beside a man in a Nazi uniform. How is it possible that I could find him attractive? This is insane. I can't accept a date with him. Gretchen would be furious and rightfully so. But he is such a gentleman, so considerate. I must be mad, but I am thinking what would be the crime? It would only be one evening, one dinner. Then he will be on his way to wherever Hitler is going to send him. And my life will be back to normal. Still, he is my enemy. If he knew who I was, he would have me arrested in a minute. He is only a gentleman because he thinks I am an Aryan. I am no fool, or am I . . ."

"Would you have me get down on my knees and beg you? I will, if that's what it would take. You see, Eva, I know what I like and what I am looking for. And, quite frankly, I don't give up easily. So, before I go and humiliate myself, please, just say yes, you will have dinner with me."

She let out a short laugh. "I've never met anyone quite like you," she said. "And you certainly do go after what you want."

"Yes, I do. I promise you that I will continue to pursue you until you say yes. So you might as well accept my invitation now."

"I suppose I must," she said.

"Then you will? You will have dinner with me?" He suddenly sounded to her like a young boy filled with excitement on Hanukkah. He was so enthused that she had to laugh.

"Yes, I will," she said. *How can I be thinking of Hanukkah? I am out here posing as a Christian. Planning to have dinner with a German soldier. A Nazi. What am I doing? Hashem, please forgive me. I don't know how to make sense of all this.*

By the time they arrived at Gretchen's flat, they had plans to meet for dinner the following evening, April 20th, Adolf Hitler's birthday. A very special day for all Germans.

Hilde was silent as she and Gretchen walked back to the apartment, but Gretchen could feel Hilde's rage. They were almost all the way home before Hilde stopped walking. She

159

stood still for a moment, then she turned to look at Gretchen. "I've been waiting to see Hann again for years. I've been hoping for a chance meeting him, like this. And finally it happened. There he was, just as handsome as ever. But did he even pay me a bit of attention? No, and that is because of your cousin. Did you see the look in his eyes, when he looked at Eva?"

"I don't know what you mean?"

"He left the restaurant right after she left. I'll bet he chased her down so he could walk her home," Hilde said. "I'm sure of it." She snorted then shook her head. "And you know what really makes me burn? I'll tell you. Look at Eva. I realize now how much Eva looks like Thea. That man certainly has a type, doesn't he?"

"They don't look anything alike. But Hilde, please don't be thinking about Hann. You are married now; you have Axel. He loves you, and he's such a nice fellow. Soon you'll have a child . . ."

"You don't understand how I feel. I told you that I never loved Axel. I've been mad about Hann for as long as I can remember. And now that I've finally had the opportunity to see him again . . ."

"Hilde," Gretchen said, putting her arm around Hilde's shoulder, "if he is interested in Eva it's only because he can see that you're pregnant and married."

"That's not it. Not at all. Eva is pretty. I am ugly. My mother always said I was ugly." The bitterness in Hilde's voice scared Gretchen.

"Don't say that. You're a beautiful woman. And Axel loves you. Don't forget that. Many women never have the kind of love you have from Axel."

"Yes, Axel loves me, but he's the wrong man."

"He's your husband."

"Yes, and I would give him up in a second for Hann." Hilde crossed her arms over her chest and set her mouth in a hard grimace. "Besides, I've been thinking about this, and I think that Eva might be a Jew. Are you sure she's your cousin? How do you know for certain? When did you first meet her? Maybe she isn't really your cousin at all. Maybe she's a Jew who stole your cousin's papers." Hilde was ranting. "I've been around a lot of dirty Jews in the camp. They are sneaky. They do things like this."

They walked for a few minutes. Gretchen tried to catch her breath. She had to think of something to say. Something that would convince Hilde that Eva was her cousin and not at all trying to sabotage Hilde. Gretchen squeezed Hilde's shoulder. "Hilde, I'm your best friend, right?"

"Of course. You've always been my best friend."

"I'm begging you to not let this upset you. Eva is my cousin. She knows things about my family that only a cousin could know," Gretchen lied. She was trying to sound as convincing and concerned about Hilde as possible. But inside she was terrified. "And you're in your seventh month of pregnancy. You need to try and take it easy. Please, for the sake of your child. Hann is nobody to us anymore. He's just someone from our past. He means nothing in our lives today."

"I suppose you're right," Hilde said, but she wasn't convinced. "But it hurts, you know?"

"Yes, of course, I know. Let's have a nice cup of tea and one of the chocolates that you brought, when we get home. What do you say, best friend?" Gretchen put her arm around Hilde's shoulder and squeezed.

"All right."

Gretchen smiled and Hilde smiled back. But Gretchen was worried about Eva. She knew how cruel Hilde could be when she felt threatened. When Hilde had set out to ruin Thea, she'd had no limits, no scruples. And the worst part of all was that Eva had a secret. Eva was a Jew. *There will be hell to pay for Eva and myself if Hilde ever finds out the truth.*

CHAPTER 32

Once Hilde was asleep in her room, Gretchen went into the living room and found Eva sitting on the sofa, reading.

"Turn off the light in case Hilde gets up to go to the bathroom then come into my room. I want to talk to you."

Eva nodded and did as Gretchen asked. Once the door was closed, they both spoke in whispers. "Did Hann walk you home?"

"Yes, he insisted. I tried to discourage him, but I couldn't."

"There is something you must know. Hilde is dangerous. When we were young, she was in love with Hann. But he was never interested in her. He was in love with another girl, Thea. Hilde was so jealous that she caused a terrible scandal that forced Thea's family to leave Berlin. She started a rumor that Thea's mother had an affair with a Jewish doctor and that the doctor was Thea's father making Thea a Jew. It was terrible for Thea. I still doubt the truth of it, but that rumor ruined Thea."

"What happened?"

"The whole town turned against Thea's family. Her father left her mother. And then Thea and her mother disappeared from Berlin."

"Why are you still friends with Hilde if she is such a

terrible person."

"She had a rough childhood. Her mother was an alcoholic and prostitute. Her father left them when Hilde was very young. Then to make matters even worse, her mother committed suicide. Hilde found her dead. It was very hard on Hilde. She is damaged, and until she met Axel she didn't have anyone else in the world but me. I just don't know what to do with her. I have often wanted to distance myself, but I always feel sorry for her. But, quite frankly, right now I am afraid of her. You must never have anything to do with Hann. Do you understand me?"

"Of course, I understand, and you're right. But I have to know what happened to Hann when Hilde did this to him and Thea?"

"He didn't care if Thea was Jewish or not. He was in love with her. He searched everywhere for Thea, but I don't think he ever found her. I don't know for sure. But he left Berlin and went to work somewhere else. Hilde tried to write to him but he didn't respond. He never had any interest in her. But you are tall and blonde, like Thea, and I can tell that he is very interested in you. You must stay far away from him because Hilde can be dangerous. When she is provoked, she is like a cobra, especially when it comes to Hann. If she ever finds out your real name or who you really are . . ."

"He made me agree to have dinner with him tomorrow night."

"You can't ever have anything to do with him. You must not. Do you understand me?" Gretchen shook Eva's shoulders. Then she caught the look in Eva's eyes. "Please don't tell me you like him. I can see it all over your face. This is more terrible than you can possibly imagine."

Eva bent her head. "I'm sorry. I didn't mean to cause all of this. I really didn't. I tried to discourage him . . ."

"Is he coming here to pick you up tomorrow night?"

"Yes."

"I'll answer the door and tell him you're not here. He'll think you stood him up."

Eva nodded. "All right."

"Oh, Eva, I am so sorry. Are you upset?"

"Please, don't worry about me. I understand. I would never put you at risk because of my own selfish feelings. It was nothing, really, with me and Hann. I just found him attractive, that's all. And you're right. It's better this way. He's a Nazi. I'm a Jew."

Eva sat on the edge of Gretchen's bed with her head bent. Gretchen looked at Eva in the semidarkness. With her wispy, wheat-colored hair falling softly on her shoulders, her long legs, her slender waist, and her full breast, Eva was even more beautiful than Thea. *She and Hann would have made a lovely couple even though the entire idea is rather absurd. But it is far better this way.*

CHAPTER 33

The following day was busy at the bakery. The hours flew by as the customers came and went. There was a line of hausfraus buying bread and any sweets that Albert had for sale. Albert told Eva they were all planning special dinners for their families in celebration of the führer's birthday.

Eva's back ached and her legs were sore. She and Albert had been working nonstop since early morning. They had not even had a moment for lunch.

There was no denying that Hann was handsome in his uniform, as he walked into the bakery in search of Eva. The eyes of the female customers, both young and old, betrayed their appreciation of his blatant good looks. Many of them knew him. They'd grown up in this neighborhood as had he. "Hann? How are you?" one hausfrau asked. She was holding the hand of her child.

"Fine."

"You look well," said another woman, with her dark brown hair in a twist.

"Thank you."

But he didn't turn to even acknowledge them. He only had eyes for Eva. He walked up to the counter.

"Eva."

"How did you find me?" she asked, her hands trembling. She wished he would go away and never come back. Warning lights were going off in her head. *Danger!*

"You said you worked in a bakery, didn't you? I've been to every bakery in Berlin looking for you. I know we have plans for tonight, but I just wanted to see you for a few minutes. I wanted to look at you."

"Hann, I am busy, but I do need to speak to you," Eva said.

In the corner of her eye, Eva could see Albert watching her. She felt sorry for him. "Eva," he said. He must have overheard her because he added, "It's all right. I can handle the customers if you would like to go outside and speak to him." Albert was jealous, but he would not restrict Eva from speaking to this man if she needed to.

"Are you sure, Albert?"

"Of course. Go on," he said.

Albert is such a good, kind man. It's a shame I can't be attracted to him, instead of Hann. But my feelings don't really matter. I can't have dinner with Hann. I can never see or speak to him again. This ends here and now, Eva thought as she walked outside. It was a little past three in the afternoon, and the hot sun blazed on the sidewalk. Before she had a chance to say a word, Hann grabbed her hand and pulled her on the side of the building where the women could not look out the bakery window and watch them. Then he quickly kissed her.

"Oh! You must not do that ever again," she said, feeling her face flush. "Never, do you hear me?" Her voice was raised.

"I'm sorry. I didn't mean to offend you. Please, don't be angry."

"Hann. I have a boyfriend. A serious boyfriend whom I am in love with. I don't have any feelings for you. I don't want to have dinner with you."

167

"I don't believe you. If you do have a boyfriend, you should break up with him. Because no man would want to be involved with a woman who could look at me the way you do. I can tell by your eyes that you feel the same about me as I do about you."

"You're wrong. I don't."

"Lie to someone else, Eva. From the first moment I glanced across the room and saw you, I was hooked. You are everything I have been searching for."

"Aren't you in love with a girl named Thea?"

"Oh, so you know that story about Thea?"

"Yes, I do."

"Thea was a childhood crush. That was years ago. There is something very special about you."

"How can you say that, when you don't know me?"

"But I want to."

"Just forget we ever met. Go away and forget me, please. Get out of my life. Go."

"Is it Hilde? Are you pushing me away because of her? Because I never had any feelings for her. There was nothing ever between us. At least not on my part."

"It's not Hilde, it's me. I can't do this. I told you I have a boyfriend . . ."

He wiped a bit of flour from the shoulder of her dress. She backed away, almost cringing.

"Please, don't be afraid of me. I would never hurt you."

"I am not available. Go away and don't come back." Eva turned away and walked back into the bakery, picked up her apron, and headed behind the counter.

CHAPTER 34

Hilde didn't believe that Eva and Hann were not meeting secretly. She was certain that Eva was out to steal her boyfriend the same way Thea had done so many years ago. Once Gretchen had gone to work leaving Hilde alone in the apartment. She went to the mirror to ask the Valkyrie what to do.

"She is trying to take Hann away from me," Hilde said. "He's finally come back after all these years, and she is trying to steal him. She's probably a Jew just like Thea."

Thea wasn't a real Jew, remember? We made up that rumor, you and I, so that we could force her and her family to leave Berlin.

"I don't remember," Hilde said. "All I remember is that Thea was a boyfriend-stealing Jew pig."

It doesn't matter. Thea is gone. Now we have to get rid of Eva.

"Do you think she feels it's all right for her to go after Hann because I am married and pregnant?"

Who cares what she thinks? It isn't all right because we still love Hann. And we know that deep down he loves us too. The Valkyrie's face was crimson with rage.

"You're right. He does love us," Hilde said.

Eva is a whore. Probably a Jew whore. I'll bet she is manipulating him with sex, the Valkyrie said. *You must catch them together, so you can tell Gretchen that Eva is evil, and she is trying to steal your boyfriend. Gretchen knows how much you and Hann love each other, doesn't she?*

"She knows I love him. But she doesn't think he loves me."

Would he have come over to your table if he didn't love you? He came over to declare his love for you, and then Eva, that miserable whore, stepped in and stole him before he had a chance to say what was in his heart. The Valkyrie glared at Hilde.

"Yes, you're right. So what do I do now?"

You catch them together. Then you tell Gretchen. It's that simple.

"How? How can I ever catch them together?"

It should be easy. You'll have to put on a disguise and follow Eva after she leaves work. I am sure she will be on her way to meet Hann somewhere.

"You're right. You're always right," Hilde said.

We're always right, the Valkyrie corrected her, and then she disappeared.

Hilde went into town and purchased sunglasses and a hat that she was able to tuck all her hair into. She put them all on in the public restroom in the park. Then she walked to the bakery where Eva worked and hid in the alleyway until she saw Eva leaving for the day. Hilde followed Eva. She was waiting for her to go into a café where Hann would appear. Once he did, Hilde would come out of the shadows, take off her hat, and accuse Eva of stealing her boyfriend. She was going to tell Eva that Hann belonged to her, but she could never have imagined what was about to happen. It was more than anything she could ever have hoped for.

CHAPTER 35

After Eva finished work she left the bakery and decided to save the bus fare and walk home. As she rounded the corner she heard a voice call out, "Rebecca, is that you?"

Her head turned instinctively when she heard her name. But she wanted run. Someone from her previous life recognized her. Her heart raced as she walked more quickly.

"Rebecca," the woman's voice called out again. There was a line of people in front of the butcher shop blocking Eva's way. She couldn't get through fast enough to escape the woman who came running up to her.

"I'm sorry," Eva said. "I don't know what you're talking about; my name is Eva."

"Rebecca, it is you. Do you remember me? Frau Heidelhoff? I worked as a maid next door to your in-laws before the laws changed, and Aryan's couldn't work for Jews anymore. Don't you remember? You were kind to me several times. You gave me money when my son got hurt at his job at the factory so I could take him to a doctor. You gave me extra food when my daughter got pregnant. Whenever you saw me on your way to the market you always had a kind word to say." Frau Heidelhoff was speaking loudly.

It was true, Eva had always been kind to the woman

because she knew that Frau Heidelhoff was below average intelligence.

Eva's shoulder's slumped. "Yes, Frau Heidelhoff, I remember," she whispered, trying to quiet the woman down.

"I knew you would! I am doing very well now. My son joined the party, and they gave him his own business. My daughter and her husband both have good jobs. I live with my daughter, and I don't have to clean houses anymore." She smiled. But what are you doing out on the streets. It's dangerous for Jews to be out on the streets. You should not be out; you could end up in a prison camp," she said.

Eva pulled the woman away from the crowd. "You must go away, and promise me that you will never tell anyone that you saw me. Can you do that for me?" Eva asked.

"Yes, of course. But you should get off the streets."

"I will, but if you see me again, please don't say hello."

"Are you angry with me?"

"No, just do as I ask."

"Are you pretending not be Jewish? Are you pretending to be someone else, Rebecca?" The old woman's eyes lit up as if she finally understood.

"Never mind all of that. Please, Frau Heidelhoff, do as I ask."

"You are, aren't you?"

"Yes," Rebecca finally admitted. "And if you don't do as I ask you could cost me my life."

"Oh! Yes, you're right. You're right. I'll do it. I'm sorry. I didn't mean to cause you any trouble. Good luck to you," Mrs. Heidelhoff said as she scurried away.

Rebecca was unnerved. She was trembling so hard that she could barely stand. Leaning against the building she took several long slow breaths. *It's going to be all right. Even though she is a bit slow, she won't say anything. She doesn't want to hurt me.*

"Are you all right?" a handsome young man asked Eva.

"Yes, thank you," she answered. Then she did her best to compose herself and started walking toward home.

CHAPTER 36

When Hilde heard the old woman call out "Rebecca" and then run up to Eva, she ducked into a doorway where Eva could not see her and listened. She trembled as she heard the woman say the words that she had always known were true. Eva was not Gretchen's cousin; she was a slippery Jewish imposter. *Poor Gretchen had been tricked by the Jew's lie. This Jewis, Rebecca, probably killed Gretchen's cousin and stole her papers, and poor Gretchen has no idea.* Hilde bit her lip and continued to watch as Rebecca and the woman separated. She felt gratification when she saw Rebecca lean against the building. *I've caught you in your lie, you Jew bitch*, she thought. Then once Rebecca began to head back to the apartment, Hilde took off the hat and glasses and stuffed them into her handbag. Then she began walking in the opposite direction.

When she arrived at the familiar apartment, she knocked on the door. An older man with thinning, gray hair and a cane answered. "Yes?" he asked in a hoarse voice.

"Is Hann at home?"

"I think he's in his room. Come in," the old man said. "Who can I tell him is here to see him?"

"Hilde."

"I'll be right back."

Hilde sat down in the sparsely decorated living room and waited. Her hands were ice cold and trembling. She was so nervous and excited at the same time. Hilde was about to share information with Hann that would change the way he felt about Eva . She was certain that what she was about to tell him would make him realize he'd made a mistake. *Perhaps once he sees that he and I are both the same, both pure Aryan, he will finally declare his love for me.*

Hann came out of the back of the apartment. His hair was uncombed, and he was wearing a white, sleeveless T-shirt and a pair of old, loose-fitting, black pants. Hilde had never seen him dressed so casually, and it tugged at her heartstrings. She began to fantasize. *This is how he will look once he and I are married. He will be busy working on the house, and I will be cooking and caring for our children. All he has to do is ask, and I will divorce Axel and marry him.*

"Hilde?" Hann's voice brought her back to the present moment.

"Yes, I came because I have to tell you something. Can we go somewhere we can talk?"

"Of course," he said, looking at her a little skeptically. "Come with me. We'll go into the kitchen. My mother is at the market, and my father won't bother us."

Hilde followed him.

"Please, sit down," he said.

They sat down at the table.

For several seconds she didn't speak. Hilde was sweating with excitement and anticipation. She was savoring the moment. *Here I am sitting across from Hann at the kitchen table. This is the way it will be every night once we are married.*

"Hilde? What is it you want to talk to me about?"

"Oh!" she stammered. "Yes, I want to tell you something very important. Something you should know. I had some suspicions about Eva. I wasn't sure she was who she said she was, so today I waited until she got off work, and I followed her. And do you know what I found out? I found out she's not Eva, Gretchen's cousin. She's a Jew. Her real name is Rebecca."

Hann glared at her. "Don't start this stuff again," he said, getting up and walking away from her. Then he stopped in front of the window and slammed his fist on the countertop. "You did this with Thea. You caused me all sorts of problems with Thea. I didn't believe you then, and I don't believe you now."

"But Hann, it's true this time. I swear it. I heard an old woman call Eva by the name Rebecca. The old woman told her that she should not be on the streets because it was dangerous for Jews to be on the streets." Hilde was begging to be heard, to be believed, to be loved.

"This time? This time! So you lied last time?"

"Hann, you don't understand . . ." Hilde said.

"Get out of my home," Hann said, his voice was raised. "Stay out of my life. Stay away from me! Do you hear me?"

Hilde could hardly speak. She wished she go to the bathroom mirror and consult the Valkyrie, but Hann was throwing her out. Tears began to fall down her cheeks. "You should listen to me. I'm trying to help you. You don't realize it, but you and I are the same. We are both Aryans. We belong together."

"I said, get out," he growled.

She stood up and dropped her handbag. He picked it up from the floor and thrust it into her hands. Then he walked to the front door. Hilde followed him. Hann opened the door. "Goodbye, Hilde," he said.

She walked out. HIlde held her belly and ran down the street. She ran until she got to the park. Then she sat down on the bench and wept.

It was then she decided to go to the Gestapo headquarters. *I'll make that Jew bitch pay for stealing Hann from me. She cast a spell on him, and that's why he has turned on me. But If Hann won't listen to me, the police certainly will.*

CHAPTER 37

April, in the Woods

There had been no sun for two days. The skies were a miserable charcoal gray. Angry bursts of lightening flashed through the air and thunder roared like a hungry beast through the forest. Wild animals let out loud, frightening cries. A cold wind whipped out of the north as torrents of heavy rain fell in sheets, penetrating the trees until the grounds were covered in mud. Moishe and Lila were drenched. Even the blankets that Lila had wrapped around Moishe were soaked. Neither Lila nor her son had eaten anything since the rains began. And every few minutes Moishe began to cry.

"I'm hungry, and wet, and cold, Mommie," he cried.

Lila held him close to her as the raindrops fell off the tip of her nose and chin. He was shivering, and his tiny teeth were chattering. She had to find a way to get him inside. And she had to put something into his belly. The only thing to do was try to walk as close to the clearing as possible and search for a farm with an unlocked barn where they could stay the night, dry off, and hopefully find food.

Moishe was coughing, a thick phlegmy cough, that scared

Lila each time she heard it. But for her child's sake she reminded herself that she had to remain calm. "Moishe, we have to walk so we can find a farm. All right? We have to get up and start walking."

He nodded. She stood up, her dress soaked and muddy sticking to her where she'd been sitting. She took Moishe's hand and they began to walk. Lila was cautious, staying hidden by the forest but close enough to the clearing to see what was up ahead. A gush of rain came down even heavier than before, blinding her. But Lila held tight to Moishe's hand, and they kept walking, going forward into the unknown. And then Moishe let out a scream. He grabbed his foot and held it as he sank down to the ground.

"What is it?"

"Hurts!" he cried, pointing to his ankle. Lila realized that he'd twisted his foot in the slippery mud.

"Oh, sweetheart. I'm so sorry." She held him close, kissing him. His shoes and socks were wet and black with mud. But as she held his foot up to look at it, the rain had already started to wash it clean. "Come on, let's try again."

"No," Moishe said. "No, Mommie."

Lila looked at him. She was ready to burst into tears or yell at him and tell him that all of this was hard on her too. But, of course, she realized, he was just a child and that would have done her no good. So she lifted him into her arms. Usually it upset her to see how light he was whenever she held him. But right now, she was glad she was able to carry him comfortably. They walked for over an hour. Lila slipped once and fell. She didn't drop Moishe, but it scared him and sent him into a fit of weeping. And although she cut her leg on a branch, she made light of it all and laughed.

"We took a slip, didn't we?" she said.

Once Moishe heard his mother laugh, he laughed too. Lila

couldn't sit down and look closely at her leg because she didn't want Moishe to notice that she was bleeding. The cut was smeared with dirt mixed with blood, but the rain was quickly washing it clean. Careful not to let him see the blood, Lila picked Moishe up and began walking again. Finally, in the distance, she saw the lights of a farmhouse. Behind the house was a big red barn. Never had she been so happy to see anything as she was right now, as she looked at that barn. It was early evening already, and it wouldn't be long before nightfall. They would have to stay back and wait in the woods until it was dark outside. But once all the lights were extinguished in the house, she would take Moishe and try to get into the barn. Most barns were not locked. She prayed that this one would be no exception. Especially tonight.

Now that Lila had a plan, she pulled Moishe back farther into the woods to wait. Every few moments he asked her when they could go inside. And every few minutes she answered "soon." Her patience was wearing thin, but she forced herself to control her temper. Moishe was only a toddler, a frightened, cold, and hungry toddler. He was just a little boy forced to endure conditions no child should ever endure.

From where they were hiding, Lila could see the light shining inside the house. Once the house was finally dark, she forced herself to wait another half hour or so before taking Moishe and heading to the barn. The darkness was a gift that she relished. They were invisible as she carried Moishe across the open path.

"Be quiet. Don't make a sound," she warned him as they passed the house, realizing after she'd said it that her voice might have been a little harsh.

"Mommie?" Moishe said, sounding terrified. "Are you angry at me?'

"Shhhh. I'm not angry, but be quiet," she warned again. There was no time right now to comfort him. No time to explain. They had to get to the barn.

Moishe began to weep. Lila, still carrying him, put her hand over his mouth to keep him silent. He wept harder and she began to run. Someone turned on a light in an upstairs room in the house and came to the window. Lila dropped down in the field and lay on top of Moishe. She whispered in his ear, "Please, my love. Please, don't make a sound." Her nerves were shattered. She was trembling with fear. If the farmer saw them or heard them, anything could happen. He might be kind and help them, give them food and shelter, or he might not believe they weren't Jewish and turn them in to the Gestapo for a reward. Her breathing was ragged, and she could hear her own frantic heartbeat.

"I'm scared, Mommie!"

"Shhh . . ." Again, she put her hand over Moishe's mouth. She knew she was adding to his terror. If she could only hold him and talk to him he would calm down. But there must be absolute silence if they were to survive. Little Moishe tried to pull his mother's hand from his mouth. And when he could not, panic set in. He began to kick his feet and pound his fists. "Shaaa, Shaaa, my child," she whispered in his ear. "Mommie would never hurt you. Trust me, please." His little body seemed to calm down with the softness of her voice and the kindness of her words. "I'm going to take my hand off of your mouth, but you must be quiet. You must not make a sound. All right?"

He nodded. The rain continued to fall heavily. Lila said a silent prayer then removed her hand. "Mommie, I'm cold," Moishe said loudly. She knew the farmer had heard something because she saw him open the window upstairs.

Lila covered her son's mouth again. "Who's out there?"

the farmer called out into the darkness.

Lila's heart was beating so hard that it felt like it might leap right out of her chest and run away on its own. In the moonlight, she could see Moishe's blue eyes wide with terror. Again, she tried to calm him by whispering in his ear. But because they wandered through the forests alone, they almost never heard the sound of anyone else's voice. So when the farmer hollered out his window, it petrified the child. He was crying softly but had stopped kicking his feet. The light was still blazing in the second-floor window. Lila knew they had better run. She whispered in Moishe's ear. "I am going to pick you up, and we are going to head back toward the forest. It's not safe for us here. Please, Moishe, I am begging you . . . don't make a sound."

They were both soaking wet and covered in mud but Lila lifted her son into her arms and began to run toward the forest. This time, Moishe was silent. She ran, but her feet slipped out from under her, and she fell in the mud, still holding her son close to her breast. Behind her she heard the door of the farmhouse open. There was a severe pain in her leg as she tried to get up, but her feet could not get any traction in the slippery mud. She couldn't trust that the farmer would be kind. Her inner voice told her that if she and Moishe were to survive they must get away from there quickly. She stood up, but she was too late. The farmer was behind her with a long-barreled gun in his hand, pointed straight at her and Moishe.

CHAPTER 38

In the Woods

Lila couldn't tell if it was the rain that was blinding her or her own tears. Moishe was pulling at her hair and tugging her sleeve with his tiny hand.

"Run away, Mommie. Let's run away."

"Wait a minute. I think I recognize you," the farmer said in a hard voice. "I was working on the roadblock last year when the crop was bad. You're the woman who was in the car with that Nazi officer who was murdered," he said, wiping the rain from his eyes. Thin wisps of gray hair were now wet and sticking to his scalp.

"We are only a woman and a child. Please, I beg you to let us go. Please, take pity," Lila begged.

Just then the farmer's wife came outside, wearing a yellow raincoat. "Who are these people?"

"I am certain that this is the same woman who was with the SS officer who was found murdered only a few miles from here. She's a killer. It's a good thing that the police are on the way," the farmer said.

The farmer's wife glanced at Lila and then turned back to her husband. "It's raining like crazy out here. I am going to go inside and put a pot of water on for hot tea. It will be ready for you when the police take them away. You'll need something hot, so you don't catch your death of a cold from standing out here in the rain." Then without a second glance at Lila, the woman turned away and walked toward her house.

"I hungry, Mommie. I want tea too. Tell her. I want tea."

"Shhh." Lila squeezed Moishe's shoulder gently. Then she turned to the farmer again. "Please, I am only a woman with a small child . . ."

"Quiet! I don't want to hear anything from you. You're a killer," he said. "Nothing, not another word, or I'll shoot you and the boy."

Lila had no choice but to remain silent and wait. Every so often, Moishe whispered in her ear, "Mommie?"

"Shhh," she answered each time.

Then she heard the terrible blaring horn of the Gestapo car. This sound was burnt into her memory from the days when the Nazis had begun clearing the Jews out of her small neighborhood, back in Poland. Ahh hut, ahhh hut, ahhh hut . . . It was a loud, petrifying sound that everyone knew meant that some poor, unfortunate Jew was being taken away from their home and from their family. Jews were being branded as criminals. But Lila was certain that the only crime any of the other people who had been arrested and taken to the ghetto had ever committed was the crime of being Jewish.

The imposing black automobile stopped in front of the farmer. Two men in long, black leather coats got out of the car. "You picked a hell of a night to call us, Sobeinski," one of the policemen said. "So what have we here?" He turned to look at Lila and Moishe. "A drowned rat and her dirty little rat offspring."

"Papers!" the other Nazi barked at Lila. "Give me your

184

papers."

"I don't have any," she said.

"No papers? That's a crime in and of itself. You must be a Jew."

"We are Polish. We are not Jews, my name is Felicia Bankowski, and the boy is my son, Anatole," Lila lied.

"So what were you doing crawling around the grounds of this man's farm in the rain?"

"Looking for food. Our farm burned down."

"She's a murderer," the farmer said. "I saw her when I was working on the roadblock last year. She was in the car with that SS officer on the same night that he was found murdered."

"A murderer? You killed an SS officer? You are in serious trouble, young lady. Get up from the ground. Take your filthy child and get in the back seat right now. Vermin! Mach schnell, I want to get out of this rain."

Lila stood up. She thought about running, but she knew she would be shot in the back. Moishe would either be killed along with her, or worse—he might be tortured. She sucked in a deep breath and carried Moishe into the car. The door slammed. Then the two policemen got in the front seat. Lila held Moishe close to her.

"Car, Mommie," he said.

She nodded.

"Where we going? Home?"

"I don't know."

Moishe laid his head on her breast. For the moment, Moishe seemed content just to be out of the rain. Lila felt sick when she looked at her son. The poor child didn't realize that the danger they were about to face was much worse than the cold and the rain. There was no reason to tell him. He would find out soon enough what was in store for them, and so would she. Right now, he was just satisfied to sit on her lap and cuddle himself into her while quietly sucking his thumb.

CHAPTER 39

Ravensbrück

Moishe screamed as the Gestapo pushed him and his mother onto the train that would transport them to Ravensbrück. She put her hand over his mouth to quiet him. But the guard was unnerved by the boy's scream and he struck Moishe, whipping his hand hard across the child's face. Moishe's lip spurted blood. The boy began shaking, but he grew quiet. He was trembling so hard that he couldn't walk. Lila had to carry him in her arms.

"Get on the train and Mach schnell. There is no time for us to waste trying to quiet your spoiled brat," the guard said.

Once inside, Lila and Moishe huddled in the corner. The boxcar was so crowded with women and children there was no room to sit. They were forced to stand. It was very dark in the train car; the only light that flickered was coming through the tiny openings in the wooden slats. There were several other children on board and most of them were crying. Some of the women were crying too. The child was growing heavy in Lila's arms as she stood, holding him close to her. Moishe put his head on his mother's breast and his thumb in his mouth. She hummed a lullaby. And then the train rocked to life and began slithering down the rails.

"Where do you think they are taking us?" one of the younger women asked, directing her question to no one in particular.

It was hot, and the smell of sweat permeated the air. The bucket in the corner that was there for excretions emitted a strong and foul odor.

"I don't know," another woman said, "but we can be sure it won't be good."

"I am a Jew. Is everyone here Jewish?" someone asked.

"No, I am Romany," a young girl's voice came from the other side of the boxcar. "They took the rest of my family too. I don't know what they did with them. But I am alone here, now."

"I am Polish. I was a partisan," another said.

The women all began declaring their backgrounds.

Lila had been silent.

"What about you?" the women next to Lila asked.

"I had no papers. I suppose you might call me a thief. I stole food for my child," Lila said.

"Are you a Jew?" the woman asked Lila.

"Yes," Lila whispered, admitting that she was Jewish for the first time since she'd left the ghetto. "But I am not going to tell them I am Jewish. I am going to tell them I am Polish. Perhaps it will save my son's life."

"Well, your papers wouldn't have helped you much. If you had papers they would say you were a Jew and as soon as the Nazis saw the star, you'd be right here on this train with the rest of us. Being a Jew is a crime in and of itself. I know; I'm Jewish."

Between the heat and noxious odors, Lila felt dizzy and sick to her stomach like she might vomit. Moishe gagged several times which resulted in dry heaves. *My poor little boy;*

he is sick to his stomach. He gags, but his stomach is empty, Lila thought. *What scares me even more is that he has stopped asking for food. His appetite is gone. All he does is lie here in my arms. His head is burning up with fever. And he is so still that I sometimes fear he has died.*

The train came to a sudden halt tossing the passengers in the boxcar around like rag dolls. Then there was a loud noise as the guards unlocked and pulled open the door. Lila was not sure how long she had been traveling, but it seemed like many days. After so much time in the darkness, the sunlight hurt her eyes. However, there was no time to adjust to the light. Female guards with dogs and whips were demanding that the prisoners move quickly. Lila heard the whips cracking and the cries from the women who'd been whipped. Moishe's eyes were half closed. He was no longer crying. Lila was carried forward in a rush of frightened people. As they were all forced into lines, the guards began to separate the children from their mothers. Moishe let out a loud wail as the guard ripped him out of Lila's arms. She didn't take the boy away, however. The guard seemed to get some sort of sadistic pleasure from watching Moishe beg to go back to his mother. He reached out to Lila. "Mommie?" he said, crying and begging her to come and get him. But there were guards standing over her, and she was unable to escape from the line of women. Again, Moishe yelled out, "Mommie?" Her heart hurt, and she ran out of the line toward her son. But one of the female guards put out her foot and tripped Lila, who fell facedown in the dirt. "Mommie?" Moishe's voice was frantic now.

"Shut up," she heard one of the guards say to Moishe.

"He's just a child and he's frightened. Please let him stay with me," Lila begged the guard who had tripped her. But instead of compassion, the woman began to kick Lila with her black boots while the other guard held Moishe firmly so that he was forced to see his mother being kicked and beaten.

"Mommie! No, please, no! Mommie!"

He was screaming in a terrible, high-pitched voice and kicking his legs in a panic. All he could say was "No," "Mommie," and "Please."

Lila tried to look up at him and smile. She had to find a way to ease his fear and to make him believe she was all right. But blood was pouring from her nose and mouth. Moishe was hollering and pushing to get away from the guard, but the guard held him tightly by the shoulders. "Hurts! Hurts!" he screamed, kicking the guard in the stomach. She released her grip on him, and he fell to the ground. The guard lifted him up by his arm and punched him in the stomach. His small body doubled over as he tried to breathe. He could not fight back anymore. All he could do was struggle to breathe. Lila tried to stand up. She had to get to her son; he needed her. But the guard's shiny, black boot came down on her back, leaving her lying in the mud with blood smeared all over her face.

A woman wearing a gray-striped uniform walked over to Lila and helped her up when the guards were busy lining the others up for their pelvic exam.

"Come on. I know you are in pain, but you must get on your feet or they will kill you. Your son is in the children's camp. He will need you."

"Who are you?" Lila asked, wild eyed and wincing with pain.

"I'm a prisoner here. My name is Ann. I was an artist before I was arrested. I'm a political prisoner from Poland. I was member of a Polish Resistance group. We tried to bomb a train but we got caught. That's how I got here."

"I'm from Poland too."

"I know. I heard you speaking in Polish."

"Where is my son? You said he is in a children's camp. Take me to him, please."

"You can't go there now. You have to go through the process for new arrivals. It's not going to be easy on you. They are going to do terrible, unthinkable things to you. They are a sick lot, these Nazis. But you must muster all your courage and think only of surviving for your son's sake. You wouldn't want him in this camp without you. Now get up and follow me. We have been talking here too long."

Ann took hold of Lila's forearm, and then putting her hand in the small of Lila's back she helped her to her feet. Then Ann walked Lila into the line.

"What happens next?" Lila asked. "And how soon can I see my son?"

"Just follow the group. Don't make trouble. Don't ask questions. Close your eyes and try to remember a better time. Do whatever you have to do to get through this. I'll find you in your barracks later and I'll help you. But I must leave you now. I have to go to my work detail."

"Work?"

"Yes. Goodbye for now."

The initiation for new prisoners was more horrifying than Lila could have ever imagined. She was stripped naked, her hair and pubic hair were shaven. Then she was vaginally examined with a dirty instrument that had been used on all the woman who were in line before her. All the while, the SS men watched. She'd never felt such humiliation in her life. If it weren't for Moishe, she would have refused to allow them to do this to her, even if it had meant death. But Moishe would need her. Ann was right.

Next she was herded like an animal, still naked, shaven, and demoralized, into a shower room, with a large group of other women. Then she was given her uniform and sent to her barracks. Lila had a Star of David on her uniform. Even without papers they knew she was Jewish.

That evening there was a roll call. Lila ran alongside the other women to line up. It was there that she saw the beautiful blonde guard with the long whip who smiled at her and said, "Aren't you a pretty little thing?"

Lila felt her skin crawl. She forced herself to remember what Ann said and kept her head down.

"You are to be assigned your work duties," the guard said. "You, you, and you, will go to the tailor shop." Then she pointed to three others. "You, you, and you will go to the carpet-weaving shop." Another three were chosen to go to work at the Siemens company. And then she pointed to Lila and two others. "The three of you will work outside, in the construction of the buildings and the roads." The blonde guard smiled. "The outside jobs are the hardest ones that we have here in Ravensbrück. You will be working outside, and you'd better hope that you are physically strong enough to work like a man. You see, ladies, I always save these special jobs for the prettiest new prisoners."

Lila's heart sank. She was not strong. Of course she would do what she could. But working on construction sounded impossible. Then the women were dismissed and sent to eat. Lila was given a bowl of watery soup which she quickly devoured. She couldn't remember the last time she'd eaten.

The women were ushered back to their blocks. When it got dark outside, Ann snuck into the barracks where Lila slept. "How are you feeling?"

"I'm all right. Achy. I want to see my son, my Moishe."

"That's why I came. I want to help you."

"Why?"

"Why do you ask? You need my help, don't you?"

"Yes, I do."

"Then accept it and don't ask questions."

"I have nothing to give you."

"I'm not asking you for anything. Come on, follow me."

Lila followed Ann to the children's camp. They were careful to stay in the shadows and not be seen by the guards. The kapo blocked the doorway when she saw them coming. But Ann stuffed a moldy heel of bread into the kapo's hand. "We want to come in," she said.

"Come on, but be quiet and hurry up." The kapo took the bread and moved out of the doorway.

Lila saw Moishe laying on a small cot surrounded by other children. All of them were as dirty as he was, and she could see that his face was tearstained.

"Moishe," Lila whispered, "it's Mommie."

"Mommie," he shouted.

"Shhh. Sweetheart, you must be quiet."

"Mommie," he whispered, and then jumped out of the bed, stepping on one of the children who didn't even move, and climbed into her arms. She held him for a long time. "Now, listen to me. Be a good boy. Mommie is going to try and find a way to get us out of here. But until I can, you must listen to what the guards tell you and do whatever they say. Don't cry and don't make trouble. Just wait for me, and I'll come back to see you soon."

After Lila and Ann were back in Lila's barracks, Lila turned to Ann and said, "I don't know how to thank you."

"No need. We are all here against our will. We must help each other. Did they assign you a work detail?"

"Oh yes, I am assigned to work on the construction outside. I don't know if I am strong enough to do it."

"The construction is bad. A brothel is worse. Be glad you aren't being sent there."

"There's a brothel, here?"

"This is hell, Lila. The Nazis built this place with every imaginable horror. However, the brothels aren't here at Ravensbrück. They send the girls away to another camp where they have brothels."

"How do you know about this, if the brothels aren't here?" Lila asked.

"Because, I have friends who tell me things. And information travels through the inner circles. Let's just say, I know."

"How are we ever going to survive?"

"By doing whatever we have to do to live another day. Whenever you want to give up, think of Moishe. Remind yourself of how much he needs you. I have to go now, before I get caught being out of my bed," Ann said.

And then she was gone.

CHAPTER 40

When Gretchen arrived home from work she saw the door was closed to the room where Hilde was staying, and she assumed Hilde was taking a nap. Gretchen went to the cupboard and took out three potatoes, several carrots, and a bag of noodles to use for dinner. Then she went into her room and changed from her work frock into her housedress.

Gretchen began to peel the potatoes when Eva arrived. Eva's face was flushed from running. She looked at Gretchen wide eyed. "Where is Hilde?" she asked.

"I think she's asleep. The door to her room is closed," Gretchen said, then she looked at Eva. "What's wrong? You look upset."

"I am. Let's go into your room. I need to talk to you where no one can hear us," Eva whispered.

Gretchen nodded and followed Eva into the bedroom. Eva closed the door and leaned against it. "On my way home from work I saw a woman from my old neighborhood. The woman called out Rebecca several times. I tried to get away from her but she ran up to me in the street. Oh, Gretchen, what am I going to do?" Eva said, on the verge of hysterics.

"Did anyone hear her?"

"I can't say for sure. She was talking loudly. She mentioned that she remembered me and that she knew I was a Jew."

"Oh my," Gretchen said. "Oh my! We have to hope that no one heard her. Can you trust her not to say anything to anyone about seeing you again?" Gretchen said.

"I think so. I was always kind to her, and I know she likes me. If she caused trouble it wasn't intentional. She's not very bright. But I don't think she would turn me in."

"We have to act as if everything is all right. We can't let Hilde know anything at all. She cannot be trusted," Gretchen said.

"I know. I know you're right. I feel horrible. I have a terrible headache. My eyes are blurry and I'm feeling sick. Do we have any medicine?" Eva asked.

"No. Would you like me to go to the pharmacy and get you something?" Gretchen asked.

"I think I'd rather go. I don't want to be alone in the apartment with Hilde when she awakens. I am afraid that she'll know something is wrong from the look on my face."

"Are you sure you can make it to the pharmacy? You don't look well," Gretchen said.

"It's only two streets away. I'll be right back."

After Eva left, Gretchen went into the kitchen to start dinner. She was unnerved by the conversation she'd just had with Eva. *Why is there such hatred in the world? How can people do these things to others? Don't they realize that we are all the same? We are all made of flesh and blood. This nonsense about Jews and all of these other races being subhuman is pure insanity. Am I the only person who sees this? Hitler has taken my father away from me, and he's taken the man I love too. And now Eva is frightened, and there is a possibility that we could be in trouble. Will this nightmare ever end?*

The water began to boil. Gretchen dropped the noodles into the water. Then there was a knock on the door. She jumped at the sound. She tried to rationalize her fears. *It's probably Hann. What a pain in the neck he is. I wish I could just crawl under a tree, lie there, and die.*

The knock was louder.

Gretchen went to the door and opened it.

"Gretchen Schmidt?"

"Yes," she said in a small voice.

"You're under arrest," one of two Gestapo agents commanded.

Then things moved so fast that Gretchen hardly knew what was happening. The Gestapo were yelling in her face, but she couldn't hear them. The voices in her head were too loud. *I wonder if they have Eli too. I wonder if they've found him. Oh God, please, I have never been one to believe in you, but I need your help now. And if you do exist, help me, please. Don't let them hurt Eli or Eva. I promise you that if you protect us, I will do anything. I will go to church.* Gretchen was pushed into the back seat of a black automobile. The Gestapo agent in the passenger's seat had a thin, skeletal face. He was glaring at her. But she was so worried about Eli and Eva, that she did not even think of her own safety.

When she arrived at the police headquarters, Eva was there, and so was Hilde. All three women were in a room surrounded by a group of Nazis. One of the Nazis had an SS on his lapel. He was doing the questioning.

"Bring in the old woman," the SS officer said.

Two guards walked out of the room then returned, each of them pulling Frau Heidelhoff by an arm. "I'm sorry, Rebecca. I didn't mean for all this to happen. The Gestapo came to my apartment. They questioned me about you. They wanted to know how I knew you. I told them that I worked next door to the Kaetzel's, your husband's family. I didn't know what to do and I was so scared. I didn't mean to hurt you," Frau

197

Heidelhoff said.

"What is going on here? Eva? Hilde?" Gretchen looked at them both, questioning. There was a cut under Eva's eye that was bleeding. It looked as if she was crying tears of blood. Gretchen wanted to ask Eva about Eli, about whether he'd been caught, but she couldn't. *What do these monsters know? And what don't they know?*

"Gretchen Schmidt?" The SS officer was speaking directly to her.

"Yes."

"You should be ashamed of yourself."

"I told you she had no idea. It was not her fault. She was tricked by this filthy Jew. She's my best friend. You can't arrest her. She is a pure Aryan. She didn't do anything wrong. She was duped by this Jew. I'm telling you, Gretchen is not at fault," Hilde begged. "You must listen to me. You must—"

"Shut up. Speak when you are spoken to," the Nazi warned Hilde. "You were hiding a Jew? This woman is not Eva Teichmann, your cousin. Her name is Rebecca Kaetzel. She is a Jew, and she is the wife of another Jew by the name of Eli Kaetzel. First of all, Eva Teichmann was not your cousin. She was never related to you at all. She was a young, sickly woman who died a few years ago."

"I know you said that I should not speak," Hilde shouted desperately. "But please listen to me, I must tell you that Gretchen did not know anything about this. She was tricked. This Jew came to her and told her that she was her cousin. Gretchen believed her."

"Is this true?" The Nazi turned to Gretchen. "Were you tricked?"

Gretchen looked at Rebecca. "Yes, it's true. I tricked Gretchen Schmidt. She didn't know the truth. Hilde is right, I tricked them all. I bought the papers and I made up the lie,"

Rebecca said. The interrogator slapped Rebecca across the face with the back of his hand. Her head flew back.

"Hilde! What have you done?" Gretchen said, putting her hands up.

"I know you were not involved. I know they lied to you. Don't be afraid, Gretchen; you won't be harmed," Hilde said.

The Nazi seemed to be enjoying the interaction between the women. He leaned back on his desk and watched them with a look of amusement on his face.

"Hilde, you should never have gotten tangled up in this. You should have minded your own damn business," Gretchen said as tears streamed down her cheeks.

"I did it for you," Hilde answered, pleading with Gretchen to understand. "You're my best friend. I love you. I can get you a good job at Ravensbrück."

For Gretchen it was as if everything stopped for a moment. The SS officer was shouting. Hilde was screaming back at him. But everything had gone silent in Gretchen's mind. She could not hear them. All she could hear was the voice in her head and the rapid wild thumping of her heart. *I can choose to say Hilde is right. I can tell them that I didn't know. I can turn my back on Rebecca and walk out of here a free woman. No matter what she had to do, Hilde would see to it that I was unharmed. But I couldn't live with myself. And, of course, I know that if I tell the truth, if I say that I knew all along that Rebecca is Jewish and that I chose to help her, I will be signing my own death warrant. I am afraid. I am so afraid. And yet I can't walk away now. I know that this is what I must do. This is the only answer that I can live with.*

Gretchen shook her head. She thought about the letter Eli had left for her. She remembered how he had asked her to watch over Rebecca. Then she turned to the SS officer and said, "I knew. I always knew. I was hiding Jews because I don't believe in what the Nazi Party is doing." She'd said it.

Her hands were trembling. All the color had drained from her face.

The SS officer turned to Hilde and said, "See? I told you she was not innocent. She is a Jew lover and no friend for you."

Hilde gasped, absolutely devastated.

CHAPTER 41

Gretchen was forced at gunpoint into a dirty prison cell where she sat on a cold concrete floor. Every few hours she was beaten and questioned about Eli's whereabouts. She did not have to worry about betraying Eli. Not that she ever would have, but she didn't know where he was. Time passed. She didn't know how many days she'd lain there in her own blood and urine. But at some point, she heard Albert Weber, Rebecca's boss from the bakery, talking to the police.

"I promise you, she is not a Jew. Her name is Eva Teichmann. She is a German."

"Shut up and go home. You are lucky we don't arrest you for having a Jew in your employ. The fact is, I believe you didn't know. You are too stupid. Go back to your bakery, and be glad we are leaving you alone."

"Is there nothing I can do to help her?" Albert said in a pathetic voice.

"She is Jew. A pretty little Jew, blonde and blue eyed like an Aryan. But don't let her fool you; she's a manipulative Jew. They are all tricky, Albert. Get out of here before you end up in a cell too."

CHAPTER 42

Hilde went back home the day after Gretchen and Rebecca were arrested. She was shocked that Gretchen would lie to her. But Gretchen was still and had always been her best friend, so she was also heartsick for what she'd done to Gretchen. Until Gretchen confessed to knowing, Hilde really believed that Gretchen was innocent. If she had known the truth, Hilde would not have gone to the police. Instead, she would have begged Gretchen to go with her and turn Rebecca in. But now, everything was a mess. Hilde packed her bags to go home. But before she left, she went to the prison and begged to see Gretchen.

"I'll let you see her, but you can't go in and talk to her."

"Yes, please, let me see her," Hilde said, holding her belly. What she saw left her cold and terrified. Gretchen, bleeding on the floor of a prison cell.

"Gretchen!" she called out. But Gretchen didn't move. She tried again, but still no reaction.

The guard turned to Hilde. "Go now. Leave. I wasn't supposed to let you in here at all. Get out before I get into trouble."

Hilde nodded and walked to the train station. *What have I done?* She asked herself, over and over, as the train carried her back home to Furstenberg/Havel, right outside of Ravensbrück.

Hilde walked home from the train station, sweating as the sun beat down on her back. *If they put Gretchen in a camp, she will be tortured. I am certain of this because I've seen how the guards treat the prisoners. I don't give a damn what happens to the Jew, but Gretchen has always been my friend. And even though she made a terrible mistake by hiding a Jew, I could never abandon her. She is the only person who has ever stood by me in my entire life. Why she would take it upon herself to hide a Jew is beyond me. If only we had some time alone, I would ask her so many questions. But what difference does it make, anyway. I don't even want to know. I'd rather believe she was somehow tricked. And now that she's in trouble, and I am the person who brought the Gestapo down on her head, I wish I could help her.*

Axel was at work when Hilde arrived home. She was glad. She didn't feel like talking to him. She was in no mood to explain what had happened over the last twenty four hours. Hilde was exhausted, too exhausted to even bathe. Her head ached as she lay down on top of the sheets and tried to sleep. The sweat ran down her face and the back of her neck. When she closed her eyes all she could see was Gretchen's face. *What have I done? I might have destroyed her. Is there a God? Could there really be a God who is punishing me?* Hilde felt the bile rise in her throat. She was nauseated, sick enough to vomit.

Then a sharp cramping in her stomach brought Hilde to her feet. Rushing to the bathroom, she felt a gush of liquid run down the side of her leg. *Have I peed myself? Has my water broken?* Her belly was so big she couldn't see her feet. But when she sat down on the toilet it was as if her heart stopped. She saw that it was rich, red blood that had run down her legs, and now she could hear it pouring into the toilet. *I'm losing the baby. No, please, not this. Not this.* The cramping in her belly grew stronger. She doubled over and fell on the bathroom floor. *I have to force myself to get up and get to the phone so I can call Axel. I am in trouble.* Hilde held on to the side of the bathtub and pulled herself up. The floor where she'd fallen was covered in blood. She stared at it for a moment. Then she forced herself to walk to the bedroom, where she picked up the phone and dialed Axel at work.

"I need help," Hilde told the secretary who answered. "I'm having a miscarriage. Please, hurry, get my husband." As Hilde waited for what seemed like a very long time for Axel to come on the phone, she wondered if the girl who answered was a paid employee or a prisoner. And if she was a prisoner, was she moving slowly on purpose to punish Axel's wife? Hilde made a mental note to ask Axel about his secretary as soon as she felt better.

"What is it, darling? Are you all right?" Axel's voice was filled with concern.

"I'm not all right."

"Where are you? Are you in Berlin with Gretchen?"

"I'm here at home. I'm bleeding, I think I'm losing the baby."

"All right. Don't panic. Don't be afraid. I'll send a car to take you directly to the Hohenlychen Clinic, and I'll meet you there."

"I'm afraid of dying, Axel. Women die in childbirth all the time."

"You won't die, my love. I'll be there to take care of you. Don't be afraid. I'm on my way. Watch outside the window for the car. I'll send it right now. I'm on my way to the hospital. I'll be there when you arrive."

"Who is going to clean up this mess?" Hilde was crying. "There is blood everywhere. Oh, Axel, I've made a mistake that might cost Gretchen her life. And there is blood everywhere . . ."

"Hilde, you're hysterical. Please, you must calm down. You are making your condition worse. Now, wait for the car to take you to the clinic," he said.

After the phone went dead, Hilde did not hang it up. She held it in her bloody hands and wept. The painful cramping in her belly was worsening. Wiping the tears away from her face, she smeared her cheeks with blood. It seemed like a lifetime before the car arrived to take her to the clinic. And by the time it came, she was almost unconscious.

Hilde woke up in a white hospital room with Axel at her side. Unable to recall how she'd gotten to the hospital, she looked into Axel's eyes for answers.

"Axel?"

"Yes, my love."

"Where am I?"

"At the hospital."

"I don't feel well at all."

"I know. You're weak. Try and rest. You've lost a lot of blood."

"The baby? How is my baby?"

Axel took Hilde's hand, and she instantly knew the answer even before he said a single word. "I'm sorry, darling. But we're young, and there will be other children."

"My baby . . ." Hilde began to cry softly. "I'm being punished. If there is a God, he has punished me. And I deserve it. I ruined my best friend's life."

"Shhh, not now. You need your strength."

When visiting hours ended, Axel left, leaving Hilde alone with her thoughts, memories, and fears.

My poor innocent baby is dead. I'll never hold him or her in my arms. I'll never sing a lullaby. Tears ran down Hilde's cheeks. *And Gretchen is in danger. I am so afraid for her. I have done so many bad things in my life. If there is a God, he is angry at me. I never believed in anything I couldn't see but now I wonder. Now I think that there might be a God, and if there is, he surely hates me. I killed my own mother. She was a mean and evil woman, but I murdered her. I am so afraid that if there is a God and he is watching me, he will take out his wrath on me and never allow me to have a child of my own. And to make matters even worse, Hann out and out rejected me. I should have known he would. My mother said I was ugly, and she was right. I am. I am ugly inside and out. And all those horrible things that Ilsa made me do in the camp with those prisoners. That would surely anger any God if he exists. God? Why am I even thinking about the existence of a God? I've grown up to believe that the only God is our führer. So why am I doubting that now?*

A nurse in a crisp white uniform, with a little white hat pinned into her freshly coiffed bun, came into the room. "How are you feeling, Frau Scholtz?"

"I don't feel well," Hilde said.

"Have you gotten any rest?"

Hilde shook her head. "I can't sleep."

"Let me give you something to help." The young, attractive girl smiled. "I'll be right back."

After the injection, Hilde slept.

CHAPTER 43

Berlin

Each night, Hann wandered the pubs, the restaurants, and scanned the outdoor beer gardens, in search of Eva. But he never saw Eva, Gretchen, or Hilde anywhere. *If I don't find Eva soon, I may never see her again,* he thought. *I am leaving to go to war. I could be dead without ever having the chance to say goodbye. Not since Thea, have I felt this way about anyone. I wish Eva would just give me a chance. I know that she won't even consider a date with me because of that damn Hilde. But there has to be a way to convince her.*

Finally, on the night before Hann was to leave Berlin, he could not stand it any longer. He was expected to report for duty at five the following morning. And as of yet he had not gone to Gretchen's apartment because he was hoping for a chance meeting. After all, Eva had outright told him she was not interested, and he was afraid that if he went to the apartment, she would slam the door in his face and call the police. But he was at his wit's end now; time had run out. His only option was to go and knock on Gretchen's door and beg Eva to talk to him.

In a last-ditch effort to find Eva and speak with her, he

walked to Gretchen's apartment.

But when he arrived, he found a wooden board nailed across the door. And a sign that warned Do Not Enter.

He sat down on the stoop and put his head in his hands in despair. *Where have they gone? And why in such a rush? I wonder if they've been evicted for not paying their rent. If Gretchen had money problems, I wish she would have come to me. But we have never been close friends, so, of course, she would never tell me. And as much as I hate to write to Hilde, I will. Hilde is the only person who might know where Eva has gone.*

The following day, Hann shipped out with the rest of his regime. As he got into the cockpit to go out on his next bombing mission he thought about his conversation with Hilde and how she'd admitted to lying about Thea. Then he thought about Eva and he trembled. Hilde was dangerous. He wondered if Eva was all right. *I should have done something. I should have said something to Gretchen about Hilde and her lies. But I did nothing to stand up for Eva, and I'm sure that somehow Hilde caused her trouble,* he thought, ashamed of his own lack of moral character.

Just as Hann's plane came out from the protection of the white, billowy clouds, two British fighter jets appeared on either side of him. The sound of bullets shattered the morning stillness. Hann was trapped. Then he heard a deafening explosion to the right of him. The plane spiraled out of control and then hit the ground bursting into flames. Hann died instantly.

CHAPTER 44

Ravensbrück

Hilde couldn't overcome the depression she felt from the loss of her baby. Before she left the hospital, the doctor had given her a bottle of sleeping pills which she found herself using far more often then she should have. That was because whenever she was awake she was either sick with guilt over Gretchen or miserable thinking about the child she'd lost. Most days she drifted in and out of a drug-induced sleep. Her dreams were still alarming, but now not only was she having nightmares about the camp, but she would sometimes wake up crying for the child she had carried almost full term and would never know. One night she had a particularly realistic dream in which Gretchen was an inmate at a camp far from Ravensbrück. In the dream, the guards had thrown Gretchen on the floor, and they were kicking her in the stomach. Gretchen was calling for Hilde, but when Hilde answered, Gretchen was unable to hear her. Hilde awakened from that nightmare trembling, sweating, and terrified. Hilde was angry. She thought of everyone she hated who had, in some way, contributed to the life she now led. She cursed her mother and cursed herself. She cursed Hann and Eva. But not

Gretchen, for Gretchen she wept. And what about Axel? She couldn't say she hated him. She didn't. But since the miscarriage he'd become little more than a servant to her. She wished she didn't find him so annoying when he was constantly trying to bring her food or comfort. Often he would sit on the edge of her bed, trying to talk with her, but she couldn't bear it, so she gave him quick one-word answers. Then she told him she was tired and begged him to leave her alone.

In her youth, Hilde had always been hefty and robust. Then she was strong, fueled by the anger of a child who felt shortchanged in every aspect of life. Her family was poor; her father had abandoned her mother, and her mother tortured Hilde. The other girls were always prettier, happier, more athletic. But now, Hilde no longer had any of the strength or anger she'd had when she was young. Life's misfortunes had left her a frail shadow of her former self. She knew she was becoming addicted to her sleeping pills. But she needed them to sleep, to try and forget. And if she was blessed with a dreamless sleep, it was the only comfort she could find in life . . . even if it was only for a short while.

CHAPTER 45

Axel could see that his wife was deteriorating. He'd spoken to several doctors who promised him that she would come out of it with time. But he didn't believe them. They were not living with her. They did not see that every day she grew worse. Early one morning, on his day off, he took a train to Berlin to meet with a doctor whom one of his friends recommended highly. This was the first doctor he'd encountered who seemed to understand when Axel told him that Hilde was sliding down deeper into depression each day.

"I don't know what to do to help her," Axel said.

"There is only one thing that will help her. She must have another child," the doctor answered.

"But she won't let me anywhere near her. I can't make her pregnant if she won't let me near her!" Axel said, wringing his hands.

The doctor was an old man with thick, gray hair and eyebrows. He had soft blue eyes. "Can you ask your superiors if you can get a child from the Lebensborn?"

"I don't think so. I'm not high enough in rank, besides it takes time to get approved. There is a lot of paperwork. And Hilde needs a child now." Axel shook his head.

"I don't know if I should suggest this to you or not . . ."

"Suggest what, Doctor? Any suggestions are appreciated. I love my wife more than anything in the world, and I am afraid I am losing her. She is living on pills. She's so skinny and sickly looking, and she cries all the time."

"You could acquire a Polish child. A child that looks Aryan . . ."

"But how? How would I get to Poland?"

"Now, I can't tell you that because I don't know. Perhaps you could get transferred to a camp in Poland?"

"I could try," Axel said.

"Then try." The doctor patted Axel's shoulder.

CHAPTER 46

Axel returned home late that afternoon. He was afraid Hilde would be worried about him. But when he got home, he found her asleep with the shades drawn. She didn't even realize he was late.

When he brought Hilde her dinner, she refused to eat as she did most evenings. And that night, when he tried to take her in his arms, all she said was, "No, Axel. Please."

He let her go and turned over to face the wall. She was dying; he could see that clearly. She was drowning, and she wouldn't let him help her.

Very early the following morning, before the break of dawn, Axel got dressed and went to work early. He was on his way to the offices in the women's camp. He had to drop off some paperwork when he saw a beautiful, blond boy in the children's camp. The child was sitting outside playing in the dirt. A pretty woman with golden hair, in a gray-striped prisoner's uniform, sat beside him. She was singing a song to the child.

For several minutes, Axel watched the woman and child. He was mesmerized.

"Anatol, come give Mommie a kiss. I have to go; it's almost time for roll call," Lila Rabinowitz said to her son, Moishe.

Axel walked forward just as the little boy ran into his mother's arms.

The woman gasped. "Please, don't hurt us. I am sorry, I know I should not be in the children's camp," the woman said, trembling. "But please, please, have mercy. I beg you . . ."

"Quiet," Axel said, putting as much authority into his voice as he could muster. "Who are you?"

"My name is Felicia Bankowski. This is my son, Anatol."

"Hmmm," Axel said as he studied the mother and her child. He thought of Hilde, and it made him feel sympathy for this strange woman. "I want to talk to you," he said, knowing full well that he could take the boy if he wanted to, and no one would notice or care. But for some reason, he wanted to tell the mother what he planned to do. He wanted to reassure her. "My wife . . ." Axel stammered. "My wife . . . just had a second miscarriage."

The woman said nothing. Her eyes were cast down. But looking closely, Axel could see that Felicia was trembling. Little Anatol was still in her lap, not moving, as if he'd been frozen in time.

Axel went on. "I want to take your son to live with me and my wife. I want to raise him as my own child."

Lila's face was a mixture of fear, mistrust, and hope. "To live with you?" she said, her voice small, questioning, unsure, frightened. Axel had to strain to hear her.

"Yes, to live with me and my wife. I want to take him. He will be safe. You want that, don't you? You want to protect him. He is likely to die here."

Lila looked from Axel to Moishe then back to Axel again. "You want to take my son?"

He nodded.

"I would never see him again?"

"I could take him without your permission if I chose to. I am trying to help you," Axel said.

She nodded. "Yes, help me," she repeated in a daze. Then she asked again, "I would never see him again?"

"Yes, that's right. No one must ever know where he came from. But if I took him, you would know that he was alive."

"Alive . . . yes . . . alive. He would never know me or his father, but he would live."

"Yes. He would live."

"You would raise him to be one of you? A Nazi?"

Axel was growing impatient. He was giving this woman an opportunity to save her child, and she was asking him questions. "I am done answering your questions. I could shoot you both here and now. You know this, of course. But I won't. Instead, I will take the boy, and you will be comforted to know he is safe."

Tears ran down Lila's face. She hugged Moishe hard and then she looked into her little boy's eyes and said, "Go with the nice man, Anatol, Be a good boy. Do what he tells you. And be good to his wife. Treat her like a mommie. Call her Mommie."

"Are you coming too, Mommie?"

"No, not now."

"Why are you crying?"

"I'm not. I have something in my eye."

"Come," Axel said, taking Moishe's hand.

"No!" Moishe screamed.

"Please, forgive him, Herr Oberstrumführer. He is afraid. He is very young. He will forget about me."

"I don't want to go. I want to stay here with you, Mommie!" Moishe cried.

"You must do what I tell you," Lila said firmly.

"Come," Axel insisted.

"No, Mommie, no, please, Mommie, please!" Moishe cried, trying to pull away from Axel and run back to Lila.

Lila turned away from Moishe. "Go," she said as harshly as she was able. "I said, go."

"I have chocolates at home. You will like my house. Of course, you will be needing a bath. But don't worry, you shall have one."

"Mommie? Mommie?" Moishe cried as Axel carried him away.

CHAPTER 47

Lila Rabinowitz lay down in the dirt and wept until she had no more tears left to cry. "Life." She assured herself. "Life is better than death. And my son, my Moishe, will have a chance to live. I have no guarantee that the Nazi is telling me the truth. Still, why would he lie? He has no reason to lie. He has the power to do as he pleases. He could have killed Moishe and me right then and there if that was his goal. He could be a bad man and want to do bad things to Moishe. Oh, God forbid. Please God, watch over my son. I must believe what he told me. I must make myself believe that my Moishe will be safe and that this man, even though he is a Nazi, has good intentions toward my little boy. If it's all true, my boy will survive this war. And once it's over, I will find him, no matter what it takes. I will find him."

CHAPTER 48

When Axel arrived home with Moishe, Hilde was asleep. He gave Moishe some bread and milk, followed by four pieces of chocolate. Then he gave the child a bath and was pleasantly surprised to find that Moishe had not been circumcised. *He will easily pass for a Polish child. No one will recognize him.*

Axel crept into the darkened room where Hilde was snoring softly and sat down beside her on the bed. The love he felt for her filled his chest and made him want to cry. She was the only family he had, the only person he felt he could trust. Hilde was like him in so many ways. He wasn't blind; he could see she was not a beauty, and like him, she was never the most popular child in the Hitler Youth. Before he'd met Hilde, his experiences with women were not his brightest memories. When he was a teenager and not yet working for the SS, girls either ignored him or laughed at him when he asked them out. Then once he began working for the party, there were a few girls who took his gifts of silk stockings and chocolates in exchange for a night of intimacy. But not one of them wanted to be his wife. From the first time he saw Hilde, he knew that she was his female mirror image. In Axel's mind, Hilde was the perfect partner for him. And he wanted to make her happy. Axel saw the opportunity for a happy home and his own family with Hilde. But since she'd lost the baby, she was so melancholic, and it hurt him when he looked at her. His mind drifted to thoughts of the beautiful, blond, little boy in the other room. Axel hoped the child, Anatol, would bring Hilde's smile back. He hoped that he would, once again, hear his wife singing along with her records as he walked out the door for work in the morning.

"Sweetheart . . ." Axel whispered as he touched Hilde's forearm. "I have a surprise for you."

Hilde stirred, half opening her eyes.

"Come with me. I have something to show you."

"I can't; I'm too tired," she said.

"It's a surprise. I promise you'll like it," he tempted her, hoping he was right.

She shrugged. In the half light he could see that she was annoyed. But she got up and followed him.

They walked into the living room. As soon as Hilde's eyes fell upon the child, her face lit up. The boy smiled as if on cue.

"Who is this little boy?" Hilde asked.

"We have been given him to raise. He is of pure Aryan blood. His parents are dead."

"What's his name?"

"Anatol. He is yours."

"Mine? How can he be mine?"

"Because he is. He is yours if you want him. And if you don't, I'll get rid of him."

"I do," Hilde said. "I do want him." She walked slowly over to the child and picked him up into her arms. He hugged her.

"Where's Mommie?" Moishe asked.

"She's your mommie," Axel said, pointing to Hilde. "And I'm your father."

"Mommie?"

"Yes, I'm your mommie."

"I want Mommie." Moishe started crying and kicking his short, little legs. But Hilde didn't put him down. Instead, she began rocking him and singing to him in German. He wept for a while, but the song seemed to comfort the boy.

"It may be a while before he forgets his mother. But he is young enough that I know he will forget," Axel said.

"How old do you think he is?" Hilde wondered.

"I don't know. He's very small, maybe four?"

Anatol was almost five, but he'd been malnourished most of his life and that kept him from growing. He'd also spent over a year of his development in the forests, having very little contact with anyone other than his mother, so he was socially awkward. His use of language was limited. All of these factors led Hilde and Axel to believe he was much younger than he actually was.

"Are you sure we won't be forced to return him?" Hilde asked. "Because I don't want to become attached to him and then . . ."

"Of course I'm sure. He's yours. We just have to give him a little time, and I am sure he will acclimate himself to our home." Axel smiled proudly.

CHAPTER 49

Axel was right, the child had a profound and wonderful effect on Hilde's attitude. She flung herself into motherhood, spending countless hours sitting on the floor and playing with Anatol. Until Anatol came into Hilde's life, she'd never had much interest in cooking but now she remembered all she'd learned about meal preparation and nutrition when she was in the Bund and she put it to use. She was so happy to have Anatol that sometimes she was even kind and affectionate toward Axel.

"Ilsa is coming to dinner," Axel said when he returned from work the following day. "I told her to come on Thursday night at seven. I hope that's all right. I bumped into her and she misses you."

"Yes, it's fine," Hilde said. She was no longer threatened by Ilsa's attentions toward Axel. She was far too happy with her child to allow this to affect her.

Ilsa arrived on time, carrying a bouquet of fresh, golden sunflowers. She hugged Hilde as soon as she saw her and seemed genuinely happy to find Hilde doing well.

"How have you been? I know you lost the baby. I am truly sorry," Ilsa said and the look on her face was so sincere that, for a moment, Hilde found it difficult to believe Ilsa was the same woman who had played those horrible games with the prisoners at the camp.

"Yes, I lost the baby."

"So who is this charming and handsome young man?" Ilsa said, looking at Anatol, who was playing with a ball on the floor.

Axel winced hoping that Ilsa wouldn't recognize the child from the children's camp. But if she did, there was no recognition in her eyes.

"We've adopted him," Hilde said.

"Charming, indeed." Ilsa smiled.

They enjoyed a lovely meal of sauerbrauten that Hilde had spent the entire afternoon preparing. After dinner, Anatol played with Ilsa. "What's your name?" Anatol asked Ilsa.

"That's your Auntie Ilsa," Hilde said.

"Auntie Ilsa." Anatol smiled, and Hilde couldn't help but feel her heart swell with pride. He was such a bright little boy.

"Let me help you in the kitchen," Ilsa said, getting up.

"No, please, you stay here and play with Anatol. I'll only be a few minutes and then we can all have some coffee and cookies."

But Ilsa followed Hilde into the kitchen. "How are you, really?" she asked.

"I'm much better than I was."

"That's what I heard. I heard you weren't doing well."

"No, I wasn't."

"Hilde, there is something I must discuss with you."

"Of course. What is it?"

"We have always been very good friends, have we not?"

"Yes, we have. Go on, please. Because I need to talk to you too."

"Your little boy. He is a lovely child. But he is a Jew."

"He is not! He's Polish." Hilde was angry and shocked.

"You're wrong. He is a Jew, I tell you. Your husband must have taken him from the children's camp. I recognize him from there because he was the only beautiful, blond-haired boy there. But he's a Jew. I know because I have spoken with a woman who was on the transport with him and his mother. But don't fret. No one knows. Only you, I, Axel, and the boy's mother."

"Then who is the boy's mother?" Hilde said, challenging Ilsa. "I don't believe any of this."

"It's all true, but I don't recall her name. However, don't worry, I can find it out. And then I will take care of her, so that she will never tell anyone your secret."

"No, you must be wrong. Look." Hilde pulled down Anatol's pants. "He's not circumcised. If he was a Jew he'd be circumcised."

"I am telling you. He is Jew. I know who his mother is, I've seen her with him.   And, I will take care of everything for you, my sweet butterball."

"You mean kill her?" Hilde asked.

"Yes, and then no one need ever know the truth."

"But it's not the truth," Hilde exclaimed with conviction.

"Yes . . ." Ilsa smiled. "It is."

A chill ran down the back of Hilde's neck, and even though she needed Ilsa, she suddenly wished she'd never invited her back into her life.

CHAPTER 50

After Ilsa left, Hilde put Anatol to bed. She felt a wave of panic come over her as she looked at the child laying quietly in his bed, sucking his thumb. Ilsa could thwart the happiness that she had finally found in Anatol. She had the power, and Ilsa knew that Hilde knew that she did. Not only that, but Hilde needed Ilsa. Without her help she could not help Gretchen. A bead of sweat ran down Hilde's back. It was dangerous to be indebted to someone as diabolical as Ilsa. As she had done all of her life when she was afraid or in need of comfort or advice, Hilde went to talk to the Valkyrie, her imaginary self in the mirror.

She checked the boy, the child who she'd come to love. He was asleep. This was the perfect time to visit with her friend. Hilde went into the bathroom and closed the door. Then she stared into the mirror. "Come to me, please," she said in a pathetic tone. "I need you desperately. I am in a terrible fix."

The warrior woman on the white horse appeared.

"What are we going to do?" Hilde asked, wide eyed and trembling. "I am afraid of Ilsa. She's telling lies about Anatol. She could have him taken away from me if I anger her."

You didn't want a child, now did you? the Valkyrie asked, shaking her head. *I told you when we decided to kill your mother that children were our reason for existence. But you didn't believe me then. You said you never wanted a child. Besides, you hate Jews. You don't want him if he's a Jew.*

"But he is not a Jew and I love him. Help me, I am afraid for him."

You're afraid of Ilsa because she is as diabolical as you. Perhaps more so.

Hilde nodded her head. "You are not comforting me. You're scaring me."

The Valkyrie laughed. *I am?*

"I should not have come to you for advice. You're making this worse."

Ahhh, Hilde. You and I are one. I am the beautiful reflection of the powerful woman who lives within you. You needn't be afraid of Ilsa. And you certainly shouldn't fear me. I am your best friend. I know you better than anyone else. And I will tell you, here and now, that you are just as strong and just as smart as that little blonde bitch. If she dares to threaten our child, we will destroy her.

"Yes, you're right. Ilsa is scarier than most, but she is not indestructible," Hilde said.

Now you are talking like the Hilde I know.

"Do you think that once she has killed Anatol's mother, I can find a way to kill her and not get caught?"

Of course. You did it with your mother, didn't you? You were brilliant there. You did the best acting job I've ever seen. No one ever suspected you.

Hilde nodded. "That's true. And it was surprisingly easy."

So, if we need to kill Ilsa we'll be just as convincing. The Valkyrie smiled and tilted her head. *You must find out what she needs and make yourself useful to her. Get close to her again. Very close. Then strike!*

"You're so right."

I am you, Hilde. I am the beautiful and brilliant Valkyrie that lives within you.

"Yes, you are, and you have always been." Hilde put her hand on the mirror. It met the hand in the reflection. She smiled.

CHAPTER 51

That night, after Ilsa left and Anatol was asleep, Hilde confronted Axel with what Ilsa told her about Anatol.

"Where did you find Anatol?"

"I told you, in Berlin."

"Liar!"

"I am not lying to you."

"Why do you insist on lying? Tell me the truth. Tell me because I already know. You took him from the children's camp at Ravensbrück, didn't you? Ilsa told me. And now she's claiming he's Jewish. You should have told me. You shouldn't have lied to me."

"He is not Jewish," Axel exclaimed. "She's making this up. He's not Jewish. But he is Polish, and I did take him from the children's camp." Axel slumped down into the living room chair.

"Why did you lie to me?"

He looked at the floor, then he shrugged his shoulders and nodded his head. "I was only trying to help you. I only did it because I love you." There was an awkward silence. Then he added, "Shall I return him to the children's camp? I can return him. But if I do, he will probably be dead in a few months."

Hilde felt her heart sink. She had come to love the child.

"No. You must not take him back there, ever. Ilsa is going to get rid of his mother, then she will never come looking for him."

"And what about Ilsa? She knows? Can we trust her?"

"I don't know. That's my biggest concern," Hilde admitted.

"We could always deny it. It would be her word against ours," Axel said.

"You don't know her as well as I do. Ilsa has very important friends. They would take her word before ours."

"Do you think she would betray you?"

"I don't think so; she would warn me first. After all, she has no reason to turn us in. But if she ever wants anything from me, she will use this knowledge to her advantage."

"You mean blackmail?" Axel asked.

"Yes, exactly. Knowing Anatol could be a Jewish child gives her power over us. And to protect him we would have to give her whatever she asks for."

"Well, let's hope there is never anything she needs or wants from us."

"Yes, maybe," Hilde said. "But knowing Ilsa as I do, I think it's just a matter of time."

CHAPTER 52

A week later, Ilsa knocked on Hilde's door.

"Hello, my friend," Ilsa said, wearing a big smile on her face. Her golden hair was lovely as it picked up the rays of sunlight. "So you don't look happy to see me?" She frowned.

"Of course I am happy to see you," Hilde said. "Come on in."

"You have a beer?" Ilsa asked.

"Sure. Let me get you one."

"I've come to tell you that you need not worry about the boy's mother anymore. I took care of her."

"She's dead?"

"Yes, she's dead. It was easy, and now my little nephew's secret is safe. Now, with his mother gone, only you and I know the truth. Everyone will see him as an Aryan." She smiled sweetly, but Hilde could see her streak of cruelty shining from behind her cold, hard eyes.

Hilde trembled. "He is Aryan."

Then Ilsa patted Hilde's hand and said, "So." She reached up and touched Hilde's cheek. "Now you are indebted to me, aren't you, dear? And, of course, I will take your secret to the grave . . . unless . . . you betray me somehow. But, of course, you would never do that, would you? And I know how you can show your gratitude for my cleaning up your little mess."

"How can I show you? What do you want?" Hilde asked. She was trembling with fear. But she was also thinking about the Valkyrie. *Get close to her. Learn her secrets.*

"In return for keeping your little secret from Axel and everyone else, I want you to help me. As you already know the Jews bring all their valuable possessions with them when they come to the camp. Before their stuff is logged in, I want you to steal everything you can that is of value and give it to me. Now you had better be sure that this little exchange of ours stays between you and I. Do you understand me? Or little Anatol will suffer the consequences of your actions."

"I've never betrayed you, Ilsa. I never would."

"Why don't you get me another beer? Where are your manners, little Butterball?" Ilsa said mockingly.

Hilde was frightened. She got up to get another beer for Ilsa and as she did she saw the Valkyrie reflected in the kitchen window. *She thinks she has us*, the Valkyrie said, smiling and calming Hilde's nerves. *But don't be afraid. Be patient. We will prevail as we always have.*

Hilde handed Ilsa the beer.

"Didn't you recently go off to Berlin to visit your friend Gretchen Schmidt, your Jew-lover friend, who you thought was so wonderful? She is far from wonderful. Yet you go to see her, but you don't come to see me."

Hilde stared at Ilsa, surprised. "How did you know that I went to see Gretchen?"

"Oh, come now, sweetheart. You know that news travels fast among my friends in the SS. I also know that she was arrested." She smiled, glaring at Hilde, her eyes devoid of emotion, looking as if they had turned to glass again.

"Do you know where Gretchen is?" Hilde asked. She was humbled.

"But, of course, I know. And you know what? I am going to bring her to Ravensbrück. She's always had so much power over you. You are like a little dog that follows her around. Now we can play games with her, and she can be the bitch dog."

"Can you really bring here here?"

"You know I can. It's whether I choose to or not—that is the question. She was going to be sent to Dachau, but once they went back into her history and found out that her father was a Jew lover too, they decided to send her to Auschwitz."

"Oh no!" Hilde gasped.

"And that Jew she was hiding? The one who was living under a fake name with Aryan papers that said she was Eva something or other? She's in Auschwitz too. They'll both probably die there."

"Oh, Ilsa, you must bring her here." Hilde was reduced to a frightened child. She needed Ilsa again.

"I'll bet Gretchen regrets her efforts to protect that little Jew now because now your Aryan friend is as worthless as a Jew. In fact, she probably shares a lice-infested bed of straw with one." Ilsa stood up and began to pace the room like a tiger about to attack. "Some of the guards say Auschwitz is so bad that it makes Ravensbrück look like a summer camp."

"Please, unless you can do something to help, I don't want to hear anymore," Hilde said.

Ilsa stared at Hilde. She was smiling but her eyes glared. "And you thought that Gretchen was a better friend to you than I? You think I didn't know that you invited Gretchen to your wedding. Everyone says you call her your best friend. Oh Hilde, I thought I was your best friend." She shook her head in mock anger. "I thought so until you planned your wedding knowing that I would not be able to attend because I couldn't get off work. But of course we both knew that you didn't want me there."

"That's not true." Hilde was lying, but her tone of voice was begging for mercy. "Please, you must believe me. I didn't do that intentionally, Ilsa. It was not possible to arrange a time when we were both able to take off together."

"Oh really! Well, you could have fooled me," Ilsa sneered. "Anyway, no matter." She smiled wickedly. Her eyes twinkled, then she added, "It certainly sounds like you had quite the visit back home to Berlin this time, didn't you? And you really should be quite proud of yourself for what you did to Gretchen."

"Proud? That is the last thing I feel right now," Hilde said, staring at the floor, defeated.

"Oh yes, word got back to Ravensbrück, and everyone is calling you a hero. After all, it was you who discovered that your friend Gretchen was a common criminal and you had the courage to turn her in." Ilsa's tone was filled with syrupy sarcasm. "Just look at you, Butterball; you look as if you are about to be sick. Well, don't you worry, I already put the papers in to have Gretchen brought here. She will be your housekeeper. I've planned it so that she'll watch the boy. That will enable you to come back to work and start paying off your debt to me."

Hilde wanted to cry. She wanted to lay down on the sofa and let the tears flow until she had no more left. But she dared not. *Ilsa is dangerous. She's always been dangerous. How could I have ever thought she would help me with Gretchen? She's cruel and heartless. I don't give a damn what happens to that Rebecca Jew bitch, but Gretchen has been my friend for so many years. And now to make matters worse, Hilde knows a terrible and frightening truth about my little boy. If she didn't have so many important friends I would kill her right now. I would take a kitchen knife and stab her. No, what am I thinking, that is too messy. I would poison her the same way I poisoned my mother. But I don't dare do anything. I am trapped. She has me where she wants me, and there is nothing I can do. I have to let her live at least until Gretchen arrives here.*

"Thank you . . . thank you, Ilsa, for everything. You'll see I'll steal plenty for you."

"Oh, please stop with the dramatics; don't be so frightened," Ilsa said. "You don't like that I have so much power over you now, do you? Well, don't let it worry you. I'm sure I'll never need to use it."

Just then Anatol came running out of his bedroom, his blond hair bouncing as his fat little legs carried him right into Hilde's arms. He gave her a kiss then turned to Ilsa and raised his arms in the air. "Pick me up, Auntie Ilsa. I want to give you a kiss," he said.

"Of course, my precious, little nephew," Ilsa said, lifting the boy and allowing him to kiss her cheek. Then she glanced over at Hilde and smiled. Her smile made the hair on the back of Hilde's neck stand straight up. Ilsa gave Anatol a kiss, but her bright blue eyes were as hard as glass.

CHAPTER 53

A Village in Poland

Eli was thin and weak. He'd lost so much weight that the skin on his face had folded in on itself, causing deep wrinkles that made him look much older than he was. He was tired, hungry, and thirsty, but he continued to walk. Often he felt alone and had to remind himself that God was always with him. Sometimes, when he was very hot and miserable, he would think of Moses in the desert. In the heat of the day he lay down beneath a tree and prayed until the sun went down and he regained enough strength to walk again. Eli ate grass, and insects. Sometimes he would smile to himself as he contemplated the farce of life. *If my friend Yossi were here, he and I could sit for hours and debate whether it is acceptable to eat insects because they are the only sustenance I have.* Eli chucked as he remembered Yossi. *My dear friend Yossi, how he loved to debate anything and everything. I wonder how he and his family are doing. I pray that they have somehow escaped. I pray that they are alive. The only thing that matters is life. But for me it is not so much my own life as the lives of those I love, my bashert, Gretchen, and my dear Rebecca.* Then he began to pray again. *Please Hashem, watch over them both. I wish I could be with them. I wish I had the power to protect them. But my presence would only bring them danger.* He prayed for hours, begging God to keep Rebecca's secret from their tormentors. He pleaded with God to help both Gretchen and Rebecca to have enough food and to remain safe.

Eli rested, then he got up and began to walk again. He reached the top of a hill. When he looked down, he saw a village. It was a small village and the sight of it and the thought of people terrified him. But if he could find work for a day, he might be able to get some real food. So, even though it was safer to stay in the forest, something compelled him to walk down the hill and into the little town. When he first arrived he was afraid that everyone would know he was Jewish. People glanced at him, and he wondered if it was because he was a stranger or because he looked like a Jew. He heard people speaking, negotiating with street vendors. And he instantly knew that even though there were Nazi flags hanging from the buildings, he had somehow traveled into Poland. *At least my father taught me to speak Polish* he thought.

The local priest was standing outside his small church. Eli walked by him, trying not to meet his eyes. But when Eli looked up, the priest was smiling at him. *I must be filthy,* Eli thought. *He feels sorry for me. I can see it in his face.*

"Hello, my son," the priest said.

"Hello," Eli answered tentatively. *I should get out of this village before I am discovered and arrested. I don't really understand why there is still a church here and how this priest is still practicing. I thought the Nazis had abolished religion. I can see that the Nazis have taken over this village because of all of their flags flying and pictures of Hitler on the walls.*

"You look awfully hungry."

Eli nodded.

"Do you need work?"

"Yes," Eli said, staring at the ground.

"I suppose I am in luck, then." The kindly priest smiled. "I could use a good handyman. How are your skills with a bucket of paint?" the priest asked.

Eli felt a shiver go up his spine. *Is this man setting me up? Does he know I am a Jew? Is he going to turn me in?* "I'm not much of a handyman. And I don't know how to paint."

"Well," the priest said with a warm smile, "there isn't really much to it. I can show you how to do it. How does a good meal sound in exchange for painting the rectory?"

Eli felt a rush of saliva fill his mouth. *I am so hungry. It's worth the risk. I can't go another day without real food,* he thought. "Yes, I'll do it."

"Well, that's good. Come on inside, and I'll find you something to eat."

CHAPTER 54

Eli wanted to show his gratitude to the priest, so he worked as hard as he could. He'd never done manual labor before, and although it was exhausting, he found it gratifying too. By the time the sun began to set, Eli had gotten halfway through painting the rectory. The priest came outside to find Eli still at work.

"That's enough for today. Come in and have some soup and bread. Would you like to stay the night? You can finish your work in the morning. There is a bed downstairs, where you can sleep."

Eli knew he should not trust anyone. He was Jew, a hunted man. All it would take was a call to the Gestapo, and he would find himself behind bars. But there was something about the priest that reminded him of his father and Eli trusted him. He remembered how his father would bring home poor and hungry people and offer them a place at the family table. "Yes, I can stay. And thank you so much for your generosity and kindness," Eli said.

"I'm a man of God. It is my pleasure to help you."

As they walked back to the main church building, Eli thought about his father. His father had never turned anyone away for dinner on the Sabbath or on holidays. Many times, poor people or travelers would come to the rebbe's house on the night of the Sabbath. And the rebbe would welcome them warmly, as if they were long lost relatives, although most times they were complete strangers. Eli's father had told Eli from the time Eli was a child that as a man of God it was his obligation to help those in need. And now, Eli found it fascinating that, this man, a Catholic priest, had the same way of thinking as his father, the rebbe. *They are both kind and decent men. They are both men of God. There doesn't seem to be much difference between them, except for what they believe. If my father had met this priest, I believe he would have liked him. So far he hasn't asked me any questions. He has no idea what I am running away from or even if I am running away at all. He doesn't know why I am disheveled or why I am traveling without clean clothes, or money. He doesn't ask if I am Jewish. He only offers me shelter and food in exchange for work. And this is exactly what my father would have done.*

What began as a two-day painting job, turned into a long-term position. Eli was grateful and relieved. He had a clean and warm place to stay, downstairs below the rectory, and enough food to fill his groaning belly. The priest was kind and found work for him around the church. Eli prayed that he would somehow be able to stay in this little village until the end of the war.

CHAPTER 55

January 1943, a Small Polish Village

Many months passed without incident. Eli began to enjoy the routine of his life. It was a simple life of work, food, and rest.

In December there had been a mass on Christmas Eve and another on Christmas Day. Eli attended, sitting in the back of the room, out of respect for the priest. He marveled at how lovely the service was. Tears filled his eyes as it brought back memories of attending the synagogue on high holidays, when he listened to the rebbe's sermon and the cantor's haunting, melodious voice. He remembered the otherworldly sound of the blowing of the shofar on the high holidays, and his heart yearned for the past.

The parishioners came to know Eli as someone who was always there to help them if they needed him. The winters were hard on everyone. Once, an old man asked Eli to shovel the snow outside his home. Eli obliged. Another time, a pregnant woman asked him to bring her milk and cheese from the store because she was too far along to walk on the icy roads. Again, Eli did as he was asked.

On a daily basis, Eli kept the church clean and the wood

polished. When things broke, he figured out how to fix them. He went to the market to purchase whatever was needed. All in all, he found ways to make himself useful.

One very cold winter night, after a fresh snow had just dusted the ground, Eli and the priest were sitting together at a table by the fireplace. They were enjoying the heat that emanated from the roaring fire as they were having their evening meal. For several weeks, Eli found he was feeling guilty for not telling the priest the truth about himself. He knew his secret might even be putting the kindly priest and his entire church in danger. *I must tell him the truth. I must let him know that I am a Jew. I can't believe he would turn me in. He has become like a father to me. However, I must remember that people act strangely toward Jews. And I have seen many people turn on their Jewish friends and neighbors. It's possible that his entire demeanor might change once he learns the truth. I find it hard to believe it would, but it might. Yet I cannot continue to lie. It's wrong. I must tell him. I cannot put this man and his church in danger out of my own selfish need.*

"Father," Eli said. The priest had asked him to refer to him as father.

"Yes, my son?"

"I have something I must tell you."

"Go on."

Eli felt his mouth go dry. He took a sip of water, determined to tell him. "I wouldn't blame you if you are angry at me, once I tell you what I have to tell you. You see, I have been lying to you . . ."

The priest nodded calmly.

"I don't know how to say this . . ."

Again, the priest nodded, still remaining silent. His hands folded neatly on the table in front of him. His eyes were warm and encouraging as he looked at Eli.

"I am Jewish. I am hiding from the Nazis. I came all the way here to Poland from Germany on foot. It's very bad for Jews in Germany."

The priest's eyes met Eli's. "I knew you were Jewish the day you appeared here, looking like a hunted animal."

"So you won't turn me in?"

"Of course not. I would never do that to one of God's children."

"I haven't seen any Jews here, in this village. Am I the first Jew you've ever met?" Eli asked.

"No. There were Jewish families living in our little village before the Nazis came. When they took over Poland, they demanded that all Jews go into the big cities to register. I have not seen them since. I don't know what's happened to them. But I've heard rumors, and the rumors I have heard are frightening. You are safe here, Eli. You are welcome to stay as long as you'd like."

"Thank you. God bless you," Eli said. Then Eli put his head in his hands and wept.

CHAPTER 56

The small village in Poland was not exempt from the keen and vicious eyes of the Nazis. Rewards were offered to those who turned in Jews. And Eli began to worry because several of the congregants in the church had warned the priest that there were some who believed Eli might be a Jew. They told the priest they loved him for his kind heart and gentle soul, but they feared for his safety. And after one of the parishioners spoke with Eli, begging him to leave, Eli went to the rectory and knocked on the door.

"Come in," the priest answered.

"I don't mean to bother you," Eli said. "I was just wondering if I could have a moment of your time?"

"Of course. Please sit."

"I see you were studying?"

"Yes, I was reading. But I always have time to listen. What's on your mind, my son?"

"Mr. Sabouski came to the church to talk to me this morning. He's very concerned that there might be people in town who suspect that I am Jewish. This, of course, would put you and the church in peril. He is worried. And so am I. I think I should leave the church and go away from this village before something happens, and the Nazis come for both of us."

The priest slowly closed the book he was reading and set it down on the coffee table in front of him. Then he took a deep breath and sighed. For a moment he was silent, looking into Eli's dark eyes. Then in a quiet voice he said, "I will never allow the Nazis to intimidate me. This is God's house, and you are a child of God. You are welcome here. I don't want you to leave."

"As long as I'm living here, you are in danger with the Nazis for harboring a Jew," Eli said. "I am afraid for you and for this church."

"I'm not afraid." The priest smiled. "As long as God is with me, they cannot hurt me. They may burn down this building, but if they do, God will always find a way to build another church."

"From what I've heard, they've murdered plenty of priests."

"Well, yes. But I am not afraid. No matter what they may have planned for us, I will not run, and I will not send you away. I'm going to stay right here and put my faith in the Lord."

"For a Jew? You're going to put this entire congregation at risk for a Jew? Father . . . you are a remarkable man," Eli said, shaking his head in wonder.

"Jesus was a Jew, Eli."

"So he was, Father. So he was."

That night, Eli waited until it was dark and the full moon rose in a starless sky. Then he gathered the few belongings that the priest had given him, an extra pair of trousers, a shirt, and the bread he'd saved from dinner. He used the shirt to make a knapsack to pack his things. There was a stillness in his room as he began to pray in Hebrew, not only for himself but for the old priest. He davened as he said the familiar

Hebrew words. Then once he'd finished, he took the knapsack and quietly walked back toward the forests, leaving the safety of the little village behind.

Eli walked as far as he could until the sun began to rise. Then he sat down under a tree and ate half of the bread he had with him. His stomach growled with hunger. He missed the priest, the warm cereal that he was given each morning, and the quiet serenity of the church. But he did not regret his decision to leave. He knew he would not be able to live with himself if he caused harm to the priest and his following. So, although he was afraid of going back out into the forests and finding his own food, he was his father's son and he would rather die trying to survive on his own than cause anyone else to suffer.

CHAPTER 57

Auschwitz

Rebecca had never faced such humiliation or fear as she did when she and Gretchen arrived at Auschwitz. They were transported to the camp in a crowded boxcar with a mass of frightened people. The smells of human waste and sweat were overwhelming. Rebecca's stomach ached from hunger. And since it was the middle of winter, it was bitter cold. She and Gretchen huddled together, trying to keep warm. However, it wouldn't have mattered, there were so many people in the train car that they were practically standing on top of each other. Most people were crying or begging for help. Some were praying, others were ranting about the cold, or the filth, or the hunger. Rebecca didn't complain. She was too overcome with guilt whenever she looked at Gretchen. The poor girl was here because she had tried to save two Jewish people. Gretchen hardly spoke, either. And when she did, she seemed to be obsessed with Eli's safety. "Do you think he was captured?" she asked Rebecca.

"I don't know," Rebecca answered.

Gretchen took Rebecca's hand and squeezed it.

Then another time Gretchen said, "I hope Eli isn't dead."

Rebecca had no answer. All she could do was squeeze Gretchen's hand.

When the train stopped, Rebecca felt her heart stop in her chest. She wanted to scream out of fear of the unknown when the door rattled open.

"Get out. Mach schnell!" the guards were yelling. There were dogs growling at them with barred teeth. Still holding hands, Rebecca and Gretchen climbed out of the train. A sign that read Work Makes You Free hung over the entrance, and around the entire camp was a wall. At the top of the wall was flesh-shredding barbed wire. The passengers from the boxcar were being herded quickly and separated into two lines. There was so much confusion, people were grasping on to their loved ones who were being ripped away. The guards were yelling in angry voices.

A meticulously groomed man with shiny, dark hair, wearing a crisp white doctor's coat, was surveying the group. He was pointing to each of the prisoners. "Left," he would say, or "Right." And the guards would follow his directions by pushing the prisoner in the line to the left or the one to the right. A few feet from Rebecca and Gretchen, a young woman, whose mother had been sent away from her, began to weep. "Please," she said, "My mother is old. She is feeble. She needs me," the woman pleaded but no one was listening. The guard pushed her forward. Then she started screaming in panic. She fell to the ground and refused to move. "Please, I am begging you. Let me take my mother with me. Please, don't separate us." She was wailing so loudly that the other prisoners began to stop and look. A guard walked over to the woman, who was on her knees, and shot her. Blood and brains splattered on Rebecca's dress. She wanted to vomit? or to close her eyes and faint. But she dared not, or she was certain that her fate would be the same as the woman who had just been shot. The one whose body she was now forced to step over as if it were a doll, and not a dead body. As she did, she looked at Gretchen who was as white as the snow on the ground that mingled with the ashes from the crematorium.

"What kind of hell is this?" Gretchen whispered as they were pushed forward.

They were forced to leave their possessions as they followed the line and were registered. Next, the women were sent to have their hair shaved. Gretchen looked devastated as she watched her long, strawberry-blonde locks fall into a huge pile of hair. Tears rolled down Gretchen's face. Rebecca was next. She sat straight and tall, never making a sound. Now they were made to strip naked and then forced into a line for the showers.

"I've heard rumors that the shower's aren't really showers at all. I've heard that they are gas and that the Nazi's plan to murder us all." A woman in line behind them told her companion. Rebecca overheard the woman and shivered as reached for Gretchen's hand. Then they were ushered into a large room filled with showerheads. Several terrifying moments passed. There were sounds of a woman weeping, praying, children crying. Gretchen looked over at Rebecca. Rebecca was praying. She swallowed hard and hugged Gretchen. "Are we going to die?" Gretchen asked. Rebecca didn't answer; she just held Gretchen tighter. Waiting . . . waiting for the gas. And then . . . the water came down. Some of the women fell to their knees and began to thank God. The water was cold but welcome. Rebecca had never felt such relief. She said a silent prayer of thanks to God.

Each woman was given a small piece of paper with a number on it. Then they were ushered into a line where the numbers were crudely tattooed into their forearms.

After the painful tattooing, Rebecca and Gretchen were

given gray-striped uniforms. Gretchen's uniform had a green triangle. Rebecca's had the yellow Star of David. One of the kapos, a Jewish woman who was broad shouldered and thick armed, told them that the green triangle was for criminals.

"What was your crime?" the kapo asked.

"I was a humane person. That is a crime to the Nazis. All I wanted to do was to save my friend's life," Gretchen said.

"You were hiding a Jew?" the kapo asked.

"Yes," Gretchen said.

The kapo nodded.

Rebecca and Gretchen, along with the rest of the new prisoners, were taken to a wooden building. "Welcome to Auschwitz/Birkenau," said a kapo, who was waiting there. Her tone was sarcastic and bitter. The room was a gray, dismal, smelly place with no windows, only a skylight on either end of the building and a chimney duct that ran the entire length of the building. There were no actual beds, only paper mattresses stuffed with a strawlike material that were piled in the corner of the room.

Rebecca gagged when she caught sight of two buckets that stood in the two stalls at the back of the barracks. They were overflowing with human excrement.

The kapo indicated the mattresses. "You'll take these down at night and line them up on the floor. That is where you will sleep. In the morning, after you line up for roll call, which you will learn to refer to as appeal, you will return to your barracks and pile your mattresses back up in the corner, the way you see them over there right now. After the mattresses are all put away for the day, you will be sent to your work duty. I'm afraid that you will find that these barracks are very crowded. Therefore, in order to make room for everyone, you must sleep on your side."

A rat scampered across the room. One of the women

screamed. The kapo laughed. "You'll get used to the rats. You'll get used to the lice too."

Gretchen stole a glance at Rebecca, who mouthed the words, "I'm so sorry that you're here. I blame myself."

"I know you do, but it's not your fault," Gretchen mouthed back.

CHAPTER 58

At roll call, or appeal as it was known in the camp, the following morning, the prisoners were counted as they stood outside in the snow. After the count was finished the guards made no move to excuse the prisoners. And they dared not move. Gretchen's teeth were chattering from the cold, but the guards seemed oblivious to the suffering of the prisoners. A young woman standing beside Rebecca was whimpering.

"Shut up," said the guard, who was wearing a heavy coat and boots.

"But I'm freezing. Please, can we go inside?"

"She's freezing." The guard turned to one of her coworkers. She was mocking the prisoner.

"Oh? What a shame. What an ingrate this girl is. She is so brazen as to complain, with all that we do for these scum." The guard shook her head. "Perhaps we should show them just how good they have it?"

The other male guard nodded and turned to the kapos. "You, you, and you, bring buckets of water. Warm water, of course. These girls say they're cold. So we must warm them up. And there is nothing like a good hot shower to do that."

Gretchen could see that one of the kapos was wearing a Star of David on her arm. She was a tall girl, and her head was bent. Quickly she ran with the rest of the kapos to get the buckets of water.

When the kapos returned with the full buckets, the guard said, "Pour the water over the prisoners. Make sure you get everyone of them. And get that one first." She indicated the girl who had said she was freezing. "Everyone of these girls should be drenched. I don't want to see a single dry uniform. Get more water if you have to, but wet them all down."

Once the kapos had poured water on all the prisoners, the guard said, "If you think you were cold before, now you'll really know what it's like to be cold. You'll all stand out here until I decide that you've had enough. If you try to run or move out of line, you'll be shot. And remember, you have your fellow prisoner to thank for this. This is what happens when you complain."

Before Gretchen was drenched with water, she'd felt the cold, but now that her uniform was wet she was truly freezing. She glanced at Rebecca who looked pale. Her body was shaking, and her teeth were chattering.

For the next two hours, the women were forced to stand in line as the guards watched them. Some of them wept, the tears freezing on the eyelashes. Others just stood with their arms crossed over their bodies, trembling. Finally, after what seemed like a lifetime, the guard who had assigned the punishment came strolling outside. He smiled at the prisoners and casually said, "Now you are ready to receive your work details."

Gretchen was sent to work at the Bayer pharmaceutical company who was using prisoners as slave labor.

While they were each being assigned to their jobs, one of the SS officers chose Rebecca to be a housekeeper for his family.

Once they were assigned their jobs, they were led off to

work.

After ten grueling hours, the prisoners returned for the final roll call of the day. Once every prisoner was accounted for, they were allowed to eat. Rebecca and Gretchen ate their bowl of watery soup and small crust of stale bread sitting together quietly. There was so much to say, yet they were both so tired and scared of what the future might hold, that they could not speak. Dinner was a short fifteen minutes, after which the prisoners were ushered back to the barracks. Rebecca and Gretchen shared a bed with four other women.

"There is murder going on here," one of the women in the bunk said, her voice barely a whisper. "Those ashes that come down from the crematorium, those are the ashes from burnt bodies. The Nazis are killing people and then burning them up."

"How do you know this?" Gretchen asked.

"Because I saw the men loading the ovens."

"That's too horrible to think about," Rebecca said.

"Sure, what do you care? You have easy work. You work in a clean house. I work outside in the cold. Soon I will be dead, then they'll put me in the oven too," the other woman said.

"I do care about you and about everyone here. I care more than I can ever express. But what can I do? What can any of us do? We take the work detail they assign to us," Rebecca said.

"And yours was better than mine because you are beautiful. So the SS officer didn't mind having to look at you in his house every day. I am no longer attractive. The war did this to me, and so I am working outside shoveling and . . ." She began to weep. Gretchen gave the woman a look of disgust. But Rebecca shook her head, and then she took her into her arms and held her.

"I am sorry for your suffering," Rebecca said. "You didn't do anything to deserve this life. But neither did I. I am as

252

much a victim as you are. Please know that. I started work today at the home of Rapportführer Ziegler. It may seem to you to be an easy job. But it's terrifying. I am being watched all day. And I am afraid that the rapportführer's wife doesn't like me. She criticizes everything I do."

"That's because you're beautiful." This came from a woman who was sitting up on the floor in the middle of the room, wrapping something around her injured foot.

"It can be a curse," offered another woman in the bunk next to theirs.

"Yes, here, in this place, beauty is a curse," said a woman in her early forties, who was sitting up on one elbow.

"But she did get an easier job because she is so attractive."

"Easier? Perhaps. Perhaps not."

"And you?" one of the women turned to Gretchen. "You were sent to work at the pharmaceutical factory? That's not the worst job here."

"No, it's not. I mean, not in comparison to some others. But today, when I was going through someone's suitcase and I saw pictures of their family, I felt terrible. I was reminded that they are human beings just like you and me. And it makes me feel so sad. All of these things that people brought with them. Things they valued. Now meaning nothing. They are just thrown onto a pile of possessions. And their owners? Who knows what will become of them? Who knows what will become of any of us," Gretchen said.

And so the weeks trickled slowly by.

At night, when everyone else had fallen asleep, Gretchen and Rebecca talked with bittersweet nostalgia about their past. They talked about Eli and about the uncertainty of their futures. Finally, one night Rebecca told Gretchen about her friendship with Esther and how Esther died.

253

"She was my best friend before you," Rebecca said. "She killed her abusive husband, then she killed herself."

"That's terrible," Gretchen said.

"Well, the only consolation I have is knowing she never got sent to one of these awful camps."

"Yes, that is something to be thankful for."

Several women around them were snoring.

"Rebecca? Do you think Eli is all right?" Gretchen asked again. It seemed as though she asked this question at least twice a week.

"I hope so."

"I miss him every day. I love him with all my heart. And every day that we are here in Auschwitz, and I don't know where he is, I feel like I love him even more."

"He is your bashert. I believe that with my whole heart," Rebecca said.

"I've often wondered if you ever resented me. I know you said you didn't, but deep down I always wondered. You can tell me the truth now. No matter what you say, I won't hold it against you."

"I never resented you. Eli and I were never in love. After a time, we became good friends. But it was never that way between us. Our marriage was a failure, and I didn't understand why until I met you. Then I knew that it wasn't anything that I did wrong. The reason he couldn't love me was because he had already given his heart to you."

"And you weren't angry or hurt?"

"No, actually I was relieved. I knew from that time on that true love was possible. And someday, somehow, I would find my own bashert."

"You are truly like a sister to me. I never had a sister, but I always wanted one," Gretchen said, squeezing Rebecca's hand.

"And you are like one to me."

CHAPTER 59

As several months passed, Rebecca and Gretchen both became accustomed to their routine. Each morning after roll call and a quick breakfast of dry bread, Rebecca was escorted by a guard to her job in the home of Rapportführer Ziegler, and Gretchen was ushered off to the Bayer pharmaceutical company.

Frau Ziegler was a cold and demanding woman. As soon as Rebecca arrived, she ordered that all the floors in the house be scrubbed. Rebecca didn't say a word. Keeping her eyes cast down she took the bucket, filled it and began to wash the floors on her hands and knees.

"And make it fast. You have a lot of work to do. So don't let me catch you being lazy or I'll replace you. There are plenty of prisoners who would give an arm to have a job like this."

Rebecca nodded, still keeping her head down, not looking up from her work.

Gretchen was busy counting tablets when a guard called out the number that had been tattooed onto her forearm: 82478.

Gretchen dropped the bottle of pills. The guard who had

been overseeing her work kicked her in the calf. A sharp pain shot up her leg. *That's my number,* she thought. After a quick glance at one of the women who shared her block, she ran forward and followed the guard outside. *Where are they taking me?* She glanced over at the crematorium and shivered. *Could this be the end?* Gretchen followed the guard. He was walking very fast. She tripped and almost fell. Terror and anticipation of what might come next filled her with anxiety, and she was having trouble catching her breath.

"Get in the truck," the guard said, without any further explanation.

"Where am I going?" Gretchen asked.

The guard slapped her across the face. "Don't ask questions," he replied.

Gretchen felt blood trickling down from her nose. It ran into her mouth. The thick, salty flavor along with her fear made her gag. *How can I get word to Rebecca? She won't know what's happened to me,* she thought as she climbed into the back of the truck. It was almost spring, but the weather had not yet broken, and it was still cold outside. A heavy rain began to pour from the charcoal sky just as the truck started to move. A heavyset guard, angry that he had to get wet, stood over her with a rifle as the vehicle slowly rolled out of the gate that read Arbeit Macht Frei.

CHAPTER 60

Rebecca lay in her bed, crushed between two other prisoners and wept that night, when her blockmate told her what happened to Gretchen earlier that day.

"Where do you think they took her?" Rebecca asked.

"No idea. But I can tell you this, wherever it was, it was not good. She might already be dead."

"Shut up, Golde. Why would you say that?" a small girl named Marta sneered at Golde.

"Because it's true. Any one of us can be called up and taken to the gas, for any reason, at any time."

"That's enough," an older woman said. "We all need to get some sleep. This conversation is helping no one."

Rebecca climbed into her bed and tried to sleep, but she couldn't. Eli was gone; he might be dead for all she knew. And now, the Nazis had taken Gretchen. Crying didn't help, yet she couldn't stop. How could all of this be happening to her and her loved ones? She'd lost her family and all the people who were close to her. What was to become of her? Perhaps it was best to just wish for death. She couldn't see anything bright waiting for her in the future. If she were dead, all of this would be over.

In the morning, when Rebecca arrived at her job, the lady

of the house was not at home. She'd gone off with her husband to a meeting somewhere out of town. It was a Wednesday. On Wednesdays Rebecca did the laundry. She took the hamper of dirty clothes and emptied them onto the floor. Then she filled a bucket with hot, soapy water and began to wash the dirty things, scrubbing them until her hands were red, bleeding, and swollen. As she knelt on the floor working, she heard a heavy tapping coming from the hallway. It was getting louder.

"Good day, Fräulein," said a tall man with a chiseled jaw, high cheekbones, deep-set, green eyes, and black hair that shone like the coat of a wild horse. He carried a wooden cane. Glancing up quickly she saw that his left leg was missing from the knee down. "You don't know me, Fräulein. I just arrived here last night," he said, sitting down at a kitchen chair. He wore a Wehrmacht uniform adorned with lots of medals. "I suppose it would be polite to introduce myself. I am the spoiled-rotten son of the powerful rapportführer," he said with a note of heavy sarcasm in his voice.

Rebecca kept her eyes on the clothes as she continued scrubbing. She dared not look up at him.

"Yes, Fräulein, this is my father's house," he said, gesturing with his hands to show the entire house. "Ziegler is my name. Jan Ziegler. And I should be proud of that name, shouldn't I? My father is such an important man. And me? I am a war hero. A cripple for life but a war hero none the less."

Rebecca didn't speak. She was afraid of him. He was ranting, and in his voice she could hear a deep-seated anger. She didn't know if she was supposed to ask him if he would like something to eat or drink. She didn't know what to say, but she was afraid to leave the room. So she sat on the floor with her head down, washing the clothes. Fearing that, at any moment, he might do something terrible to her. Since she'd been at Auschwitz she'd seen the cruel tricks the Nazis would often enjoy playing on the prisoners. Sometimes they would pretend to be friendly, only to turn on the poor inmate in a terrible and vicious manner.

"What is it, Fräulein? You can't bear to look at me because I am crippled? Ahhh . . . so that must be it. Go ahead; say it. Say that you find me repulsive. Of course you do, a man missing a leg . . ." he said, a look of melancholy coming over his face.

Rebecca glanced up at him, and when her eyes met his, she believed he was sincerely feeling bad. Against her better judgment, she answered him. "It's not that," she stammered, scrubbing faster now. "I am a Jew. A prisoner here. Please, let me be. I do not want any trouble. I just want to do my work and be left alone." Tears threatened to fill her eyes.

"I ask nothing of you, Fräulein. I am a lonely man who just returned from the front. I can't talk openly to my friends or my family. They don't care how I really feel. I need someone who will listen. Someone who won't expect me to be proud to be my father's son, or proud to have blown my leg off. I need a friend who won't be repulsed by me, either, like my ex-fiancée, who broke off our engagement because she said she couldn't bear to sleep with a one-legged man." He laughed bitterly. "War hero, indeed," he said, then he added, "I would like to be your friend."

"Friend?" She stared at him in disbelief. *What am I supposed to say? I wish he would leave me alone.*

"Yes, in case you didn't hear me earlier, my name is Jan. You can call me Jan," he said smiling. There was less sarcasm in his voice now. "What's your name?"

"Rebecca."

"Is it all right if I call you Becky?"

She nodded, still very frightened of him.

"I can see that you're afraid of me. Please don't be, Becky. I really just need someone to talk to. Sometimes I am so disheartened. I find myself overcome with anger and confusion. Before my father insisted that I march off to war, I had what was considered a bright future ahead of me, a beautiful fiancée, a family with money and influence. But here is the secret: Even while I had all of those things, I was uncertain that they were what I truly wanted. Now, I don't have the fiancée anymore, and my father's position has become repugnant to me. I am a cripple, and I know there is something that I am searching for, but I don't know what it is," he said.

Rebecca looked at him, her eyes wide.

Jan took an apple from a crystal bowl on the table and polished it on his shirt. "The truth is, I don't care about losing my fiancée, or my career as a soldier. But I am heartsick over losing my leg. Do you know that in my dreams I can still feel my leg?" He shook his head.

Rebecca wasn't listening because she couldn't take her eyes off the apple. Saliva filled her mouth. *I am so hungry; what wouldn't I give for just one bite.*

Jan took a bite. Then he studied her. He seemed to know what she was thinking. "Would you like an apple?" he asked gently.

She was afraid to answer, yet at that moment, the very idea of the sweet fruit in her mouth seemed more important than living "Yes. Yes, please." *He might be teasing her. This could be the cruel joke. This was just the kind of thing Nazis did to Jews. Show them the apple, then take it away.*

He picked up the largest, reddest apple in the bowl and handed it to her.

She took it carefully, watching him fearfully out of the corner of her eye.

"Go on, eat it, please. No one is home but us," he said.

She took a bite and closed her eyes. The sweet juice filled her mouth and seduced her senses. Rebecca gobbled the apple while Jan watched.

"Good?" he asked.

She nodded. "Yes, thank you."

"I don't hate Jews. In fact, I've never hated anyone. I got swept up in all of this. I was sent off to war. I never wanted to do that, either. But, of course, my father would not have been able to live with me, had he thought for a single minute that I was a coward. So, to please him, I enlisted. His opinion was so important to me when I was young. I don't care what he thinks of me anymore." He smiled but it was a sad smile. "See these medals? I didn't really earn them. They were given to me because of my father. Not because of what I did but because of who my father is."

She finished the apple, eating the entire core.

"You were hungry?" he said. "Please take another one for later."

"I dare not," she answered, her voice barely a whisper.

"You're afraid of getting caught?"

"Yes." Rebecca found herself talking to him in spite of her fear of anyone wearing a Nazi uniform.

"I'll bring it to you. In fact, I'll bring you several. What block are you in?"

Rebecca wished he would go away. He was kind, but his friendship could be deadly for her. After all, if he were caught bringing her an apple, she would get in trouble, not him. "It's all right. Really. I would rather you didn't."

"Then you shall have some extra food each day when you come to work."

"That's very nice of you, but if your mother sees you giving me food, she will be very angry. And I am afraid . . ."

"So we'll just have to make sure she doesn't see it. Don't

worry, leave everything to me. Can you do that?" he asked, his blue eyes twinkling as he smiled at her.

"Yes, I can try. And you are very kind. I am very grateful," she said.

"Am I? I suppose." He smiled wistfully. "Being maimed has made me a mixture of rage and despondence. Disinterest and compassion. How can that be? I am a mess of contradictions . . ." He let out a short laugh.

Again, she glanced up into his eyes. She searched them for cruelty, for the lust for power she'd seen in the faces of so many of the guards, but all she saw was a man who seemed to have given up on happiness, yet she could see a spark in his eyes that said he was still searching. A mixture of black and white, of yes and no, of opposites.

"My family and friends don't want to hear the truth about my time at the front. They want to hear that I am a war hero. They want to believe that I fought bravely. But it's not the way it really was. You see, Becky, I was a coward. I hid in the trenches more often than I fought. It made me sick to fire the gun and see men fall bleeding and dying even if they were the enemy. And my leg? It got blown off by a landmine. Do you know that I sometimes reach down to feel for my leg because I can't believe it's really gone?"

She shook her head.

"Yes, I do. But when I reach down, there is nothing. My leg is gone. I am a cripple for life. And this, my father refers to as heroism. I would trade that foolish little title to have my leg back."

A month passed, and almost every day, Jan found a way to talk to Rebecca when she was working. He always came to her at a time when his parents were either busy or out of the house and presented her with a piece of fruit, a hunk of bread, or a sausage. She was so grateful that she couldn't help but like him. He was kind and unassuming. He asked nothing of her, only that she listen to him. And as the days wore on, he told her more about himself, his dreams, his pain, his hopes, and his fears.

"I wanted to be a writer when I was a young boy. I loved to read, you know."

"I love to read too. But my family was religious and I wasn't allowed to read very much that wasn't religious text," she admitted.

"Then I met Gerda at a party. Gerda was very pretty, vivacious, and charming. She wanted to marry a wealthy man. What woman doesn't. All of my friends wanted to date her. I have to admit, I was surprised when she accepted a dinner invitation from me. One thing led to another and I proposed. At the time, I was a struggling writer. Not earning much. So, my father, who never had much confidence in my writing, was planning to help me open a shop of some sort. We were discussing it, when I was commissioned to go to war. My father was not unhappy about my going off to fight. He thought it would be good for me. He said I was too soft, and war would make me grow up. Do you think I am too soft, Becky?"

She shook her head "No. I think you are a good person."

"I tell you so many things about me. But you hardly ever tell me anything about you."

"You know that I am prisoner, that I am Jew. What else do you want to know?"

"Did you have a boyfriend before the war? Where are you from?"

"I'm from Berlin. I was married. I don't know what has happened to my husband or my family. I have a best friend; she was here in Auschwitz with me, but one day, when I returned to the barracks, she was gone. One of the other inmates said she was taken away in a truck. She is not Jewish. I am so worried about her."

"You are married?" he asked. Rebecca noticed that he didn't acknowledge anything she said about Gretchen.

"Yes, I am married."

"Oh." He seemed a little put off.

"My marriage is hard to explain. We were more like friends than husband and wife." Rebecca didn't know why she felt compelled to tell him that.

"Yes, but you were husband and wife."

"Legally, yes. But he was in love with my friend. She is the one I told you about, who was taken away in a truck. Her name was Gretchen, and she was arrested for hiding us."

"You must be very angry with her. You probably hate her for ruining your marriage."

She smiled and shook her head. "Actually, she is my best friend. I never loved my husband in the way a wife loves her husband. As I said, he is my friend. I care deeply for him. But we had a very different kind of a marriage."

"I can see that," he said. "And you don't know what's happened to your friend?"

"All I know is that she was arrested with me. We were here together in the same block. Then one day, I returned from work and she was gone. The other women in my block said she was taken away. She could be dead for all I know. For a person in my position, it's best not to think about loved ones or the way my life was before all of this began."

"I'm sorry. Sometimes I find myself ashamed of my own people. I can't understand how the Germans could be doing these terrible things. My own father? How can my own father, the man who took me fishing when I was a boy, how can a man who has compassion for his family, be involved in the murder of innocent people? If you want to know the truth, I hate all of it. I hate the war, I hate the Nazi Party. And I hate Adolf Hitler. His ruthless ambitions are the reason I lost my leg."

"I'm sorry." Rebecca glanced at him then quickly looked at the floor. She was afraid. Frightened that he'd said too much and perhaps he would realize that he'd committed treason. Then he might kill her to keep her silent. After all, she was the only person who had heard him say these things that proved he was disloyal to the Nazi Party.

"Becky"—he broke her out of her thoughts and brought her back to the present moment—"don't be afraid of me. I can see in your eyes that you're afraid that I have told you too much. But please, don't worry. You're safe."

She nodded.

"When I look at you, I can see that you don't believe me. But you should. I would not hurt you. However, if it makes you feel any better, I know that if you told any of the guards what I said they would not believe you. And we both know that they would punish you. So I know my secret is safe with you." He smiled, not a mean or vicious smile, but a very real and sincere smile. "Now, I want you to know that any secret you share with me is safe as well. And . . . I want you to trust me."

She looked at the floor.

"Becky?" he asked. "Would you like me to try to find out what I can about your friend?"

"Would you really do that for me? This is not a trick, is it?" she asked, pleading, as tears formed in her eyes.

"It's not a trick. And I'll try to find out what I can about your friend. I can't guarantee anything. But, yes, I would really do that for you. What is her name?"

"Gretchen, Gretchen Schmidt."

CHAPTER 61

February, in the Woods

Eli made a poor thief. He felt guilty for stealing the pieces of fruit or vegetables that he was able to find during the night. He took only what he needed from the barns that left their doors open. And he reminded himself constantly that this was the only way he had of surviving. During the day, he stayed hidden and tried to keep moving because he was certain that if he stopped, he would freeze to death. The frigid weather left his fingers and toes numb. The little toes on both of his feet had already turned black and fallen off. His coat was hardly warm enough. When he felt the chill shoot through his chest, he thought of Gretchen, and a moment of warmth spread through him. He missed her, and he missed Rebecca too. They were his family in many ways. One afternoon when he couldn't walk anymore he sat down and propped himself up against a tree. His feet ached with cold, and he feared to look at them in case more of his toes had fallen off.

I am probably going to die here, he thought. *Hashem, are you with me? Answer me? I need to know that I will not die alone.* But there was no answer, only the stillness of the forest. *I have not served any purpose for being here on earth, and I feel that I have not only failed my father, but I have failed you too. I wanted to lead my people like my father. I wanted to do something for the Jews, to help them. Yet my entire life, I have done nothing. And even worse, I sometimes regret the only noble thing I have ever done, leaving the church to protect the priest and his congregation. It was the right thing to do, the noble thing for sure. But I had food and warmth when I was there. Look at me now: dying, starving, and freezing here in the middle of some dark woods. I don't even know where I am, not even what country.*

Eli put his head in his hands and wept. The tears froze as they hit his cheeks. *I will lie down here and try to fall asleep. Perhaps I will dream of Gretchen and Rebecca, and the pain will finally cease forever.*

But just as Eli lay his head down on the snow, he heard a sharp cry break through the silence.

"Help. Help me, please. Someone help me." It was a young boy's voice. He was speaking in Polish.

Eli jumped up and ran toward the voice, keeping himself hidden by the trees. The cry was followed by weeping. He followed the sound, until he saw a young boy of seven or eight, laying curled up in the snow with a pool of blood beside him. Without a thought for his own safety, Eli rushed to the boy's side.

"What happened?" Eli asked in Polish. *I must still be in Poland,* he thought. *How far have I walked?*

"I'm hurt. I was going hunting and I slipped on the ice. I cut my arm on my knife."

"Let me see," Eli said.

The boy showed Eli a deep cut. Eli nodded his head. "Here, let me help you." He took the knife that was laying on the snow-covered ground and reached under his coat to cut a piece of his shirt. He took the material and tied it around the boy's arm. "You have to get home and get to a doctor. It looks

268

deep," Eli said. "Let me help you get up."

Eli took the boy's arm and put it around his shoulder, then he lifted the child until the boy was on his feet.

"Thank you," the boy said.

"You're most welcome. By the way, what is the closest city to where we are?" Eli asked, not wanting the boy to know that he was shocked to be in Poland but wanting some idea of his location.

"Warsaw." The boy was trembling with pain.

"Your arm hurts, I know."

"Yes, very badly."

"We have to get you home as soon as possible because you're still bleeding. I'll walk you to your gate just to make sure that you arrive safely. Show your parents what happened right away; they will help you."

The boy nodded. Eli walked him to the gate of his farmhouse then he left.

That was the first person I have spoken to in weeks, Eli thought. *Poor child. He should be all right though once he gets home.*

Eli lay down. He was so tired, and once again he prepared to go to his eternal sleep. He lay his head on the snow and thanked Hashem for putting the boy in his path and thereby giving him the opportunity to perform one last Mitzva before he died.

Sleep came upon him easily. He felt his body shivering, but he didn't feel the cold. It seemed almost as if he were outside of his body, watching himself. His head was no longer heavy, and he drifted off without pain, to dreams of Gretchen and Rebecca.

CHAPTER 62

Ravensbrück

The ride to Ravensbrück was frightening and terrible. It was the middle of winter, and the women in the back of the open-air truck huddled together, trying to keep warm. When Gretchen arrived at Ravensbrück, she was taken out of the crowd who were all lined up to be admitted, and she was sent to a private room, where she was greeted by Ilsa.

"Hello, Gretchen Schmidt," Ilsa said. "I am Commandant Guhr, and it just happens to be your lucky day."

Gretchen didn't say a word. She knew better than to stare. She glanced at the pretty, young Nazi officer, with her curly, blonde hair and perfect uniform. She felt a wave of fear shoot through her as she tried to hide her disdain.

"Don't you want to know why you are so lucky today?" Ilsa asked in a teasing tone.

Gretchen continued to look at the floor.

"You don't answer? Either you're a mute or you're afraid of me."

Gretchen didn't say a word but she was trembling inside. At any moment, this woman might hit her with the whip she carried on her belt, or worse.

"Ahhh"—Ilsa threw her hands up—"I'm tired of toying with you. It's a waste of my time. Come, follow me. We are going to see a friend of yours."

Gretchen had no choice but to follow, and so she did.

Again, she was loaded into the back of a truck with an armed guard, while Ilsa sat in the cab with the driver. After a quick ten-minute drive, the truck stopped in front of a small, white house. The guard pushed Gretchen out of the back of the truck, and she fell, headfirst, into the snow. Ilsa came around and looked at her. "Get up. Let's go," she said impatiently. Then she waved the guard away. "Go sit in the cab of the truck. I'll be back in a few minutes."

Ilsa knocked on the door.

A cold wind rushed and penetrated Gretchen's thin, gray-striped uniform, chilling her bald head.

The door opened.

Gretchen almost fainted when she saw Hilde. Hilde's face was as pale as the snow outside. "Gretchen," was all she said.

"Well, it's cold out here. Aren't you going to invite me in?" Ilsa said.

"Yes, yes, of course," Hilde said. "Please, come in."

Ilsa pushed Gretchen forward. Then they were inside. Warmth filled Gretchen. The smell of something cooking made her mouth water. The sounds of a child at play made her want to cry with joy, with sadness, with memories.

"See, I told you I could do it. I said I would talk to some of my friends, and I'd find her and get her for you. Here she is." Ilsa smiled, cocking her head as if to say, *I have the power. Now you owe me.* "She'll be your housemaid and babysitter. And . . . since you have someone to watch the boy, you'll have no excuse but to come back to work at Ravensbrück and to fulfill your promise to me."

"I promised you I would return to work and I will. I am

grateful to you, Ilsa," Hilde said, but she hated Ilsa and wished she had the power to kill her and make it look like an accident. Again, she reminded herself that Ilsa had friends.

"Well, I want to see that gratitude, Hilde, not just hear about it. You know what we discussed."

Hilde nodded. "I'll be back at work starting next week. And I will do what I said I would do for you. Would that be all right?"

"Of course. I expect you on Monday morning."

"Yes," Hilde nodded.

After Ilsa left, Gretchen and Hilde stood looking at each other for a long time. Then Hilde said in a small voice, "Can you ever forgive me?"

Gretchen stared at Hilde. She was angry at her, yet she saw the regret in Hilde's eyes. Hilde had caused so much trouble. And because of her, Rebecca was still in danger. She wanted to mention Rebecca. Perhaps that blonde guard might be able to help bring Rebecca here. But she knew that Hilde was terribly jealous of Rebecca, and she didn't want to open that floodgate. Not just yet. Poor Hilde stood wringing her hands. Gretchen felt the anger begin to fade. She'd always pitied Hilde. And even with all that Hilde had done, she pitied her now. "Oh, Hilde," Gretchen said.

Hilde came forward gingerly and hugged Gretchen. Just then a little boy with a head full of blond hair and a bright smile, came into the room. He pulled at the bottom of Hilde's skirt.

"This is my son, Anatol."

Gretchen knew not to question.

CHAPTER 63

Auschwitz

Jan continued to bring Rebecca extra food. While she ate, they talked. He told her about the poetry he had written and the books he loved.

"Would you like to know a secret?" Jan asked Rebecca one afternoon, while she was eating a sausage on a thick hunk of bread.

She looked up at him. "If you want to tell me, then yes."

"I wrote a book. Not just a book of poetry. But a book. It's not published, of course, or it wouldn't be a secret." He smiled.

She smiled back at him. "Can I ask what it's about?"

"My life. Growing up with my powerful, often power-hungry father. And how my love for him turned to disillusionment."

Rebecca didn't respond. Sometimes she was still a little afraid of him even though he had never given her any reason to be.

"Would you like to read it?" he asked.

She nodded. "I would, but I can't. I don't have anyplace where I can read. When I am here, at your home, I have my work to do. And when I am back at my block, I must sleep. I would have no place where I can hide a manuscript."

"Ahhh, that's so true. I never thought about it," he said. "I can imagine that life is very hard for you. I wish I had the power to make things better."

"You already have. I can't tell you how much the extra food helps."

"I've made some small inquires about your friend, but I haven't been able to find out much. I might be able to, if I dig deeper. But then someone might tell my father that I am asking about the whereabouts of a prisoner, especially a girl who came in with you; he could put two and two together and send you away from our house to another work detail. I don't want to risk that. And the worst part of it is that if my father suspected we were friends, he might have you assigned to a more difficult job."

She nodded. Rebecca didn't care what happened to her if it meant she might be able to help Gretchen. But even though Jan was kind, she still dared not push him too hard. At least not yet.

"My parents are going on a holiday in a couple of weeks. They will be gone for five days. Would you like to have a bath during that time?"

"A bath?" Rebecca said. Her face turned red with modesty. "A bath?"

She longed for a bath. It would be wonderful to be clean again. But was this man expecting more from her in exchange for the luxury of a bath?

"You're blushing." He smiled. "I don't expect anything in return. I pride myself on being a gentleman. I am offering a bath, nothing more."

"Yes, oh yes. I would love a bath," she said.

"Very well, then, it's settled. You shall have a bath in our

274

tub when my parents leave."

CHAPTER 64

Jan began opening up to Rebecca by reading his poems to her.

She never asked him any questions about why he'd written a specific piece. She just listened and nodded. As time passed, his episodes of sarcastic rants gave way to heartfelt pain. He finally admitted how hurt he'd been when his fiancée told him that she couldn't marry a man with one leg even if he was a war hero. Jan told her how repulsed he was by his own body. He explained that the absence of his leg cost him in more ways than he'd ever admitted to anyone. It made him feel insecure and sometimes worthless. Occasionally, he told her a little about the war.

Then he asked about her life. She told him about Eli and Gretchen. And each day she found it easier to talk to him. He was a good listener. Not judgmental at all. Never once did he make any derogatory reference to the fact she was Jewish. Rebecca explained that she came from a religious family and her marriage to Eli had been an arranged marriage. She admitted to him that she had agreed to the marriage to please her parents. However, she told him, she'd known that Eli was not her bashert from the very first time they met.

"Your hair is growing back in. It's very pretty," he said one day, as he touched her head.

She shivered. No man other than Eli had ever touched her in such a tender way. She was suddenly ashamed of her head with the tiny sprouted curls. "I had long, blonde hair before my head was shaved."

"It must have been terrible for you."

Rebecca shrugged. "I had less of a shock than some of the other girls. You see, as a Hasidic Jewish woman, it was my mother's responsibility to come and shave my head the day after my wedding. So I had seen myself bald before. And I guess it wasn't as traumatic for me as it might have been if I had never seen it."

"Your mother shaved your head?"

"Yes, it's customary."

"Well, if it's any consolation, I think you are quite beautiful, even without your long hair."

"Oh," she said, blushing and looking away from him, "thank you."

"Now I've embarrassed you. I'm sorry. I didn't mean to. I just . . ."

"No, it's all right. I am flattered."

Jan smiled.

CHAPTER 65

The following Monday, Jan's parents left for their vacation. A guard delivered Rebecca to Jan's home immediately after breakfast, as he had done each day since Rebecca was assigned to work for Rapportführer Ziegler.

Once Jan was sure that the guard was gone and he and Rebecca were alone, he led Rebecca to the bathroom where he handed her a clean, fluffy towel and a bar of soap. "Here, enjoy your bath."

"But my housework?" she said.

He smiled. "If we do it together it will take half the time. And I will help you."

"Oh no, you must not," she said.

"Of course I will. I insist."

She looked at the kindness in his eyes and wanted to cry. How could such a good man be the son of a Nazi SS officer? As she filled the tub with hot water and the steam filled the bathroom, she remembered something her father-in-law, the brilliant rebbe, once told her. "You cannot ever blame a man for the sins of his father, Rebecca."

Now she understood what that meant.

Her body relaxed in the warm water. For several minutes, she just lay there, luxuriating in the pure pleasure of it. Then she scrubbed herself from the top of her head to the tips of her toes.

After Rebecca's bath, Jan offered her cheese sandwiches for lunch. And for the first time they ate together. He'd never dared to sit down at the table and eat with her before. If his parents had caught him, he knew they would send Rebecca to another work detail, or worse.

"Don't think me forward, but I should have tried to find you a clean uniform. I am sure it was uncomfortable to put those dirty clothes back on after your bath. It was thoughtless of me."

"You are anything but thoughtless" she said. "You are so kind . . ."

He held up his hands in mock protest of the compliment.

"Jan"

"Yes?"

"I don't want you to think I ungrateful, but I am afraid that if I wear a clean uniform it might raise suspicions."

"Don't worry. I will tell the guard who brings you each day that I secured a clean uniform for you because you are preparing my food, and I didn't take well to the dirty uniform while I was eating. Would that be all right?"

"Thank you," she whispered, her voice choked with emotion. "Thank you." A single tear fell from her eye and made it's way down her cheek.

Jan glanced at Rebecca. *She is truly lovely, both inside and out. I don't know what else I can do for her. How else I can help her. But there must be a way. I can't stand what my father is doing, not only to Jews but to all those poor, defenseless people in that terrible camp. It's murder. There is no other word for it. It's just plain and simple . . . murder. And I can't imagine this beautiful, delicate flower of a girl suffering such a hideous fate. But how can I help her? How?*

"Have I done something wrong?" she asked.

"No, why do you ask?"

"You're staring at me."

"My apologies. I just . . . well . . . I just. I don't know."

She looked down at the floor. He saw what he thought was fear pass over her delicate features. "Are you having regrets about allowing me to bathe in your home? Because, I promise you, I will never tell a soul."

"I am not sorry for any kindness I have shown you. I only wish I could do more. But I don't know what I can do to make things better for you. I feel so helpless," he said. Then it was as if God tapped him on the shoulder, and he remembered something that had happened before the war. Something with the power to change everything.

CHAPTER 66

In the Woods, Somewhere in Poland,

"Is he dead?"

"He looks dead."

Eli felt something hard and even colder than the ground poking at his ribs. Somewhere in the distance he heard someone speaking, but his head was too clogged to understand their words. His eyes felt frozen shut, and he found it difficult to open them. But once he did, the world around him came into terrifying focus.

"He's alive. He'll be worth a fine reward. Runaway Jew, I'll bet."

"I'm sure he is."

A tall mountain of a man stood over him. Next to the man was the boy who had cut his hand. The boy whom he had bandaged. *Am I dreaming? I am so clouded that I can't tell what is real and what is not?*

"I'm sorry," the boy said. "I'm sorry, mister. I didn't mean for this to happen. My father asked me who helped me bandage this cut. I didn't know that—"

"Shut your mouth," the huge man said, hitting the boy across the back of the head. "You don't have to explain anything to him. He's a Jew."

"But he helped me, Father."

"Shut up. If I didn't need you to show me where he was, I would have left you at home with your mother. You're a baby, not a man."

Eli pulled himself up to a sitting position. The boy's arm was rebandaged. It looked better, but the boy was crying.

"Get on your feet," the tall man said. "Let's go."

The man shoved the boy forward, then he walked behind Eli, keeping his gun pointed directly at Eli's head. They walked for several minutes, and during that time Eli could hear the boy whimpering. *He feels guilty. He didn't mean it, but he knows he caused my arrest. Poor child. I can see what happened. He made the mistake of telling his parents that a man in the woods was kind enough to help him. When they came back here to find me sleeping, they figured I was probably a runaway. If I have a chance to speak to the child, I will tell him that I forgive him. I think I heard the father mention something about a reward. He must be turning me over to the Nazis. I don't fear death anymore. I've come to terms with it. But I do dread being tortured. Hashem, stay with me and please give me the strength to endure whatever comes next.*

They arrived at a small, run-down farmhouse. A woman was watching through the window. She opened the door.

"The Gestapo is on the way," she said.

"Mother, what will they do to him?" the boy asked, his voice filled with terror.

"Did I say to keep your mouth shut, boy? Did I tell you that you were not to speak anymore?" The father slapped the boy across the face, sending him flying across the room where he hit the wall with a thud.

"Son," Eli said, "it was not your fault. Whatever happened, you didn't do it on purpose. I forgive you."

"Brave bastard, aren't you? Well, let's see how brave you

282

are when the Nazis come for you," the father said, hitting Eli across the shoulders with his gun butt.

Eli fell to the ground. He didn't try to stand up. The boy was looking at him, his eyes filled with fear and regret. Eli mouthed, "It's all right. I know you didn't mean it. I forgive you . . ."

The mother put her arm around the child and took him into another room, while the huge man waited for the Gestapo, with his gun trained on Eli.

CHAPTER 67

The Gestapo took Eli to the Nazi headquarters, where he was thrown into a cell for a few hours. Then two guards pulled him out and beat him severely until he passed out. When he regained consciousness, he found himself on a train, stuffed into a boxcar with other people all around him. It was a good thing in a way because the car was so full, the crowd was holding him upright. Had there been less people he might have been trampled. The ride was not long, but it was perilous. Children screamed, women cried, and the smell of feces, vomit, and urine permeated the air. There was no food or water. His right eye was swollen shut, and his head and body ached from the beating.

Finally, the train rolled to a stop. The doors opened, and Eli was carried out by the force of the crowd. The women and men were separated into lines. Then followed by guards with guns and attack dogs, the prisoners were forced to move forward.

"We are going to our deaths," said an old man, with white hair and a map of wrinkles covering his face.

Eli saw a small boy holding tight to his father's hand. His eyes were filled with terror. "I would have sent my son away to live with his mother. She left me and went to France with some man. But she died a year ago. So you see, he has no one but me." The man offered this strange testimony to no one in particular.

"Your ex-wife is probably better off dead. Look at the women over there. So many of our women. Poor things. And you want to know what is going to happen to them? They will die too. The children too. Everyone . . ." a tall slender man said in Yiddish. "You know what's up at the front of the line? Gas. A gas chamber. They are going to gas us all to death. We are in the death line."

"How do you know this?" another man asked.

"I know."

Eli began to pray. He prayed for them all, as he followed in line. *A gas chamber where we will all be killed; can this be true? Hashem? Hashem? Can this be true? I don't understand. Help me, please, to know your will and to know what you want me to do.*

The line continued to move forward. Then one of the guard's dogs began to chase a squirrel. The guard ran after the dog. "Come back here. Come back here now, Kara," he yelled.

Another guard asked, "Is she your dog?"

"Yes, she is mine, and that squirrel is rabid, I think."

"Well, go on and shoot it before it bites your dog and you have to shoot her too."

For just a few seconds, the guards were completely distracted by the dog and the squirrel. During those very precious moments God answered Eli's prayer. A man in a striped uniform with a yellow Star of David on his arm grabbed Eli's hand and pulled him out of the line. He held on to Eli's hand as the two of them ran through the camp. The man led him to the barracks. Once they were inside, the man, out of breath from running, turned to Eli and said, "Eli Kaetzel. Don't you recognize me?"

"I am sorry, I don't." Eli was bent over at the waist, trying to catch his breath. "Do I know you?"

"Of course you know me. I was a member of the shul where your father was the rebbe. My name is Joseph Goldstein. I remember you. You used to come to shul with Yossef, the chubby boy. I can't remember his last name."

"Yes, Yossi. Of course. He was my best friend."

"Your father was a good man. A very good man. And even though the last time I saw you, you were still very young, you always showed a lot of promise. You were the apple of your father's eye. His son!"

Eli smiled. "My father was a good man. I miss him all the time." Then Eli looked down at the floor, which was covered in dirt and sawdust. "You saved my life today, didn't you?" he said.

"Yes, that line you were in was headed for the gas chamber. It was lucky that guard's dog ran off. He loves that dog. Treats it like a queen. He once told us that it's named after a Valkyrie. I have often wondered how a man can have such compassion and love for an animal and yet shoot a child or a woman without showing any emotion at all. You see, Eli, this is not a work camp. This is a death camp. Those of us who are alive are only alive because we are part of the killing machine."

Eli stared at him in disbelief. *Am I in hell?* he thought. "Killing machine?"

"Yes, transports come in every day, and they are sent right to the gas chambers. Those of us who are alive either shovel bodies into the ovens, or we sort through the belongings and put them in piles for the Nazis. All the positions are full right now; no one on your transport was needed. So they were sending all of you to the gas."

"One of the men in line told us that we were going to be gassed. I found it hard to believe."

"He was right. It's true, Eli."

"But when they find me here, with you in the barracks, and I have no job, won't they just take me to the gas?" Eli asked.

"They would have. But the man who slept in that bunk over there died this afternoon. I've hidden his body. When you go to roll call, you'll use his number. Then tonight under the cover of darkness, you and I will drag his body over to the pile of dead bodies waiting to be burned. No one will be the wiser. You will take his identity and live. You will sleep in his bunk from now on."

Eli nodded, but inside he felt sick. All those men he'd been in line with would be dead in a few hours. That little boy he'd seen holding his father's hand, was just a child. His life had not yet begun, and soon he would be dead too.

"Where am I?" Eli asked. "What is this place called?"

"Treblinka," Joseph said.

Eli didn't speak. Instead, he went to his bunk and lay down. *Did Joseph Goldstein do me a favor? Or would I be better off dead than living here in this hell, where human life is worth nothing?*

Eli closed his eyes and prayed to Hashem for guidance. Then in his mind, he heard his father's voice. *Where there is life, there is hope. It is your turn to lead our people, my son. In this place. In this man-made hell, you will grow to become the leader you were always meant to be. The opportunity will present itself for you to serve our people and you will not fail. The time is near. God has an important purpose for you. You will soon see it very clearly. Mark my words, Eli Kaetzel.*

CHAPTER 68

Auschwitz

Jan went to his father's closet and took out one of his father's clean and crisply pressed SS uniforms. He put it on. It was no surprise that it fit him perfectly. From the time he was very young, everyone had always said he looked exactly like his father. They'd marvel at what an attractive boy he was. So tall and well built just like his father. What they didn't know was that he looked like the man, but that was where the similarities ended. Jan was nothing like the sadistic SS officer who, when Jan was just a boy, had fooled him into thinking he was the kindest and bravest man alive. It wasn't until Jan grew up and saw the way his father treated people whom he considered inferior that Jan knew his father's true nature. The rift between them started small, but the more Jan learned about his father, the more he found him despicable. However, strangely enough, even though he hated what his father stood for, there were times when childhood memories of days out on the lake fishing, or playing soccer, could almost bring him to tears. Can you love and hate someone at the same time? He often wondered.

Jan hated this uniform and all that it stood for. He lived

outside of Auschwitz. He smelled the burning bodies and brushed the ash from the crematorium that fell on his shoulders. They were murdering people in there, and he knew it. His father's excuse was that the Jews and the Gypsies were subhuman, and in order to cleanse Europe, they must be destroyed. "We are only doing what must be done," his father said in a gentle tone when Jan asked him how he could be involved in such despicable things.

But Jan didn't believe him. The idea that his father could murder made him sick. "Subhuman, Father? I went to school with Jews. They were the same as the rest of us."

"You don't know them the way I do. You were too young to remember what happened, because of them, during the Great War. When you are older, you will understand why we had to do what we did. The Third Reich will be remembered for all the good we did for the world."

Jan knew his father was talking about the Reich cleansing Europe of undesirables. And he was sure that his father believed all the nonsense he spewed. But he was still young, and he found that arguing with his father did him no good. So he tried to ignore what went on at Auschwitz.

However, it is much easier to ignore horror when one does not see it with their own eyes.

As a boy, Jan had never been allowed into the camp. Then one afternoon, when Jan returned from fighting in the war, he went through the gates of Auschwitz in search of his father. And it was then that the reality hit him. He saw the walking corpses and the piles of dead bodies. He saw the uniformed prisoners shoveling the dead into the ovens, their vacant eyes staring at him. Jan looked around him at what the Nazi Party was doing, and he knew for certain that he'd gone to war for nothing. This was a cause he would never support. And for this, he'd lost his leg.

Jan combed his dark hair back with a little of his father's hair grease. He looked in the mirror and assessed his appearance. Even with his cane he was an intimidating sight. He knew that in order to achieve the goal he was setting out to accomplish, he must appear authentic. Jan looked at the SS emblem on his lapel, the death head on his hat. All of it was frightening. And he knew that in order to get what he wanted today, he had to be frightening.

Satisfied, he took the keys to his father's car and drove off. He'd never done anything like this before, and it was difficult for him to play the role of the SS officer. He'd seen his father interact with many farmers. It was important that they found him powerful and intimidating if he was going to succeed. And he was quite certain that if he didn't succeed, Rebecca would end up dead. So he mustered all his inner strength and drove ten miles to the little farm he remembered. He'd been to this farm with his father many years before he'd gone off to fight.

CHAPTER 69

Jan slept late the following day. Rebecca heard him getting up at around noon, so she prepared his lunch. He came out of his room stretching.

"Where is your plate?" he asked.

"I . . ." Rebecca didn't know what to say. "My plate?"

"We take meals together since my parents are gone, don't we?"

She nodded.

"Are you hungry?"

"Yes."

"Then come on, make up a plate for yourself."

She quickly made up a plate for herself.

"Becky, sit down." He motioned her to the table. She had been taking meals with him since his parents had gone on vacation, but she dared not presume that she was welcome to sit beside him. She was still afraid of him, and each day she waited to sit down until he asked her to join him. His parents would return in two days, and then all of this should stop. But until then, she enjoyed bathing each day, wearing the clean uniforms that Jan was able to secure from the camp, and eating at the table like a human being.

She was surprised to find that Jan still had not tried to

seduce her or compromise her in any way. He was, as he'd promised, a gentleman in every way. And she had long since stopped noticing his missing leg. Each day he read a poem to her from the book of poetry that he wrote and promised that one day he would allow her to read his memories.

"Becky." He loved calling her this name. Even though his parents must never hear him call her any name at all. "Do you remember I told you that I had an idea, a very special plan that would change everything?"

"I remember. How could I forget?" She nodded.

"Well, I've checked things through, and let me just say that I believe the plan will work."

"How? In what way? I am confused. What do you mean?"

"All right, let me explain. Years ago, before I went off to fight, my father used to insist that I accompany him when he went to the neighboring farms. The Nazi Party always takes the lion's share of their produce for the war effort."

"Yes, go on."

"Did you know that? Did you know that the Nazi Party took most of the harvest that the farms produced? So, even though the farmers had plenty of food, they were forced to give it to the fatherland, and consequently, they never had enough. Many of them stole food and hid it in their cellars, barns, or in the attics."

"Hmmm, I never knew."

"Anyway, my father would go from farm to farm to make the produce collections. When we arrived, he would have the trucks loaded while I was sent to look for any hidden stashes that the farmers might be trying to steal."

"Oh dear. Did you find any?"

"Yes, I am ashamed to say, I did. I didn't understand the repercussions at the time. But later I found out that the farmers were punished severely. They were imprisoned in a camp like this one for stealing from the party."

"Oh no, Jan."

"Yes, and I was wrong. So very wrong. I regret my part in it. But there is nothing I can do to change the past. The reason I am telling you about this is because once, when my father sent me off to look for hidden food, I found a secret room under the floor. I found it quite by accident. The cat scratched the rug, and when the rug was moved out of the way, I saw an opening, a sort of crawl space. And then peeking up at me through an opening in the floorboards was a child. But not just any child. It was a little girl who had the facial features of a mentally retarded person. I knew, of course, why the farmer and his wife had hidden her. Himmler had declared that all mentally handicapped people were to be sent away. And later we learned that they were destroyed. This little girl was looking up at me, and she was so innocent. A line of drool ran down her chin. I suddenly felt a wave of pity. I knew I wasn't going to tell anyone about her. At that time, I didn't know that the mentally deficient were being euthanized. But something told me to keep my mouth shut. So I quickly replaced the rug and moved the table over so that the cat couldn't move the rug back again and reveal the opening. Then I went to my father and told him that I found nothing."

"That was very kind of you. Did you ever see the child again?"

"Not until yesterday. Do you recall that I went out for a few hours yesterday afternoon?"

"Of course, you left right after lunch and returned right before I went back to my block." She looked away.

"What is it?" he asked, reaching over and touching her shoulder. "Are you all right?"

"Yes, I was just thinking about something."

"What?"

"Never mind. It's not important."

"Yes, it is. It's important to me. Anything that could make your expression so dark is important to me. Tell me what's wrong. Please."

"When you left yesterday, you were wearing an SS uniform. Have you joined the SS?"

He laughed.

She looked at him, puzzled. "I didn't think that was funny."

"I would never join. I thought you knew me better. It was my father's uniform. I was wearing it to look intimidating."

"You're not making any sense. Where did you go?"

"I went to see that farmer. The one with the mentally deficient daughter."

"Why?"

"To make a deal with him."

"What kind of a deal? You don't need any more food. You have all you could want, don't you?"

"Yes, of course I do. You know that. But I need a place to hide you. A place where you will be safe. Becky, I have to get you out of Auschwitz. So I told the farmer that I knew about his daughter. At first he panicked, begging me to have mercy on the child."

"Oh"—she sighed, her hand flying up to her throat—"the poor man."

"I told him his daughter was safe as long as he would do as I asked. He agreed. He said he would do anything. I told him I wanted him to take you in and hide you under the floorboards with his daughter. I told him I would fix the opening in the slat so no one would be able to see that there was a room beneath the floor. He readily agreed. I promised him I would come at least once a week with extra food to be sure you had enough to eat."

"Jan? Why? Why are you so kind to me?"

"Can't you guess?"

She shook her head. He smiled and looked at her with a warmth she'd never seen in the eyes of any man before. "I care about you, Becky. I don't believe all this nonsense about Jews being subhuman. You are the sweetest, gentlest creature I've ever seen, and well . . . you've stolen my heart."

Rebecca looked down. "I don't know what to say."

"Say you care for me too."

"I don't know what I feel. I've stifled my feelings for so long and now, well, I don't know. I am so afraid all the time, Jan."

"No matter. We will have plenty of time to get to know each other. I will come to see you each week and we will talk, and eat, like we do now. And before you know it, all your fears will go away."

"What will your parents say when I don't come to work?

"I will tell my parents that you became ill while they were gone, and so rather than possibly catch something from you, I took another maid from the camp. My mother won't care, and neither will my father."

"What about when I don't show up at roll call? They will send out dogs looking for me, won't they?"

"They might. But who cares? You'll be safe at the farm, and no one will ever know where you are."

She looked at him. "You've arranged all of this for me?"

He nodded.

"Thank you," she said. "How can I ever thank you?"

CHAPTER 70

Later that afternoon, before the evening roll call, Jan tucked Rebecca into the trunk of his father's car. Then he passed the guards at the gate with a quick wave and headed toward the farm. Once they arrived, Jan pulled the car around the back. Then he helped Rebecca out of the trunk.

"Are you all right?" he asked, his voice filled with genuine concern.

She nodded. "Yes, I am all right." But her back and legs ached from being confined in the small space. Jan and Rebecca went into the house, where the farmer's wife was waiting. She looked at Jan skeptically, as he was not wearing the SS uniform. The farmer's wife moved the rug and then carefully opened the trapdoor. She led Rebecca and Jan into the secret room under the floor. There, huddled in a corner, was a small girl with chubby cheeks, a flat face, slanted eyes, and a worried look.

The farmer followed them all into the secret room and looked at Rebecca suspiciously.

"This is Rebecca," Jan said, forcing a note of authority into his voice. "Why don't you introduce yourselves to her?"

"I am Henryk, and this is my wife Felka. The little girl is Anke."

"And now, tell her your surname."

"Gorski," the farmer said. "But, please, I do wish you would go away and not get us involved in this thing you are doing. You see, we are only humble people. We don't want any trouble with the Nazis," Henryk said, wringing his hands on the tail of his well-worn work shirt.

"But you must remember, Herr Gorski, you have already broken the law, now, haven't you? You have been hiding a deformed child."

"Yes, please, I beg you; don't let any harm done to our little Anke. She is a harmless, sweet, little creature. And we love her so much. Anke was born this way. She can't help it. I beg you . . ."

"I understand how you feel. You love your daughter. I care very deeply for my friend, Rebecca. So, if you want to keep Anke safe, then you will make sure that you don't do anything foolish like turning my friend in to the Gestapo. Anke will be safe as long as you protect Rebecca as if she were your sister. Do you understand me?" Jan demanded an answer.

Rebecca had never heard him sound like this. She knew he was playing a role, but it scared her to see how easy it was for him to act like a Nazi.

"Yes," the farmer nodded. "I understand. And believe me, we will not do anything foolish."

"That's very wise. Now, leave us alone. I would like to speak to Rebecca alone."

The farmer nodded then took his wife's arm. Turning back for a moment he said, "Must I take Anke out of here with us?"

"No, leave her. She's fine," Jan said.

After the farmer and his wife were gone, Jan turned to Rebecca. "Everything is going to be fine. You'll see. Trust me, please."

"I do," she said. She was glad that he was no longer acting like a Nazi, and he was once again the caring and wonderful man she'd come to know.

"I will return tomorrow afternoon. I'll bring you some regular clothing. I want you to change out of that uniform. I think it's best. My mother has a bag of clothing she is preparing to donate. I'll just take a couple of dresses from the bag. She'll never notice that they are gone."

Rebecca nodded.

"And I'll bring enough food to carry you through the week. I wish I could stay with you, but I must go now. Please, don't worry, everything will be fine," he said, clumsily touching her shoulder. She knew he wanted to embrace her, but the child was watching, and it was an awkward moment.

After Jan left, Rebecca was alone with Anke.

"Hello, Anke," she said.

Anke hid behind a chair, a trail of drool running from her lips to her chin.

"It's all right, you don't have to be afraid of me," Rebecca continued. "My name is Rebecca. But you can call me Becky if you would like. My friend, Jan, that man who was just here? He calls me Becky."

"Becky," Anke said.

"Yes, Becky." Rebecca smiled, then she continued. "I am going to be staying here, with you. I'll tell you stories, and we can sing songs. Won't that be fun?"

The little girl peeked her head out from behind the chair and smiled. When she smiled, Anke was beautiful. And her beauty touched Rebecca's tender heart.

CHAPTER 71

It didn't take long for Anke to warm up to Rebecca. By the time Jan returned the following evening, carrying clothing and food, Anke was lying with her head on Rebecca's lap. He came down to the secret room without the Gorskis and put the pile of things he'd brought down, on a small table.

"It seems that the two of you are getting on well," he said smiling at Rebecca.

"We are. She is a sweet little marvel. She has the beauty of a child's innocence. Such a kind heart, she has."

"I'm glad."

"Did they send out a search for me?" Rebecca asked, worried.

"They didn't bother. I am not questioning it. And I am certainly not complaining," he said then added, "By the way, I brought you something."

"Oh?"

He handed her a package wrapped with pretty paper and a bow. "This is for you," he said, his voice husky.

She cocked her head. "You didn't need to bring me anything, Jan. I am so grateful for all that you've done already."

"Open it."

She took the package and carefully removed the wrapping. Inside she found a thick, neatly arranged pile of papers. "What is it?" she asked, but she already had an idea.

"It's my manuscript. I wrote about growing up with my father. I have never shown it to anyone before. But I would like you to read it. That is, if you want to."

"Of course I want to."

He looked down. "I hope you won't find it too boring."

She smiled at him and rubbed his lower arm. "I am sure I will find it very interesting."

"And here. I brought you something else too." He smiled broadly as he took a smaller package out of his pocket and handed it to her.

Rebecca took the package and opened it. "A toothbrush?" She held the toothbrush to her chest.

"I thought you might need one," he said.

She put her arms around him and hugged him, as the tears ran down her cheeks.

CHAPTER 72

June, Treblinka

By the beginning of summer, Eli had seen enough at Treblinka to know that it truly was a man-made hell on earth. He'd witnessed the shooting of a child, the beating of an old man, and the constant smoke from the crematoriums. He'd heard grown men cry with fear, and even worse, he'd seen others who were too weak and dead inside to cry at all.

Eli's job was shoveling dead bodies into the ovens. For each dead person he would recite a silent prayer. It took him over a week to get used to the smell. At first he retched and gagged all day. But he knew he had to keep working or he, too, would be dead, and someone would be shoveling him into an oven.

When Joseph Goldstein had introduced Eli to the other Jewish men in his block as the son of a great rebbe, Eli found that some of the men were desperately in search of miracles. They needed hope, something to grasp on to. They needed God, and they needed Eli to assure that there was a God. These men began to follow him. They asked him when this would all end. They asked him what to do. All he could do was tell them to pray.

And then there were others who were filled with anger. Sometimes they took their anger out on Eli. They would rage at him. Often they would shake him or strike him. Always demanding some explanation for why the Jews were suffering the way they were.

"I lost my family," one said. "Why? If there is a God, why would he let this happen to me? My wife and I did nothing wrong. We were simple people. We never broke God's commandments."

Another man demanded, "I lost my wife. They separated us when we first got here. They tore her away from me. She tried to run back to me but they shot her. I watched her die. Why, Eli, son of a great rebbe? Why?"

A young man in his twenties said, "My child died on the transport. No air, no water. He was only a baby. What could he have done to offend your God? Then my wife was gassed. Why did this happen? What's the explanation, Eli? I beg you, tell me?" The young man wept.

Eli hung his head and admitted to having no answers.

Then one night he was approached by a Polish engineer who was well respected even among the Jewish population.

"Katz, is it?" the engineer asked Eli if that was his name.

"Kaetzel," Eli replied. "Eli Kaetzel."

"You're the one the Jews talk about, the man whose father was a rabbi?"

"A rebbe, but yes, I think I am the man you're looking for."

"Good. I'm glad I found you. I need to talk to you. Do you know who I am?"

"I have an idea. You work in the extermination area, don't you?"

"Yes, my name is Wiernik, Jankiel Wiernik."

"I've seen you around. Why do you want to talk to me?"

"I've been watching you for a while. I think it's a good

thing that you're a man of God. That means you have a conscience."

"You are a religious man?"

"No." Jankiel laughed. "But I was a carpenter, just like Jesus, before I became a guest of the Nazi Party."

"A guest, huh?" Eli smiled. "And . . . you have a good sense of humor."

"You have to know how to laugh if you're going to survive here."

Eli nodded. "I suppose you're right. You need a sense of humor and a lot of hope."

"I'll get right to the point. I, along with others, are trying to organize an uprising, here in the camp. It is our goal not only to disrupt this systematic murder going on here at Treblinka, but we are hoping that during the chaos some of the prisoners might escape."

"And what is it you want from me?"

"I want the help of the Jewish prisoners. And most of them trust you. Most of them will follow you."

"You want us involved in the uprising?" Eli studied the man.

"Yes. We recently lost a man. Did you know Chorazycki?"

"He was a doctor, wasn't he?"

"Yes. He was trying to buy weapons outside the camp. The camp's deputy commandant caught him, and rather than endure the torture he knew they'd put him through, he committed suicide. I believe he didn't want to be forced to turn any of us in."

"So you want the Jewish prisoners to help you buy weapons from outside?"

"Have you talked with any of the prisoners that have been coming in on the recent transports? The ones from the Warsaw ghetto? They staged an uprising there, in the ghetto, by buying weapons from the Poles. A handful of Jews held the Nazi bastards off for a month."

"How can the Jewish prisoners buy weapons from outside. We can't get out of here, except for work details, and when the men are on slave-labor details; they are being watched very closely."

"I don't expect them to buy weapons. I, along with a group of others are buying the weapons. Of course, if they have any way to buy weapons, it would be very helpful. But what I want is for you to organize a group of men who, once the command is given, are willing to storm the camp arsenal, take the guns and any other weapons they can find then attack the Ukrainian and German guards."

"How will we get in? It's always locked."

"That's true, Kaetzel. But . . . we have a key. One of the men in my group was a locksmith; he was able to make a key."

"Brilliant," Eli said.

"Oh yes, there is no lack of talent here in Treblinka. The prisoners here come from all walks of life." He smiled wryly. "Sad, isn't it? Each one of us has something to contribute to the world. Look around you, Kaetzel; there are doctors here, scientists too, teachers. You just name the profession, and they have been through the gates to this miserable place."

"Yes, I know," Eli said.

"Ah, well, there is nothing we can do except rise up against them. The Nazis don't want the good things that we have to give. They'd rather see us all dead." He shrugged his shoulders as if it didn't matter, but his eyes said that it mattered to him more than he could ever express. Then in a sad voice he continued to speak. "Anyway, the signal to begin is a gunshot. Once this is sounded, a group of our men are scheduled to start all the buildings on fire. Of course, the Nazi bastards aren't expecting this, so we will have the element of surprise. That was how the uprising in the Warsaw ghetto was so effective. The Nazi guards were completely unaware of what was coming. And I must tell you that it will give me such pleasure to see these bastards squirm. I hope we can kill them all. The Warsaw ghetto uprising proved one thing to us: that the Nazis are a lot tougher when the other side isn't fighting back, yes?"

Eli nodded. "Yes, Jankiel, we have been passive for too long; it's time for us to fight back."

"And with luck, some of us will be able to escape into the forests. Others, I know, will die. But at least we will go down fighting. I would rather die watching this whole camp burn to the ground, than live as a prisoner here and shovel dead bodies like those." He pointed to the pile of bodies waiting for Eli to shovel into the ovens.

"Who else is involved in this? Are there any Jews?"

"Yes, some. Others, not. It doesn't matter here. We are all victims of the Nazis, Jews, not Jews. We must all work together. So what do you say? Are you in?"

Eli thought for a moment. As a Hasidic he should refuse. But after all he'd seen and endured in this terrible place, he felt certain this man, Jankiel, had come to him with the message he'd been waiting for. This was his calling. He was to lead his people, not in the way he'd originally thought, but in a powerful and effective way, nonetheless. Men who might have died would escape, and live. They might have children and grandchildren, all because of his efforts. And even if the uprising only saved one life, it all would have been worth it. "Yes," Eli said firmly. "Yes, you can count me in. Do you have a date set for this revolt?"

"August second."

"It's June already. We don't have much time." Eli rubbed

his chin as he considered this.

"Then we'll have to work fast," Wiernik said, winking. "Welcome aboard, Eli."

CHAPTER 73

Over the next month, Eli went to secret meetings with Wiernik. He met the others and learned that each of them wanted the same thing, to destroy Treblinka and all the misery it caused.

Eli became active in every aspect of organization. Eli, who had never believed in stealing, who had to be pushed to the brink of starvation in order to take a few apples or a bunk of asparagus, a man who would never have stolen jewels or money for his own sake, was now taking everything he could from the suitcases of the newly arriving prisoners. If he were caught, it would mean death. But if he lived, he could sell the things he stole, and that would mean more guns, more ammunition, and a better defense for the prisoners against the guards.

Eli had never believed it was up to him to decide if a man was worthy of life. He had been taught to leave that decision to Hashem. But now he felt certain that Hashem had chosen him to lead his people in this revolt, and when it came to the Nazis, he was prepared to shoot and to kill.

At night, when Eli lay on the straw where he slept, the lice nipping at his skin, his thoughts would not allow him to sleep. He was haunted by memories of everyone in his past.

He remembered his best friend Yossi's wedding when he married Ruthie, whose Yiddish name was Rivka. And then came the children. Eli could still see Yossi's face turn white when the mohel cut each of his little boys at their bris. All the old men had laughed at Yossi, but Eli understood his best friend and took him into the kitchen to get him a glass of sweet wine. As he lay there, thinking of Yossi, Eli whispered a prayer for him and his family and hoped they were safe. When he closed his eyes, he often saw the faces of his parents, and he was glad they had not lived to see this. The idea of his mother and father in a camp like Treblinka was horrific.

He was filled with regret when he had recollections of the day he had married Rebecca. Not because he didn't care for her—he did, very much—but because they had wasted so much time in the beginning of their marriage trying to fulfill other people's dreams for them. If only they had been able to speak their minds and their hearts. Both of them knew from the beginning they were never meant to be husband and wife. But things did turn out all right for them. They became the best of friends, and he found that he often missed that friendship. He wondered where Rebecca was now and whispered a prayer that Hashem would keep Rebecca safe.

Then came his deepest thoughts—his thoughts of Gretchen. These tender recollections came to him all day and all night. *My love, my life,* he thought. *Gretchen is the woman in my heart. My bashert. The other half of my once searching soul. It was a blessing from God to be given a love so deep. Not every man will have such a gift. And although I might die in this uprising, my heart will be with her forever. This much I know. Oh, Gretchen, I wish I had one more opportunity to speak to you. Just one more moment to hold you in my arms. If I live through all of this, when it's over I will find you and never let you go. You will never be unhappy, not for one day.* Then he whispered a Hebrew prayer for Gretchen. And on many nights, his eyes began to close just as the morning bell rang for him to report to roll call and then to work.

On a hot evening in early July, after working a twelve-hour day sweating over the hot ovens, Eli ate his watery soup quickly. Then he gathered several of the men who had also been working on the uprising.

"I need to ask a favor of you," he said. "It's very important to me."

"What is it, Eli?" Joseph Goldstein asked.

"If I should die during the uprising, and any of you survive, you must promise that you will find these two people and tell them what happened to me."

"Of course I will, if I survive," Aaron Levin said.

"Yes, I will do what I can as well," Samuel Minowsky said.

The others nodded. "Yes of course," they voiced in unison.

"Rebecca Kaetzel and Gretchen Schmidt. Please, remember these names. Do you promise me?"

"Yes."

"Yes."

"I promise."

"Tell them that they must go on with their lives, marry, have children . . ."

The men were all nodding just as a guard walked over. He slammed his club against the table. "No talking," he said.

The men separated. But Eli felt a wave of relief pass over him. He had not been afraid to die before this. It if was Hashem's will, then he accepted it. But now, he felt an even greater inner calm.

CHAPTER 74

July, Auschwitz

Each week, Jan brought gifts when he came to see Rebecca. He brought clothing, food, and some children's books for Anke, who ran into his arms hugging him whenever he arrived. She was a delight, but also a distraction. And there were times when Jan wanted to talk to Rebecca without disruption. So, one week in late July, when he came to see Rebecca, he brought a special gift for Anke.

The little girl jumped into Jan's arms as she always did. He kissed her forehead as the food and a package he'd brought dropped out of his hands.

"Anke," he said, and picking up the package, he handed it to her. "This is for you."

"For me?" she asked.

"Yes, all for you. But there is a little catch."

"What does that mean, a catch?"

"Well, it means that if you take my gift, you have to try to do as I ask."

She frowned. "What do I have to do?"

"When I am here visiting, you can play with your gift, but only if you allow me and Becky to have some time to talk about adult things. Would that be all right?"

"Can I talk too?"

"No, you have to play while we talk. But before I leave, I will spend some time talking to you. Just to you. When it's our time to talk, you will have all of my attention. Does that sound all right?"

"I don't know. Let me see the gift."

He laughed. "I think you'll like it," he said, handing her the package.

Anke ripped the paper open and five fat crayons fell out. There was a thin block of paper as well. "What is this?" she asked.

"Watch." Jan winked at her. He set the paper and crayons on the table. Then he picked up a blue crayon and began to draw a little girl. Anke was fascinated. He drew red hair with another crayon.

Rebecca watched Jan playing with Anke, and a wave of tenderness came over her. *How can I feel this way? His father is a Nazi, an SS officer. He should be my enemy. Yet he is not. He has been my savior. I know a man is not responsible for his father's crimes . . .*

"I promise to play with this while you and Rebecca talk. And I won't bother you at all," Anke said, picking up a green crayon.

Jan winked at Rebecca and motioned for her to come to the other side of the room. They sat down on the floor.

"Where did you get those?" she asked him.

"The crayons? They were mine when I was a child. I thought she might like them."

"She loves them. That was so nice of you, Jan."

"I like her. She is a sweet little thing. And I enjoy doing nice things for her. But I must admit, bringing her a gift to keep her busy wasn't all for her enjoyment. It was also so I could have a little time with you."

"I know that." She smiled.

He smiled back. "I like you, Rebecca. I like you a lot." When he took her hand, she didn't flinch. "I know we are from different worlds. And there is a sea of hatred between us, deep enough to drown the whole world. But my feelings for you are real. I've never felt this way about anyone before."

She turned away for a few minutes to compose herself. Then she turned her head back to look in his eyes. "I've never felt this way about anyone before, either." She hesitated for several minutes, while he gently massaged her hand with his thumb. Then she added, "I've been reading your manuscript. I know a lot about you. You aren't like your father."

"That's not entirely true. I am not like the Nazi in my father. But I am like the man I knew who was my father when I was a child: the man who took his son fishing because he knew his boy wanted to go, even though he had no idea how to fish."

"I read that part. I laughed. It was very sweet. He tried so hard."

"Yes, he did. And I can see myself in my father when he taught me to play soccer and to throw a ball. But this man who claims to be my father, the one who spends his time killing innocent people? I have nothing in common with that man. I don't know where that man came from or how my father ever became that way."

"Look at my picture," Anke came running over with a paper scribbled with color.

"It's lovely," Rebecca said.

"It's for you." Anke handed it to Jan.

"Thank you." He smiled. *If my father would have had his way, little Anke would already be dead*, he thought, and a shiver ran up his spine. *And so would my sweet, beautiful Rebecca.*

CHAPTER 75

Ravensbrück

Ilsa kept her promise. She never interfered in Gretchen's position as Hilde's housekeeper either. Hilde was grateful to Ilsa, so she and the Valkyrie decided to put the plans to murder Ilsa on hold. Besides, Hilde could not be sure if she would ever need Ilsa again.

Hilde went back to work at Ravensbrück. She stole jewelry and anything else she could find of value, all of which she gave to Ilsa. The SS officers were pulling in the reins at Ravensbrück. They had begun to watch the guards more closely. Hilde knew that if she were caught stealing from the Reich, she would be arrested for treason. The penalty was death, or worse to be imprisoned in the camp. She trembled when she thought of herself as one of the inmates sleeping beside those she'd once been guarding. And there was no doubt that if the prisoners could get their hands on her, they would make her suffer.

Hilde had never been one to be so unselfish, but there was something about this child that made her feel complete. She'd never believed that motherhood could be an important part of her life, but now it was the most important thing in her life.

And not only motherhood, but she truly treasured her friendship with Gretchen. Since Gretchen had come to Ravensbrück, and they were together every day, Hilde found less need to talk to the Valkyrie in the mirror. However, she still resorted to her childhood coping mechanism of making believe she had become invisible when she had to steal for Ilsa. So far, she'd been lucky the invisibility had worked. She had not been caught.

CHAPTER 76

August 2nd, 1943, Treblinka

No wind filtered through the open windows in Eli's block that night. There was nothing to break the oppressive heat, only the heavy, odorous air that hung over the room as the dirty, sweaty men tried to sleep.

Eli couldn't sleep a wink. Tomorrow was the day of the uprising. And he felt certain that no matter what happened, things would never be the same. He sucked in a deep breath of air and began to pray. Not for his own safety, but for clarity as to what God's purpose for him was and the strength to carry it out. He prayed for his people and for an end to the Nazi oppression. Then he said a prayer for Rebecca. And then he thanked God for Gretchen and for the joy she'd brought to him even if it was only for a short time. Eli begged God to protect Gretchen. If he should die tomorrow, he asked that Gretchen be spared and that she be blessed with happiness with another man once this war ended. Everything was in place for tomorrow. Everyone knew what they were expected to do. He'd gone over the plan with his men more times than he could remember. It was simple. The signal to begin was a gunshot. They were to keep their ears open and listen closely for it. There had been construction work near the arsenal for the last several weeks. The chaos due to the construction had allowed the resistors to enter the arsenal unnoticed and steal twenty hand grenades, twenty rifles, and a few guns. The rest they would get on the day of the uprising. Each morning, one of the prisoners was assigned to spray the camp with disinfectant. He used a hose. Last night, two men removed the disinfectant and replaced it with gasoline that they siphoned out of one of the guards trucks. The guards would not know that the buildings were being sprayed with gasoline instead of disinfectant. Once all the buildings were doused with gasoline, Eli was to gather some of his men, and they were to move as quickly as possible, throwing grenades at the buildings to start them on fire, while others took the rest of the weapons from the arsenal. Eli went over the plan one more time in his head. Then he allowed himself the luxury of envisioning Gretchen. He remember the first day he saw her. How beautiful she was, with her hair like silky strands of rose gold blowing in the wind. He smiled at the thought as he lay quietly, waiting for dawn.

The following day Eli could sense the nervous energy that was flowing through the camp. But he was relieved to see the guards remained oblivious to any of it.

Two prisoners, who had been friends for several years, had plans of their own. They were a part of the Resistance, but they wanted to ensure that if they survived they would have enough money to begin a new life. So, while the others were readying themselves for a fight, these two men stuffed their uniforms with stolen money that they'd stolen from the suitcases of incoming prisoners. This should not have been a problem except that one of the guards noticed the bulges in their pants. He called over another guard. They forced the prisoners to take off their clothes. When they found the stolen money, the guards began to beat the prisoners. From across a field, one of the resistors heard the prisoners crying out as they were beaten. He ran over to see what was happening. The two inmates were lying on the floor, and the guards were kicking them. The man who had come over to see what was happening was a part of the Resistance. He was afraid that torturing prisoners would break them down, and they would tell the guards about the planned uprising. So to prevent the possibility of the prisoners revealing the plan, the man took a stolen gun out of his pants that he had been carrying and shot both prisoners.

The shots rang out through the camp. But this was a mistake. It was too early. Still, the gunshots set everything into motion. Eli's heart was thumping as they ran to get the grenades. He realized the gunshots had gone off earlier than expected, but everyone acted according to plan. However, no one knew what had happened. The man with the hose had not yet finished his morning spraying. He hurried to be sure the gasoline was distributed before the men came with the grenades. The buildings burst into flames as Eli and his group tossed the grenades at the lice-infested barracks, the ovens, the administration buildings.

All of it was burning as if God had pointed a finger at the Nazis and set their terrible death factory ablaze with the fire and light of righteousness.

Eli ran from building to building throwing grenades, until a guard caught him by the shoulders, throwing him to the ground. The guard kicked Eli hard in the stomach, flipping his body over. Then came a deafening explosion as the arsenal blew up. The earth trembled. The guard who had been beating him was momentarily paralyzed by fear. Eli looked out in front of him, and he saw men escaping. They were climbing over and through the barbed wire. Under his breath, he said a prayer for them, in hopes that they would survive.

"You dirty Jew," the guard said. Then he pulled out his gun.

Eli held his breath, waiting for the shot that would end his life. But instead he felt the guard fall on top of him. Then Eli saw the gray-striped uniform of one of the prisoners. He had shot the guard, and now he pulled Eli from beneath the dead man.

"Let's go, Katz." It was Wiernik.

Eli smiled at him and began running beside him. "You still can't get my name right, can you?" Eli said. "You still call me Katz." Eli should have felt some fear, as bullets were flying all around him and men were falling. But in the distance, he could see men were escaping, climbing through the barbed wire to freedom. Eli's feet felt as if they'd taken flight. He glanced over at Wiernik and laughed.

Wiernik laughed too. "Your name is Katzel or something like that, right?"

"Yes, right. Thank you for saving me," Eli said.

"We did it, Katzel. We did it. Look at all those men running for the forest. God bless 'em."

"Yes, may Hashem bless them with freedom and life. Look, there goes one of the Jewish men from my group. May he bring plenty of healthy, happy Jewish children into the world."

"May they all live long and happy lives," Jankiel said.

"Yes, oh yes," Eli replied. He was laughing and crying at the same time. Tears were streaming down his face as he and Jankiel reached the barbed wire at the gate. Eli held the wire open for Wiernik. He felt the sharp wire slicing through the flesh of his hands, and he saw the blood dripping down. Behind him, there was a loud explosion. He never looked back, only forward. And in spite of the pain in his hands, his heart was filled with joy. As Wiernik began to climb through, a bullet found him, and he fell without a sound. Eli dropped to his side.

"Wiernik," he said, holding the man's head in his arms. "I'm going to try and get us through the wire."

Wiernik nodded. Blood was pouring out of him. Eli knew Wiernik was dying, but he refused to leave him to die alone. Then as Eli stood up and began to tug at Wiernik's shirt, trying to pull him through the wire, he felt the hot lead of a bullet soar through him. It was as if his body was ripped apart. He fell forward. And as he did, he saw an ocean of blood surrounding him. *I'm dying*, he thought. And then as his eyes closed, he whispered these words to Gretchen:

"Gretchen, my one and only. Please know that I finally found my purpose. I know now why I was born the son of a great rebbe. I finally led my people to a victory. A small victory, but a victory it was because a few men escaped, and they now have a chance at life. I helped to give them that chance. And so, I can go to my rest easily. But know always that my heart is with you. You are never alone, my love. And someday, when it is your time to join me, we will once again be together as one, my twin soul, my bashert. My true love."

CHAPTER 77

August 3rd, Ravensbrück

Gretchen had no way of knowing what happened to Eli on that fateful day in the summer of 1943. But as Eli fell, she felt something change inside her. In the living room of Hilde's home, Anatol was on the floor playing with a toy truck his father brought home for him. When he looked up at Gretchen, he asked her if she was feeling all right.

"Yes, sweetheart," she said, but she didn't feel well at all. Her heart was beating out of sync and she felt dizzy. Anatol, who had become very close to her, ran over and took her hand.

"You don't look well," Anatol said. "Maybe I should go over to the neighbor's house and ask for help."

"No, no, please. Don't do anything. We have talked about all of this before. I am a prisoner in the camp, remember? The people who are your friends in the neighborhood and at school would not like the fact that you see me as your friend. If they think I am sick, they will take me away from you. I don't want you to be scared, but you must remember the things I tell you."

The child looked at her with wide eyes older than his years.

"Why would you die there? The doctors will help you. When I am sick, my doctor helps me."

"No, my little love, the doctors in the camp won't help me. I am a prisoner. If I get sick, they might kill me."

"But why would they do such a terrible thing to you? You are so kind and good to me. You are such a good friend to my mother. I don't understand all of this."

"Your mother, Hilde, is a very good friend of mine. She has made it possible for me to survive in this camp. But we, you and I, must be very careful. We must never trust anyone. We must never tell anyone that I am a friend of your family. They must see me as little more than a housekeeper. Do you understand?"

Anatol nodded. Then he said, "You should lie down. You are looking so pale. Can I get you anything to eat or drink?"

"No, I'll be all right," Gretchen said. "But I do think I will lie down for a few minutes. You can play until I get up. Then we will do some more of your schoolwork. I want to go over your reading assignment with you."

"Yes, Gretchen. I will do as you say. I won't leave the house. I will just sit here on the floor and wait for you."

"That's a good boy," she said, and feeling worn out, she went into the bedroom and lay down. Her head ached, and when she closed her eyes, she saw Eli's face. "Something has happened to Eli," she whispered aloud. Miles away from Ravensbrück, in Poland, life began to leave Eli's body. Gretchen trembled. She couldn't explain how she knew at that precise moment Eli had left the earth, but she knew. As death took him under her warm, dark wing, Gretchen felt the other half of her soul leave the planet, taking a piece of her heart with it. She forced herself to get up an hour later to help Anatol with his studies. She only did this because she knew how attached he was to her, and she didn't want him to be afraid that she was seriously ill. But that night, as she tried to sleep in the terrible cramped quarters, where she shared a bunk with three Jewish women, she wept. *Eli,* she whispered his name in her mind. *I love you. I will always love you.* Then she heard his voice in her head. *Gretchen, my one and only. Please know that I have finally found my purpose. I know now why I was born the son of a rebbe. I finally led my people to a victory. A small victory, but a victory it was because a few men escaped, and they now have a chance at life. I helped to make that chance happen. And so I can go to my rest easily. But know always that my heart is with you. You are never alone, my love. And someday, when it is your time to join me, we will once again be together as one, my twin soul, my bashert. My true love.*

"Are you all right?" the woman who slept beside her asked.

"Yes, thank you," Gretchen said.

"You were crying."

Gretchen nodded.

The woman did not persist with any more questions. She just gently touched Gretchen's cheek then turned over and closed her eyes to sleep.

CHAPTER 78

January, 1945
Auschwitz

It was late at night when Jan arrived at the farmhouse. Quite often, Jan made his visits at night because he wanted to speak to Rebecca while Anke was asleep. This time, he brought a pile of blankets for Rebecca and Anke. The temperature kept dropping, and Anke had been coughing and sneezing for over a week.

As quietly as he could, he climbed under the floorboards, carrying a single candle. There were never any complaints from the farmer or his wife about his visits. They were even more accommodating than he had hoped, giving him a key to the house, so he could come and go at night when they were both asleep.

Jan found Rebecca and Anke cuddled together, lost in slumber. Jan took a moment to gaze at Rebecca before awakening her. She looked angelic by the light of the candle. Her golden curls had grown back, framing her lovely face in wisps. Gently, he touched her shoulder, stirring her awake. When she saw him, a sweet smile came over her face. Unwinding herself with gentle care from the child's arms and legs she stood up and went to the other side of the room, where Jan waited.

"I brought some extra blankets."

"Thank you," Rebecca said smiling. She took two of the blankets and spread them over Anke, who continued to sleep, snoring softly.

"I have news," he said.

"Bad news?"

"No, good news. As I have been telling you, Germany has been losing the war. Now it looks as if Hitler is going to surrender very soon."

"That is very good news." She breathed deeply.

"And I have more."

"Yes?" she said.

He took her hand in his. "Remember long ago you asked me to see if I could find out anything about your friend, Gretchen Schmidt?"

"Yes, of course, I remember."

"She's alive, Rebecca. She's been at Ravensbrück working as a housekeeper for one of the guards."

"Oh!" Tears filled the corners of Rebecca's eyes. "My sister."

"She's your sister? You never told me that."

"Not blood. But close enough."

"Once this is all over, we will find her. I promise you."

"I would love to see her again."

"You said she was your husband's girlfriend. I thought that was rather strange. But I accepted it. You are a very wonderful but unusual girl."

Rebecca smiled. "Gretchen was Eli's bashert. Anyone could see that when they were together."

"Bashert?"

"That means the one person that is meant for you in this

world," Rebecca said. "I knew from the day I met Eli that he was not my bashert."

"No, I don't believe he was."

"And why is that? You never knew him," she said.

"Because I am," he said. "I am your bashert."

Rebecca looked into his eyes. They had never kissed before. But she'd thought of kissing him and wondered what it would be like.

"Yes, I think you might be right. As strange as all of this is, I believe that you are my bashert. And maybe I had to come to Auschwitz so I could find you. God can work in very strange ways."

Jan took Rebecca's face gently into his hands and kissed her lips. "When this is over, I want you to be my wife."

"I will," she said.

"I will become a Jew if that proves to you that I am not like my father."

"Let's wait and see. I want you to know more about Judaism before you even think about committing to it."

"Fair enough," he said. Then he kissed her again. "As long as I can commit to you."

CHAPTER 79

Ravensbrück

Hilde came home from work one afternoon, with her hair disheveled. Anatol was sitting next to Gretchen on the sofa. He was reading from his book and she was helping him.

"Go to your room for a few minutes, please, Anatol. I need to speak to Gretchen," Hilde said.

Anatol stood up and walked to his room. He didn't argue just gazed at her with that wise expression he often had.

Hilde waited until the door to Anatol's room had closed. Then in a quiet but desperate voice, she said to Gretchen, "Hitler surrendered. Ilsa ran away last night. She never came to work today. When the SS officer in charge went to her room, it was empty. All of her things were gone. I don't know where she went, but she told me that if things went sour with the Reich she was going to leave. And now she is gone. Axel and I are planning to run away too. We are going to take Anatol with us. But if we are caught we will be arrested. I would ask you to come with us, but you'll be better off here. The camp will be liberated soon. The Russians, British, and Americans are storming through and liberating the camps," Hilde said. Her eyes were glassy with unshed tears. "It's all over, Gretchen. Our beloved Reich has fallen."

"Hilde," Gretchen said, hesitating for a moment, "perhaps it would be best for Anatol if you left him with me. I mean, if you and Axel are fugitives on the run, wouldn't it be safer for him if he were here, with me?"

"Oh, Gretchen!" Hilde said, sighing deeply. "I've never been an unselfish person. But I have never loved anyone the way I love that boy. Somehow, he made up for everything that was wrong in my childhood. Not only in my childhood, but in my life. Being a mother fulfilled me. I know it sounds crazy, but it gave me everything I was missing. And I know you're right. But if I leave him, there's a very good chance I will never see him again."

"I understand. And you do know that I care for Anatol too. I want what's best for him," Gretchen said. A thought of Eli and Rebecca raced across her mind, but she pushed it aside for the moment. She didn't feel the same way as Hilde about the Reich. In fact, she rejoiced that it had fallen. But why tell Hilde that? There was no point in it. Right now, she had to find a way to save Anatol.

"Do you think they would blame a child for what Axel and I did?"

"I don't know what they will do. But if he is with you, he will carry the stigma of being a Nazi. If you leave him with me, I will say he is mine."

Now the tears ran down Hilde's cheeks. She wanted to run to the mirror to ask the Valkyrie what to do. She longed to cloak herself, Axel, and Anatol in a veil of invisibility. But the truth was that she knew none of this was the answer. The only right answer was to leave Anatol with Gretchen, and if she and Axel could find a way to get back, they would come back for him later. "You're right," Hilde said, her shoulders slumping. "You're right. You should take him."

Gretchen nodded. "You know that I will care for him as if he were my own. You do know that?"

"I know you will. Axel and I are leaving tonight."

Gretchen took Hilde in her arms and held her for a long time. Then Hilde broke away. "Help me pack?"

"Of course."

Later that afternoon, when Axel returned, Hilde told him what she had decided. He agreed, but he wanted to speak to Gretchen alone. Hilde, who had taken a pill to calm her nerves leaving her too exhausted to question him, allowed it. She called Gretchen into her bedroom and told her that Axel wanted to speak with her. Then Hilde left.

"There is something you must know about the boy," Axel said.

"Go on, tell me, please," Gretchen said.

"He wasn't taken from a Polish family. I took him from the children camp. He was born a Jew. Hilde never knew that I knew he was Jewish. I denied it to her. However, Ilsa told me the truth about the child a while ago. Ilsa said she tried to tell Hilde too, but Hilde refused to believe her. HIlde was afraid that Ilsa would tell the SS and have Anatol taken away. She was desperate for a child when she lost the baby. He was not a baby when we took him. But he was blond and looked Aryan. So Hilde did whatever Ilsa asked of her in order to protect Anatol. Ilsa told me Anatol's real name. It was Moishe Rabinowitz. His father was Benjamin Rabinowitz; his mother was Lila. Ilsa admitted she killed Anatol's mother to protect the secret, but I don't know anything at all about his father. Someday, when he grows up, Anatol might ask you for his story. And now you can tell him if you want to."

"Anatol will be safe with me, and that's all that matters now," Gretchen said.

Axel nodded. "Thank you for taking Anatol, Gretchen. It is

328

a comfort to me to know that he will be in your care. Take him and go home to Berlin. Hilde and I have done some terrible things. I don't know what is in store for us."

CHAPTER 80

January, 1947 Berlin

Anatol lay with his head on Gretchen's lap while she was reading to him. She gently ran her hand over his golden hair. *He is such a treasure,* she thought. *But I feel so bad for him. It's been two years and he still asks if Hilde and Axel are going to return.*

As Gretchen stroked his head, Anatol looked up at her and asked, "What is going to happen to the world now that the war is over?"

"Well, Anatol, before this terrible nightmare began, I remember my father talking to my uncle. My father said that when Hitler was taking over, he could see that Hitler was causing a small crack in the right-thinking minds of our people, here in Germany."

"What does that mean?"

"It means that people started to lose track of right and wrong. A foundation that had once been firmly in place was now cracked. Then my father said that if the German people allowed that small crack to go unrepaired, it would grow until it would become a dark canyon."

"A canyon?"

"A huge, dark hole. The crack went unrepaired and so it grew, and people forgot what was right and what was wrong. At first, only a few people followed Hitler. But by the time the war ended, many people had lost themselves in his empty promises.

"Where are my parents, Aunt Gretchen? When are they coming back?"

"I don't know," she lied. How could she tell him that they were arrested and would be standing trial in Nuremberg? If they were found guilty, they would face execution. How does one tell a child that the only parents he can remember might be killed? Or that the people who raised him had his birth mother killed? Gretchen decided he was too young to comprehend all the evil that Axel and Hilde had done. *Where do I begin to tell him about the camps and that the people he loved, who were kind to him, were guards—cruel and horrible guards? They were Jew haters. And then if I am going to tell him the truth, should I not tell him the whole truth? Does he not deserve to know that his birth parents were Jews? I don't know the fate of his father, so when he asks, I will have no answers. He could be dead, or alive.*

"Is it a real canyon? Where is it? I can't see it."

Gretchen was pulled back into the present moment by Anatol's question. "It's not a real canyon that you can see. It's a deep crack like a wound in the fabric of humanity."

"I don't I understand what you're talking about, Auntie Gretchen."

"I know," Gretchen said. "It's very complicated."

"Are we doomed? Can we fix the hole?"

"I believe we can," she said.

"But how? How do we fill a big hole like that?"

"With one pebble at a time, Anatol." She touched his hair.

There was a knock at the door. Anatol sat up. He looked worried. *He's been through so much. It is such a shame that a knock on the door can spark such terror in the eyes of a child so young,* Gretchen thought. Then she smiled at him trying to reassure him. "It's all right. I am going to see who is there," she said, walking to the door. She too was worried about who might be at the door. After all, once the Russians had marched into Berlin, it had become very unsafe for German women. Terrible things had happened to Gretchen at the hands of those Russian soldiers. Things she would never tell Anatol.

She took a deep breath, glanced back at Anatol for a single moment. Then she opened the door.

"Rebecca?"

Millions Of Pebbles

Book Three in a Holocaust Story series.

Benjamin Rabinowitz's life is shattered as he watches his wife, Lila, and his son, Moishe, leave to escape the Lodz ghetto. He is conflicted because he knows this is their best chance of survival, but he asks himself, will he ever see them again?

Ilsa Guhr has a troubled childhood, but as she comes of age, she learns that her beauty and sexuality give her the power to get what she wants. But she craves an even greater power. As the Nazis take control of Germany, she sees an opportunity to gain everything she's ever desired.

Fate will weave a web that will bring these two unlikely people into each other's lives.

AUTHORS NOTE

First and foremost, I want to thank you for reading my novel and for your continued interest in my work. From time to time, I receive emails from my readers that contest the accuracy of my events. When you pick up a novel, you are entering the author's world where we sometimes take artistic license and ask you to suspend your disbelief. I always try to keep as true to history as possible; however, sometimes there are discrepancies within my novels. This happens sometimes to keep the drama of the story. Thank you for indulging me.

I always enjoy hearing from my readers. Your feelings about my work are very important to me. If you enjoyed it, please consider telling your friends or posting a short review on Amazon. Word of mouth is an author's best friend.

If you enjoyed this book, please sign up for my mailing list, and you will receive Free short stories including an USA Today award-winning novella as my gift to you!!!!! To sign up, just go to...

www.RobertaKagan.com

Many blessings to you,
Roberta
Email: roberta@robertakagan.com

Come and like my Facebook page!

https://www.facebook.com/roberta.kagan.9

Join my book club

https://www.facebook.com/groups/1494285400798292/?ref=br_rs

Follow me on BookBub to receive automatic emails whenever I am offering a special price, a freebie, a giveaway, or a new release. Just click the link below, then click follow button to the right of my name. Thank you so much for your interest in my work.

MORE BOOKS BY THE AUTHOR

AVAILABLE ON AMAZON

Not In America

Book One in A Jewish Family Saga

"Jews drink the blood of Christian babies. They use it for their rituals. They are evil and they consort with the devil."

These words rang out in 1928 in a small town in upstate New York when little four-year-old Evelyn Wilson went missing. A horrible witch hunt ensued that was based on a terrible folk tale known as the blood libel.

Follow the Schatzman's as their son is accused of the most horrific crime imaginable. This accusation destroys their family and sends their mother and sister on a journey home to Berlin just as the Nazi's are about to come to power.

Not in America is based on true events. However, the author has taken license in her work, creating a what if tale that could easily have been true.

They Never Saw It Coming

Book Two in A Jewish Family Saga

Goldie Schatzman is nearing forty, but she is behaving like a reckless teenager, and every day she is descending deeper into a dark web. Since her return home to Berlin, she has reconnected with her childhood friend, Leni, a free spirit who has swept Goldie into the Weimar lifestyle that is overflowing with artists and writers, but also with debauchery. Goldie had spent the last nineteen years living a dull life with a spiritless husband. And now she has been set free, completely abandoning any sense of morals she once had.

As Goldie's daughter, Alma, is coming of marriageable age, her grandparents are determined to find her a suitable match. But will Goldie's life of depravity hurt Alma's chances to find a Jewish husband from a good family?

And all the while the SA, a prelude to the Nazi SS, is gaining strength. Germany is a hotbed of political unrest. Leaving a nightclub one night, Goldie finds herself caught in the middle of a demonstration that has turned violent. She is rescued by Felix, a member of the SA, who is immediately charmed by her blonde hair and Aryan appearance. Goldie is living a lie, and her secrets are bound to catch up with her. A girl, who she'd scorned in the past, is now a proud member of the Nazi Party and still carries a deep-seated vendetta against Goldie.

On the other side of the Atlantic, Sam, Goldie's son, is thriving with the Jewish mob in Manhattan; however, he has made a terrible mistake. He has destroyed the trust of the woman he believes is his bashert. He knows he cannot live without her, and he is desperately trying to find a way to win her heart.

And Izzy, the man who Sam once called his best friend, is now his worst enemy. They are both in love with the same woman, and the competition between them could easily result in death.

Then Sam receives word that something has happened in Germany, and he must accompany his father on a journey across the ocean. He is afraid that if he leaves before his beloved accepts his proposal, he might lose her forever.

When The Dust Settled

Book Three in A Jewish Family Saga

Coming December 2020

As the world races like a runaway train toward World War 11, the Schatzman family remains divided.

In New York, prohibition has ended, and Sam's world is turned upside down. He has been earning a good living transporting illegal liquor for the Jewish mob. Now that alcohol is legal, America is celebrating. But as the liquor flows freely, the mob boss realizes he must expand his illegal interests if he is going to continue to live the lavish lifestyle he's come to know. Some of the jobs Sam is offered go against his moral character. Transporting alcohol was one thing, but threatening lives is another.

Meanwhile, across the ocean in Italy, Mussolini, a heartless dictator, runs the country with an iron fist. Those who speak out against him disappear and are never seen again. For the first time since that horrible incident in Medina, Alma is finally happy and has fallen in love with a kind and generous Italian doctor who already has a job awaiting him in Rome; however, he is not Jewish. Alma must decide whether to marry him and risk disappointing her bubbie or let him go to find a suitable Jewish match.

In Berlin, the Nazis are quickly rising to power. Flags with swastikas are appearing everywhere. And Dr. Goebbels, the minister of propaganda is openly spewing hideous lies designed to turn the German people against the Jews. Adolf Hitler had disposed of his enemies, and the SA has been replaced by the even more terrifying SS. After the horrors they witnessed during Kristallnacht, Goldie's mother, Esther, is ready to abandon all she knows to escape the country. She begs her husband to leave Germany. But Ted refuses to leave everything that he spent his entire life working for. At what point is it too late to leave? And besides, where would they go? What would they do?

The Nazis have taken the country by the throat, and the electrifying atmosphere of the Weimar a distant memory. The period of artistic tolerance and debauchery has been replaced by a strict and cruel regime that seeks to destroy all who do not fit its ideal. Goldie's path of depravity is catching up with her, and her secrets are threatened. Will her Nazi enemies finally strike?

Book Four in A Jewish Family Saga

Coming Early 2021….

The Smallest Crack

Book One in a Holocaust Story series.

1933 Berlin, Germany

The son of a rebbe, Eli Kaetzel, and his beautiful but timid wife, Rebecca, find themselves in danger as Hitler rises to power. Eli knows that their only chance for survival may lie in the hands of Gretchen, a spirited Aryan girl. However, the forbidden and dangerous friendship between Eli and Gretchen has been a secret until now. Because, for Eli, if it is discovered that he has been keeping company with a woman other than his wife it will bring shame to him and his family. For Gretchen her friendship with a Jew is forbidden by law and could cost her, her life.

The Darkest Canyon

Book Two in a Holocaust Story series.

Nazi Germany.

Gretchen Schmidt has a secret life. She is in love with a married Jewish man. She is hiding him while his wife is posing as an Aryan woman.

Her best friend, Hilde, who unbeknownst to Gretchen is a sociopath, is working as a guard at Ravensbruck concentration camp.

If Hilde discovers Gretchen's secret, will their friendship be strong enough to keep Gretchen safe? Or will Hilde fall under the spell of the Nazis and turn her best friend over to the Gestapo?

The *Darkest Canyon* is a terrifying ride along the edge of a canyon in the dark of night.

Millions Of Pebbles

Book Three in a Holocaust Story series.

Benjamin Rabinowitz's life is shattered as he watches his wife, Lila, and his son, Moishe, leave to escape the Lodz ghetto. He is conflicted because he knows this is their best chance of survival, but he asks himself, will he ever see them again?

Ilsa Guhr has a troubled childhood, but as she comes of age, she learns that her beauty and sexuality give her the power to get what she wants. But she craves an even greater power. As the Nazis take control of Germany, she sees an opportunity to gain everything she's ever desired.

Fate will weave a web that will bring these two unlikely people into each other's lives.

Sarah and Solomon

Book Four in a Holocaust Story series

"Give me your children" -Chaim Mordechaj Rumkowski. September 1942 The Lodz Ghetto.

When Hitler's Third Reich reined with an iron fist, the head Judenrat of the Lodz ghetto decides to comply with the Nazis. He agrees to send the Jewish children off on a transport to face death.

In order to save her two young children a mother must take the ultimate risk. The night before the children are to rounded up and sent to their deaths, she helps her nine year old son and her five year old daughter escape into a war torn Europe. However, she cannot fit through the barbed wire, and so the children must go alone.

Follow Sarah and Solomon as they navigate their way through a world filled with hatred, and treachery. However, even in the darkest hour there is always a flicker of light. And these two young innocent souls will be aided by people who's lights will always shine in our memories.

All My Love, Detrick

Book One in the All My Love, Detrick series.

Book One in the All My Love, Detrick Series

Can Forbidden Love Survive in Nazi Germany?

After Germany's defeat in the First World War, she lays in ruins, falling beneath the wheel of depression and famine. And so, with a promise of restoring Germany to her rightful place as a world power, Adolf Hitler begins to rise.

Detrick, a handsome seventeen-year-old Aryan boy is reluctant to join the Nazi party because of his friendship with Jacob, who is Jewish and has been like a father figure to him. However, he learns that in order to protect the woman he loves, Jacob's daughter, he must abandon all his principles and join the Nazis. He knows the only way to survive is to live a double life. Detrick is confronted with fear every day; if he is discovered, he and those he loves will come face to face with the ultimate cruelty of the Third Reich.

Follow two families, one Jewish and one German, as they are thrust into a world of danger on the eve of the Nazis rise to power.

You Are My Sunshine

Book Two in the All My Love, Detrick series.

A child's innocence is the purest of all.

In Nazi Germany, Helga Haswell is at a crossroads. She's pregnant by a married SS officer who has since abandoned her. Left alone with the thought of raising a fatherless child, she has nowhere to turn -- until the Lebensborn steps in. They will take Helga's child when it's born and raise it as their own. Helga will now be free to live her life.

But when Helga has second thoughts, it's already too late. The papers are signed, and her claim to her child has been revoked. Her daughter belongs to Hitler now. And when Hitler's delusions of grandeur rapidly accelerate, Germany becomes involved in a two-front war against the heroic West and the fearless Russians.

Helga's child seems doomed to a life raised by the cruelest humans on Earth. But God's plan for her sends the young girl to the most unexpected people. In their warm embrace, she's given the chance for love in a world full of hate.

You Are My Sunshine is the heartfelt story of second chances. Helga Haswell may be tied to an unthinkable past, but her young daughter has the chance of a brighter future.

The Promised Land:

From Nazi Germany to Israel

Book Three in the All My Love, Detrick series.

Zofia Weiss, a Jewish woman with a painful past, stands at the dock, holding the hand of a little girl. She is about to board The SS Exodus, bound for Palestine with only her life, a dream, and a terrifying secret. As her eyes scan the crowds of people, she sees a familiar face. Her heart pounds and beads of sweat form on her forehead…

The Nazis have surrendered. Zofia survived the Holocaust, but she lives in constant fear. The one person who knows her dark secret is a sadistic SS officer with the power to destroy the life she's working so hard to rebuild. Will he ever find her and the innocent child she has sworn to protect?

To Be An Israeli

Book Four in the All My Love, Detrick series.

Elan understands what it means to be an Israeli. He's sacrificed the woman he loved, his marriage, and his life for Israel. When Israel went to war and Elan was summoned in the middle of the night, he did not hesitate to defend his country, even though he knew he might pay a terrible price. Elan is not a perfect man by any means. He can be cruel. He can be stubborn and self-righteous. But he is brave, and he loves more deeply than he will ever admit.

This is his story.

However, it is not only his story; it is also the story of the lives of the women who loved him: Katja, the girl whom he cherished but could never marry, who would haunt him forever. Janice, the spoiled American he wed to fill a void, who would keep a secret from him that would one day shatter his world. And...Nina, the beautiful Mossad agent whom Elan longed to protect but knew he never could.

To Be an Israeli spans from the beginning of the Six-Day War in 1967 through 1986 when a group of American tourists are on their way to visit their Jewish homeland.

Forever My Homeland

The Fifth and final book in the All My Love, Detrick series.

Bari Lynn has a secret. So she, a young Jewish-American girl, decides to tour Israel with her best friend and the members of their synagogue in search of answers.

Meanwhile, beneath the surface in Israel, trouble is stirring with a group of radical Islamists.

The case falls into the hands of Elan, a powerful passionate Mossad agent, trying to pick up the pieces of his shattered life. He believes nothing can break him, but in order to achieve their goals, the terrorists will go to any means to bring Elan to his knees.

Forever, My Homeland is the story of a country built on blood and determination. It is the tale of a strong and courageous people who don't have the luxury of backing down from any fight, because they live with the constant memory of the Holocaust. In the back of their minds, there is always a soft voice that whispers "Never again."

Michal's Destiny

Book One in the Michal's Destiny series.

It is 1919 in Siberia. Michal—a young, sheltered girl—has eyes for a man other than her betrothed. For a young girl growing up in a traditional Jewish settlement, an arranged marriage is a fact of life. However, destiny, it seems, has other plans for Michal. When a Cossack pogrom invades her small village, the protected life Michal has grown accustomed to and loves will crumble before her eyes. Everything she knows is gone and she is forced to leave her home and embark on a journey to Berlin with the man she thought she wanted. Michal faces love, loss, and heartache because she is harboring a secret that threatens to destroy her every attempt at happiness. But over the next fourteen tumultuous years, during the peak of the Weimar Republic, she learns she is willing to do anything to have the love she longs for and to protect her family.

However, it is now 1933. Life in Berlin is changing, especially for the Jews. Dark storm clouds are looming on the horizon. Adolf Hitler is about to become the chancellor of Germany, and that will change everything for Michal forever.

A Family Shattered

Book Two in the Michal's Destiny series.

In book two of the Michal's Destiny series, Tavvi and Michal have problems in the beginning of their relationship, but they build a life together. Each stone is laid carefully with love and mutual understanding. They now have a family with two beautiful daughters and a home full of happiness.

It is now 1938—Kristallnacht. Blood runs like a river on the streets, shattered glass covers the walkways of Jewish shop owners, and gangs of Nazi thugs charge though Berlin in a murderous rage. When Tavvi, the strong-willed Jewish carpenter, races outside, without thinking of his own welfare, to save his daughters fiancée, little does his wife Michal know that she might never hold him in her arms again. In an instant, all the stones they laid together come crashing down leaving them with nothing but the hope of finding each other again.

Watch Over My Child

Book Three in the Michal's Destiny series.

In book three of the Michal's Destiny series, after her parents are arrested by the Nazis on Kristallnacht, twelve-year-old Gilde Margolis is sent away from her home, her sister, and everyone she knows and loves.

Alone and afraid, Gilde boards a train through the Kinder-transport bound for London, where she will stay with strangers. Over the next seven years as Gilde is coming of age, she learns about love, friendship, heartache, and the pain of betrayal. As the Nazis grow in power, London is thrust into a brutal war against Hitler. Severe rationing is imposed upon the British, while air raids instill terror, and bombs all but destroy the city. Against all odds, and with no knowledge of what has happened to her family in Germany, Gilde keeps a tiny flicker of hope buried deep in her heart: someday, she will be reunited with her loved ones.

Another Breath, Another Sunrise

Book Four, the final book in the Michal's Destiny series.

Now that the Reich has fallen, in this—the final book of the Michal's Destiny series—the reader follows the survivors as they find themselves searching to reconnect with those they love. However, they are no longer the people they were before the war.

While the Russian soldiers, who are angry with the German people and ready to pillage, beat, and rape, begin to invade what's left of Berlin, Lotti is alone and fears for her life.

Though Alina Margolis has broken every tradition to become a successful business woman in America, she fears what has happened to her family and loved ones across the Atlantic Ocean.

As the curtain pulls back on Gilde, a now successful actress in London, she realizes that all that glitters is not gold, and she longs to find the lost family the Nazi's had stolen from her many years ago.

This is a story of ordinary people whose lives were shattered by the terrifying ambitions of Adolf Hitler—a true madman.

And . . . Who Is The Real Mother?

Book One in the Eidel's Story series.

In the Bible, there is a story about King Solomon, who was said to be the wisest man of all time. The story goes like this:

Two women came to the king for advice. Both of them were claiming to be the mother of a child. The king took the child in his arms and said, "I see that both of you care for this child very much. So, rather than decide which of you is the real mother, I will cut the child in half and give each of you a half."

One of the women agreed to the king's decision, but the other cried out, "NO, give the child to that other woman. Don't hurt my baby."

"Ahh," said the king to the second woman who refused to cut the baby. "I will give the child to you, because the real mother would sacrifice anything for her child. She would even give her baby away to another woman if it meant sparing the baby from pain."

And so, King Solomon gave the child to his rightful mother.

The year is 1941. The place is the Warsaw Ghetto in Poland.

The ghetto is riddled with disease and starvation. Children are dying every day.

Zofia Weiss, a young mother, must find a way to save, Eidel her only child. She negotiates a deal with a man on the black market to smuggle Eidel out in the middle of the night and deliver her to Helen, a Polish woman who is a good friend of Zofia's. It is the ultimate sacrifice because there is a good chance that Zofia will die without ever seeing her precious child again.

Helen has a life of her own, a husband and a son. She takes Eidel to live with her family even though she and those she loves will face terrible danger every day. Helen will be forced to do unimaginable things to protect all that she holds dear. And as Eidel grows up in Helen's warm maternal embrace, Helen finds that she has come to love the little girl with all her heart.

So, when Zofia returns to claim her child, and King Solomon is not available to be consulted, it is the reader who must decide…

Who is the real mother?

Secrets Revealed

Book Two in the Eidel's Story series.

Hitler has surrendered. The Nazi flags, which once hung throughout the city striking terror in the hearts of Polish citizens, have been torn down. It seems that Warsaw should be rejoicing in its newly found freedom, but Warsaw is not free. Instead, it is occupied by the Soviet Union, held tight in Stalin's iron grip. Communist soldiers, in uniform, now control the city. Where once people feared the dreaded swastika, now they tremble at the sight of the hammer and sickle. It is a treacherous time. And in the midst of all this danger, Ela Dobinski, a girl with a secret that could change her life, is coming of age.

New Life, New Land

Book Three in the Eidel's Story series.

When Jewish Holocaust survivors Eidel and Dovid Levi arrive in the United States, they believe that their struggles are finally over. Both have suffered greatly under the Nazi reign and are ready to leave the past behind. They arrive in this new and different land filled with optimism for their future. However, acclimating into a new way of life can be challenging for immigrants. And, not only are they immigrants but they are Jewish. Although Jews are not being murdered in the United States, as they were under Hitler in Europe, the Levi's will learn that America is not without anti-Semitism. Still, they go forth, with unfathomable courage. In

New Life, New Land, this young couple will face the trials and tribulations of becoming Americans and building a home for themselves and their children that will follow them.

Another Generation

Book Four in the Eidel's Story series.

In the final book in the Eidel's Story series the children of Holocaust survivors Eidel and Dovid Levi have grown to adulthood. They each face hard trials and tribulations of their own, many of which stem from growing up as children of Holocaust survivors. Haley is a peacemaker who yearns to please even at the expense of her own happiness. Abby is an angry rebel on the road to self-destruction. And, Mark, Dovid's only son, carries a heavy burden of guilt and secrets. He wants to please his father, but he cannot. Each of the Levi children must find a way to navigate their world while accepting that the lessons they have learned from the parents, both good and bad, have shaped them into the people they are destined to become.

The Wrath Of Eden

The Wrath of Eden Book One.

Deep in them Appalachian hills, far from the main roads where the citified people come and go, lies a harsh world where a man's character is all he can rightly claim as his own. This here is a land of deep, dark coal mines, where a miner ain't certain when he ventures into the belly of the mountain whether he will ever see daylight again. To this very day, they still tell tales of the Robin Hood-like outlaw Pretty Boy Floyd, even though there ain't no such thing as a thousand dollar bill no more From this beautiful yet dangerous country where folks is folks comes a story as old as time itself; a tale of good and evil, of right and wrong, and of a troubled man who walked a perilous path on his journey back to God.

The Wrath of Eden begins in 1917, in the fictitious town of Mudwater Creek, West Virginia. Mudwater lies deep in mining country in the Appalachian Mountains. Here, the eldest son of a snake-handling preacher, Cyrus Hunt, is emotionally broken by what he believes is his father's favoritism toward his brother, Aiden. Cyrus is so hurt by what he believes is his father's lack of love for him that he runs away from home to seek his fortune. Not only will he fight in the Great War, but he will return to America and then ramble around the United States for several years, right through the great depression. While on his journey, Cyrus will encounter a multitude of colorful characters and from each he will learn more about himself. This is a tale of good and evil, of brother against brother, of the intricate web of family, and of love lost and found again.

The Angels Song

The Wrath of Eden Book Two.

Cyrus Hunt returns home to the Appalachian Mountains after years of traveling. He has learned a great deal about himself from his journey, and he realizes that the time has come to make peace with his brother and his past. When he arrives in the small town where he grew up, he finds that he has a granddaughter that he never knew existed, and she is almost the same age as his daughter. The two girls grow up as close as sisters. But one is more beautiful than a star-filled night sky, while the other has a physical condition that keeps her from spreading her wings and discovering her own self-worth. As the girls grow into women, the love they have for each other is constantly tested by sibling rivalry, codependency, and betrayals. Are these two descendents of Cyrus Hunt destined to repeat their father's mistakes? Or will they rise above their human weakness and inadequacies and honor the bonds of blood and family that unite them?

One Last Hope

A Voyage to Escape Nazi Germany

Formerly *The Voyage*

Inspired by True Events

On May 13, 1939, five strangers boarded the MS St. Louis. Promised a future of safety away from Nazi Germany and Hitler's Third Reich, unbeknownst to them they were about to embark upon a voyage built on secrets, lies, and treachery. Sacrifice, love, life, and death hung in the balance as each fought against fate, but the voyage was just the beginning.

A Flicker Of Light

Hitler's Master Plan.

The year is 1943

The forests of Munich are crawling with danger during the rule of the Third Reich, but in order to save the life of her unborn child, Petra Jorgenson must escape from the Lebensborn Institute. She is alone, seven months pregnant, and penniless. Avoiding the watchful eyes of the armed guards in the overhead tower, she waits until the dead of night and then climbs under the flesh-shredding barbed wire surrounding the Institute. At the risk of being captured and murdered, she runs headlong into the terrifying, desolate woods. Even during one of the darkest periods in the history of mankind, when horrific acts of cruelty become commonplace and Germany seemed to have gone crazy under the direction of a madman, unexpected heroes come to light. And although there are those who would try to destroy true love, it will prevail. Here in this lost land ruled by human monsters, Petra will learn that even when one faces what appears to be the end of the world, if one looks hard enough, one will find that there is always A Flicker of Light.

The Heart Of A Gypsy

If you liked Inglorious Basterds, Pulp Fiction, and Django Unchained, you'll love The Heart of a Gypsy!

During the Nazi occupation, bands of freedom fighters roamed the forests of Eastern Europe. They hid while waging their own private war against Hitler's tyrannical and murderous reign. Among these Resistance fighters were several groups of Romany people (Gypsies).

The Heart of a Gypsy is a spellbinding love story. It is a tale of a man with remarkable courage and the woman who loved him more than life itself. This historical novel is filled with romance and spiced with the beauty of the Gypsy culture.

Within these pages lies a tale of a people who would rather die than surrender their freedom. Come, enter into a little-known world where only a few have traveled before . . . the world of the Romany.

If you enjoy romance, secret magical traditions, and riveting action you will love The Heart of a Gypsy.

Please be forewarned that this book contains explicit scenes of a sexual nature.

Made in the USA
Las Vegas, NV
28 December 2020